LEO'S CHOICE

BY

OTIS L. SCARBARY

For Janie -
Merry Christmas !
from Ms. Shirley
Hope you enjoy the book.

Otis Scarbary
P.S. Thanks for taking
care of Mom.

Leo's Choice
Otis L. Scarbary
Copyright 2018 Otis L. Scarbary

ISBN: 978-0-9898648-4-8

First Edition

Layout by: Cheryl Perez, yourepublished.com
Front Cover art: Carl Graves, extendedimagry.com

DEDICATION

This book is dedicated to those brave men and women of law enforcement who have served and continue to serve their communities often without acknowledgement of their sacrifices.

It has been a privilege to know and work with so many over the course of my life. Thanks to all of you.

CHAPTER ONE

The woman heard the bartender say last call for anyone interested, and she debated with herself whether to honor the offer. She had already consumed three martinis over the last two hours, but was her buzz enough to get through another night alone? She wasn't scared in the least of being stopped by the cops and was more concerned if sleep would come after getting into bed. More often than not, alcohol consumption was important in that regard.

Since Maxine Moore's divorce two years ago, she had started frequenting bars near her home. Now at one of the three places she visited most often, the staff knew her name and her drink of choice.

"One more dirty, Maxie?" asked the slender black-haired guy named Mike.

Maxine regarded the man in front of her. He was thin-lipped, clean-shaven and all arms and legs. Besides that, he was an asshole who thought he was cool but made weak drinks.

Nothing redeeming about him, she thought.

While contemplating her answer, a boorish customer on the opposite side of the u-shaped bar hollered for a draft causing the stick man to frown as he grabbed a pilsner glass to fill. Maxine's smirk went unnoticed as she watched the jerky movements signifying the employee's displeasure for having to do his job at the direction of someone he probably felt was beneath him.

Maxine took the moment as a sign that she needed to leave. She fished the tab out of an empty cocktail glass in front of her and left enough money inside to pay the bill that included a healthier tip than he deserved. Gathering her purse, she got off the wooden stool and headed with slight unsteadiness toward the rear of the establishment. A quick pit stop would be necessary just in case it took longer than the normal ten-minute drive to make it home.

The ladies room door contained a standard picture of a circle above a triangle. It made her think of geometry and triggered a fleeting thought of the nerd who taught the subject back in high school. She giggled at the memory of the guy and the ever-present slide rule he often wore like some kind of weapon on his wide leather belt.

As she started to push it open, loud voices could be heard coming from inside the room causing her to pause. The slurred cursing indicated that someone was accusing the other one of messing with her man. She sure as hell didn't want to get in the middle of some drunken argument between two women.

Maxine backed from the door and turned around. While jumbled thoughts bounced around her juiced brain she noticed a man staring at her. He was partially hidden by a shadow in the corner of the room where he sat. There was no doubt in her mind he was looking her way even as he diverted his attention discretely in another direction.

Part of her was a little bothered, but another part was just plain curious. She hadn't met anyone new in months; so a little interest from a stranger might be welcome. Maybe she should go over and flirt with him a bit.

Before she could act on the impulse, the bathroom door was flung open and struck a glancing blow to the right side of her body. It was enough of a force that it caused Maxine to stumble on the cork wedge heels she sported.

A peroxided blonde strode past Maxine as she fell to the floor on both hands and knees. Pain akin to electric shock ran from her joints as they all struck concrete covered by cheap indoor/outdoor carpeting. The woman resembling her hairdresser because of her spiked hair kept a fast pace without hesitation or saying she was sorry. There was another woman chasing after the bleached queen who gave Maxine even less acknowledgement.

Maxine stayed down a few seconds that seemed longer than they probably were, and she felt a little pee seep into her panties. She shook her head side to side like a dog with an ear infection trying to get her bearings.

How in the hell did I get here, she thought.

Nobody made an effort to help her up. After a moment of realization that wasn't happening, she stood up and noticed red coloring oozing from the right knee like ketchup on a big French fry. The left one was only throbbing like a bad toothache.

Son-of-a-bitch!

How she got to this point became unimportant. Maxine needed to take care of herself because no one else would. That was the reality of her life and had been for too long.

As an afterthought, she glanced to the area where the mysterious man had sat the moment before. He was no longer there. *No Sir Galahad,* Maxine said to herself with a sad giggle.

She gathered herself and stood up trying not to sway. Now more sober than before, Maxine went into the bathroom not only to find a toilet seat, but to attend her injuries as well.

She dabbed at her scrapes with paper from a thin single ply roll near her seat and rubbed the contusions as if she could stop bruising by the efforts. Maxine shed some tears as she nursed her body.

Everything was a mess. How did I end up this way?

Only a few years ago, it seemed she had it all. A cute framed house with a white picket fence was so symbolic of her life back then. Such a portrait was what she had always wanted and dreamed of when she was younger. The perfect husband, the perfect job, and the perfect kid were all fantasies that became true. Now they were just memories that sometimes didn't seem real.

It was all gone and she was a pathetic shell as a result. Now she was alone looking for something, but didn't know what. Whatever it might be wouldn't be found in a lonely stall in a dingy bathroom.

She got off the toilet and wiped herself with an abundant amount of the thin tissue paper. Teardrops continued to run down her face and sniffles failed to stem the tide as she walked to the sink and looked in the mirror above it.

Gazing into the cloudy surface that needed more than Windex to make it clear, Maxine felt a deep sense of remorse. The starkly lit incandescent tube above the glass showed her face in a light that was less than flattering even reflected as it was in the opaque glass. Others would probably still find her attractive, but she saw all the premature wrinkles and tired lines she wanted to forget because they represented failure.

Maxine snatched a couple of brown paper towels from the mounted dispenser. She wet one of them and dabbed at eye makeup running down her face and then dried off the area with the other.

After washing her hands, she looked once more at her image and exited the restroom. Though she thought herself sober, the vodka consumed earlier still played tricks with her brain.

Maxine noticed the club was nearly empty as she headed toward the rear entrance. Her main desire was to get home. She thought she might even soak in the hot tub and turn on the jets before crashing.

Home first, and forget this night.

Her hands trembled slightly while getting the keys out of her purse. She had parked farther away than she thought and the misty night made the black Honda look as if it was fading into the gloom. It made her nervous, and Maxine thought about going back inside to ask for an escort to the car.

No need for paranoia. My emotional health is already screwed up enough.

She clutched the key ring tightly with her fist so that a couple of the keys jutted out between her fingers as a makeshift weapon. It was something Maxine had seen on the Internet as a form of self-defense, and for some reason it seemed necessary as she walked across the murky parking lot.

Upon arrival at her car, Maxine relaxed. She got inside and started the engine. With the doors locked, she took a few deep breaths and fastened the seatbelt before driving away. She never saw the car that followed.

CHAPTER TWO

Leo was stretched out and comfortably warm. He loved everything about the scenery although for some reason it reminded him of an old battleground. The blue sky was decorated with a few fluffy clouds and dotted with occasional birds found near the ocean. A line of pelicans flew silently by resembling vintage B-52 bombers in formation while noisy gulls reminded him of fighter planes darting and scrambling mid-air. Sandpipers scurried around his secluded beach spot and appeared as infantrymen. It was all something out of his departed grandfather's era, and the thoughtful grandson smiled at the memory of the WWII vet.

Salty smells of the azure water clung in his nose hairs and he couldn't help but breathe in gulps with gusto. Waves lapped the nearby white sandy shore and could be heard even with his ear buds providing the pounding of classic rock and roll Rascals' style.

Good lovin', indeed, he thought.

The prosecutor was at peace in this place and thought he might never leave. There none of the grind that permeated his reality back home. Never ending court and the necessary preparation that was required for such was non-existent here. Leo couldn't help but smile as his right foot kept rhythm with the music pumping through his brain.

In the distance Leo thought he heard a ringing noise that became persistent and annoying. He tried shaking his head to the east and then to the west in an effort to discover the source. His wife, Dee, started talking to his right.

"Hello…hello, is anybody there?"

The spell was broken, and Leo awakened from the colorful dream he had been experiencing. Momentarily disoriented, he found himself in the bed shared with Dee as she spoke into the phone located on the stand beside her.

He stared at the alarm clock to his left and let it register that it was 4:16 a.m. Anybody ringing at this time of the morning couldn't be calling about anything good. Happy news and these types of Ma Bell notifications didn't go hand-in-hand in his experience.

Even in the dim light that escaped through the partially cracked open bathroom door, Leo could see concern on his wife's face. She took the phone from her ear and sneaked a quick look at the displayed caller's name. Her lips pursed and then opened in a slight movement that caused Leo to reach his hand from underneath the covers to Dee's exposed shoulder.

She glanced his way and then responded into the mouthpiece, "Maxie, what's wrong?"

Leo only knew one Maxie. It had to be her old friend, Maxine Moore. They had been friends as long as Leo could remember. Recent personal problems had caused increased contact between the two, and Leo wasn't exactly happy about it.

As his eyes became more adjusted to the early morning, he watched Dee's expressions as she listened to the caller. She had a way of chewing on her lip when she was in deep thought that he found endearing. It was just one of many little things he loved about her.

"Don't worry about it. Just tell me what's wrong," she said.

Leo's attitude only intensified as he listened to the one-sided conversation, and now his bladder was screaming for relief leading to his deepening discomfort. He slid out from underneath the covers and headed toward the bathroom.

Leaving the door open between the two rooms, he could still hear his wife talking after finishing the early morning toilet. The concern in her voice was even more disconcerting because of the time that would be better suited for sleep and pleasant dreams involving beaches.

"Give us thirty minutes or so, and we'll be there. Don't worry, we won't call the police."

Dee hung up the phone and got out of the bed as Leo pulled up his shorts. She joined in the bathroom suite as he flushed.

"What's going on, baby?" he asked as she brushed past him and sat on the seat he had just placed back down.

"I'm not sure. I'm still half asleep and not certain what's going on. Maxie is a mess and not real coherent. She kept saying she had been attacked, but was insistent she doesn't want the police involved. I told her we would come over. Are you okay with that?"

Leo thought about it for only a second. "You know I'll do whatever you ask, but it sounds like she needs the very help she's avoiding if she's been hurt in some way."

"I know, I know. She wasn't making a lot of sense, but she's been under so much stress lately," she said while chewing her lip again.

Their adjacent walk-in closet to the master bathroom was humming and glowing with incandescent light as always since Dee never turned off the overhead fixture. Leo and Dee searched to find suitable clothing and dressed quickly while lost in their own thoughts. Leo slipped on his favorite jeans and a long sleeved faded Buffett tee shirt while his wife chose a soft pair of capri pants and an oversized pullover she had purchased the last time they had gone to Blue Heaven, their favorite Key West restaurant.

"It's a good thing Mindy is spending the night with Mama," mumbled Leo as he placed a baseball cap on his head.

"Yeah, I can't imagine her wanting to do that much longer now she's a teenager," replied Dee.

Leo found himself absently nodding in agreement one minute and wondering if he was still awake the next. As he pondered, he slid his bare feet into well-worn boat shoes and watched Dee as she sat down in front of the mirror above her sink.

"I'm just going to put on a little war paint and whup my hair up. I'll be ready in ten minutes if you want to go check on Tiki," she said.

"Time for a cup of ambition?" he asked.

Dee only nodded as Leo shuffled back through the bedroom down the hall to the kitchen. Their coffee maker had been set the night before with the usual four scoops and he turned it on. In a few seconds gurgling erupted which signaled the device was working, and Leo continued his trek to find the four-legged member of the family. Usually he would've fixed a cup before finding the dog, but there was not enough time for that now. Routines were a big part of Leo's existence. Morning rituals always included taking the Jack Russell terrier outside for a potty break while picking up the morning paper. Later after a couple of cups of hot brew and digesting the morning news, he would take Tiki out again for a run if it were a weekend day. Otherwise, a half-mile walk before work would suffice as the entire exercise the hyper animal got during the typical weekday morning.

The household dog had his favorite places to bed depending on the season and whether Mindy was at home. Since it was still late winter and a little cool in the middle Georgia area, Leo found Tiki curled up on his soft blanket near the front door. If Mindy were at home, he more than likely would be asleep in her bed. Once spring sprang in a couple more weeks, the pet would move to cooler hardwood or tile flooring found in other areas of the house. Another favorite spot was Leo's chair.

"Hey, buddy. You want to go outside?" Leo asked as he bent down to stroke Tiki. "I don't have but a minute."

The tan and white terrier rolled slightly onto his back and enjoyed the rubbing of his belly evidenced by his hanging tongue. Leo noticed the traces of gray around the animal's snout and knew the dog was slowing down some because of age. He didn't jump as high, run as fast or as far as he did even a year ago. Leo saddened for a moment as he thought of the day when

Tiki would no longer be a part of the Berry clan and then put it out of his mind as something not to be contemplated now.

As soon as his master quit petting him, Tiki sat up on his haunches. He waited patiently as Leo secured him to the leash that hung by the front door. It was a habit both knew well.

They walked out the storm door into the crispy cool morning air. A nearly full moon lit the concrete driveway, and Leo could easily see that the newspaper contained in a clear plastic bag had already been delivered. As he walked to its location, Tiki veered into the front yard and hiked his right leg near a hedge that bordered the area.

The dog turned in his tracks with ears perked as the sound of cracking branches broke the morning stillness. Leo tensed as well as he crouched to pick up the paper. Since being involved in threats to his life a few years before, he found he had become much more cautious, even fearful on occasion. Some counseling had taught him that was normal.

Peering toward the wooded area beside his front yard, Leo didn't see anything at first. When Tiki snuffed and blew out air, a deer jumped from the darkness and bounded across the cul-de-sac through the neighbor's place across the street. Tiki initially strained against the leash, but made no real effort to follow.

Leo laughed to himself and felt his heart return to a natural rate. The canine joined him and received a pat on the head.

"I'm awake now for sure, Teek," said Leo calling the dog by his nickname. "Let's get inside."

As Leo closed the front door and unleashed the dog, he heard Dee announce from the kitchen she was ready to go. He couldn't believe how quickly she had prepared herself to leave the house since he knew her penchant for achieving just the right look before being seen in public.

Leo got Tiki a jerky treat. Then he poured a cup of coffee for himself and Dee into matching Tervis tumblers to take with them on the early morning journey. Dee's index finger poised near the touch pad ready to arm the alarm system while her husband completed those tasks. Her demeanor and constant lip chewing was out of character and caused Leo a heightened sense of uneasiness. He couldn't help thinking he should call one of his contacts at the Sheriff's Department before they headed out of the house.

CHAPTER THREE

The established neighborhood looked like many of the other middle-class ones located in the central Georgia area. The black asphalt street had a pockmark or two, but was otherwise fairly pristine. Residents generally believed in the concept of keeping their yards cut and weed-free, and if one saw a wayward fast food cup thrown out the window of a teen's vehicle, they didn't hesitate to pick it up with only a slightly disgusted shake of their head.

The tree-lined street was dark in the predawn hour, but in no way appeared sinister as lights illuminated the driveway where the dark sedan pulled into. Its driver touched a garage door opener fastened on the visor above his head before the car reached the final destination, and the double white aluminum entrance revealed an organized space inside.

While placing the transmission in park and shutting off the engine, the door was sent down again. The driver didn't exit the car until that task was complete and the only light remaining came from an overhead fixture within the enclosed structure.

He exited his nondescript sedan and took a quick inventory. Everything appeared to be in order, just like he preferred. If there was one thing he sought in his existence, it was order. Everything had its place, as it should be.

He knew some people would think that was weird. In his mind, for others to think that way was strange itself. His was the superior knowledge.

As he walked from the car into the spotless environment that was his garage, a smile formed on his thin lips. It had been a good night and he felt satiated. It was the kind of night he'd relive many times in the future before the need to do something similar arose again.

Morgan Thomas was a smart man. In fact, in his humble opinion, he was the smartest guy around. He did what he wanted when he wanted. He didn't need other people to tell him what to do. Morgan had his own ideas on just about any subject and had found over the years those ideas were far better than those of most others. He just chose not to share them with most people.

He did consider himself rather fortunate for several reasons besides possessing his superior intellect. For one, his father had left him financially secure enough that he didn't have to work. A healthy bank account provided him with more opportunities to do as he pleased. Money certainly had its benefits, and he thought those who were constantly striving for the legal tender were at a distinct disadvantage in this cruel world. He was smart enough not to flaunt it, though. His lifestyle didn't suggest his true net worth. It was good not to draw too much attention to himself. So, he maintained a steady job and was good at it even though he didn't need the dough.

Not only did he have smarts and money, Morgan wasn't tied down with emotional baggage. He saw on a daily basis how personal relationships dragged people down. Even some people he thought otherwise had the potential to be close to his equal on some levels fell short because of ties they had to their families. They were hamstrung and didn't even know it. He would never let himself fall into such a trap.

Family, what a crock, he thought with a grimace.

Part of Morgan felt the hole inside due to the fact he had none left, but he had been alone for so long, it didn't matter. He didn't know one without problems. His had been no different, but now it was only him, and he was glad. They had always gotten in his way when they were still around.

No more restrictions for me unless I impose them.

Morgan entered the house after using a small remote attached to his key chain that disarmed the sophisticated security system. The resulting chirping sound reminded him of something out of *Star Wars.*

He carried a small black nylon bag in his left hand. Using his other hand, Morgan hung the keys used to unlock the door on a functional rack just inside the frame.

Walking down the short hallway, he took a turn into his kitchen and set the bag on an island in the middle of the room. He turned to the refrigerator and removed a soft drink, popped the top, and drank half the can before closing the door. If pressed, he might admit sodas were a personal weakness since he consumed several every day.

Weaknesses. Everybody's got them. Some worse than others.

Morgan smiled at his thoughts before finishing the drink. He felt adept at recognizing the soft spots in people and his enjoyment of caffeinated colas seemed tame compared to most.

He unzipped the bag and dumped the contents on the counter. Plastic ties, a mag light, an open box of medical gloves and pre-moistened cleaning cloths spilled out. There were other items also. Ones more associated with his pleasure seeking.

Maybe that was his major weakness. A compulsion to look for excitement.

Suddenly he was hungry. Sex made him that way, and he had enjoyed his share during the previous night. He smiled again to himself as he relived part of it.

Even though she might not want to admit it, he bet Maxine liked the thrill, too.

Of course. She's been served by the best now. Her whimpering proved it.

CHAPTER FOUR

Leo and Dee arrived at her friend's residence within thirty-five minutes of first receiving the early morning call. They had barely spoken on the ride over, each lost in their own thoughts. Leo's centered on how to get Maxine on board with calling in law enforcement. He couldn't yet imagine what had happened to her, but knew leaving them out of the equation was not a good option.

The northwestern Macon home was of a cookie-cutter style that was one of four basic choices in the contained neighborhood. Although not a gated community, it had the feel of security that other parts of town often lacked. In the early morning light the small house didn't appear any different than those others nearby except for the green color of the front door. That entrance magically opened just before Dee was about to knock on it.

The two women hugged fiercely within the doorway as Leo stayed behind them on the stoop. He felt awkward and out of place while his wife whispered something in Maxine's ear. A fresh stream of tears trickled from Maxine's eyes as Dee's murmuring continued.

When they separated there was a protracted look between the two of them until broken up by Maxine glancing past Dee and attempting a smile at Leo. He noticed her splotched face looked scrubbed and makeup free notwithstanding the recent tear tracks. Her brown hair was damp and spikey as if it had just been washed and further enhanced the appearance of vulnerability.

"Thanks for coming. Both of you. I didn't know who else to call."

"Hey, what are friends for?" replied Dee as Leo nodded in agreement.

"Please come in."

Maxine led the couple through a foyer into an open area that was comfy and inviting. His wife had been a guest a few times, but Leo had never visited and surveyed the room with furtive admiration. While definitely feminine inspired, the over-stuffed couch and contrasting colored chairs would lure anyone to sit and stay awhile.

"I brewed some coffee. Y'all want a cup?" asked Maxine in a shaking voice while wringing her hands.

"No, thanks. Not for me," replied Dee. "Leo made us some before leaving the house."

"I'm fine, too," said Leo.

She tightened the sash holding her terry cloth robe together and then reached out to take Dee's hand. Maxine pulled the other woman toward the sofa where they both sank. Leo took a seat opposite from them and resisted the notion to start questioning.

Once Maxine began talking, the Berrys listened with rapt attention. She commenced relaying the events of the previous evening avoiding eye contact with Leo and only doing so with Dee at short intervals during the monologue. He felt somewhat like an uninvited interloper.

She started by talking about how lonely she had been lately. It was as if Maxine was trying to justify why she had gone out to a nightspot by herself. Leo wanted to interrupt and tell her neither of them would ever place blame under the circumstances, but continued to hold his tongue. Over the course of his years as an attorney, he had found it was often a good idea to let witnesses tell their stories the first time he heard them without questions. You could always clarify later with further inquiries as necessary to flesh out the testimony.

Maxine then rambled for sometime; at least it seemed so to Leo, about falling and injuring herself. She explained at least three times that she wasn't intoxicated and that it was the fault of a couple of women embroiled in an argument.

I wonder if she protests too much, he thought.

"I saw a guy watching me just before I fell down," mumbled Maxine.

"What?" asked Dee.

"I think he was the same guy who came here and attacked me. I-I-I'm not sure."

This started Maxine sniffling, which led to Dee gently pulling the friend into her arms. They stayed in the embrace for only a few moments when Maxine backed away to arms length.

"I'm so damned stupid. I didn't pay attention that somebody was following me to my own front door."

"Don't beat yourself up, Maxie," replied Dee in hushed tones as she patted her friend's arm.

"There's no reason for you to think like that. Did the guy hurt you?" Dee asked.

There was a pregnant pause before Maxine answered. When she did, it was directed in Leo's direction.

"I know what you're thinking, but I'm not shot, cut, beat up, bleeding, or even bruised, at least not from what he did to me. There's not a single mark on me to prove what he did. All I got to show from the night came from me being knocked down at the bar by some Blondie bitch. That's why I can't report this to the police. I know you're thinking I should. I couldn't bear the scrutiny. The embarrassment. Humiliation is what I'm feeling right now, and I can't help believing it would only be worse to talk about the experience with strangers."

Leo couldn't avoid responding. "I gotta tell you, Maxine. That's not different from how a lot of victims think after a sexual assault. Many feel as if some how it was their fault. You haven't exactly said you were attacked in that way, so I'm only guessing at this point. If it's true, I bet you wouldn't want somebody else to go through what you did and you would want to help prevent him from doing it again. Criminal behavior like that is often repeated. A trained officer can walk you through the process of taking your statement and collecting evidence. There's no telling how much forensic evidence can be found. I just hope you haven't compromised that already. I can call somebody to help you through it."

Maxine's face turned scarlet as she blurted, "Yes, I was raped! And he did other things to me, too. But, you've got to understand. There's no evidence, and it's not because I took a shower that he made me take, by the way. He took every precaution to leave no DNA. He wore a condom and surgical gloves. He was completely hairless as far as I could tell. He had on a mask and made me wear one most of the time, too, so I couldn't see his face. He wiped everything he touched with disinfectant towels while still wearing those damned gloves. He even made me put the sheets in the washing machine."

"Oh, my God," exclaimed Dee.

Maxine slumped back in her seat as her face turned from red to white. She looked defeated as Leo momentarily sat speechless on the edge of his chair.

"It's not even the worse part of it," she whispered and then closed her eyes as if to block the memory.

Leo searched for the right words to say that would encourage the woman to cooperate. He didn't know if there was an active serial rapist in the area, but it sure seemed that way. The prosecutor side of him wanted to ask what she meant by the "worse part of it," but dared not to ask now.

"That's an awful experience you've been through, Maxine," he finally responded. "But, look. All of those things he did provide a unique set of facts that may very well establish a pattern of behavior the police and ultimately a prosecutor can use to bring a sadistic animal to justice. Let me help. I know detectives working in the Persons Crime Unit, and I'll call one to meet you here. They will be discrete and professional. What do you say?"

Just before it appeared she wouldn't answer, Maxine opened her eyes that now showed something different than before. Her voice quivered along with her lips.

"I guess you're right. But, I don't know how it's going to sound if I have to admit I've got no proof other than my word. I don't want to be a face in a movement like *#MeToo*. Have you seen how some people react to women making accusations like that? Even other women don't believe them. I never thought something like this could happen to me," she said barely above a whisper before pausing.

After several moments that included looks back and forth at Dee and Leo, Maxine spoke again, "Okay, I'll at least talk with somebody you know and trust, Leo. I'm not making any promises about how much I can or will help," she said.

Reaching into his pocket, the prosecutor retrieved his ever-present cell phone. He used his thumbprint to access the main screen and opened the contact list. Scrolling through the names quickly, Leo found Captain Jimbo Barbour's number.

Yep, he's the one to start with, Leo thought. *Been on the job for forty years and has seen it all. He'll know what to do.*

CHAPTER FIVE

Leo sat at his desk that contained several stacks of files. One comprised cases in which plea offers were outstanding and defense attorneys hadn't got back to him with acceptance or rejection. Another had cases in various states of incompleteness whether awaiting additional evidence, discovery or other such issues. One had cases with motions pending either a hearing or a ruling by the court. The biggest heap was the one that had just been added at the beginning of the workday, the new cases that needed to be reviewed for a decision about whether to file formal charges. There was not much open area available to place anything else except for the mug he held in his right hand.

Such was the norm in the busy environment of the Bibb County Solicitor-General's office Leo named his other home. He had been calling it that for the last fifteen years of his professional career since leaving the private practice of law. When he started, the younger version of himself had seen the assistant prosecutor's job as a chance to make a difference in the middle Georgia community he had never strayed far from and where his real home was located. It hadn't hurt that the steady paycheck provided for more financial stability than the roller coaster of running a private practice.

A few days had passed since he and Dee had been to Maxine Moore's house, but the meeting wouldn't leave Leo's brain. As a criminal trial lawyer for the majority of time since passing the bar, he had seen his fair share of deviant behavior. What Dee's friend had described as happening to her was near the top of the list he had witnessed over those years. It distressed him that there were so many women victims of crime.

It had begun when he was an idealist fresh out of Mercer Law School, and he had hung out his law office shingle. Always a goal setter, the budding attorney had a vague notion back then he would save the world and make a million bucks while doing it, all within the first year. Both sides of his family were life-long residents for at least a couple of generations, and he felt there were enough connections in the community to help him reach the marks he had set.

He knew it would take hard work, but that never bothered him. His parents had instilled a strong work ethic. Leo had labored all his life and had started at an early age cutting grass, throwing newspapers, and working other part-time jobs in order to earn money. The fact that he had never known any other attorneys, not worked in a law office, or knew much about running his own business were minor considerations at the early stages of his practice. Leo was convinced his determination to succeed would get him through.

The experiences gained during those first few years proved to be invaluable. Although the young lawyer had thought he knew a lot about human conduct, he soon found out it was not as much as he had believed. That was particularly true with respect to people who found themselves in the criminal justice system.

Because all newly admitted lawyers back in the day were required to represent indigent defendants for at least three years upon becoming bar members, Leo had been thrust right away into handling all sorts of criminal cases. They became more serious as his experience progressed, and he showed skill in that area of the law.

Within the first three years of starting his practice, Leo found himself graduating from the defense of simple probation violations and various misdemeanors to representing individuals charged with armed robbery, aggravated assault, rape, and homicide. One thing that didn't change was the defendants seemed often to minimize their conduct and to be less than truthful about what they had done, no matter how strong the evidence pointed to their guilt.

Some of his clients were just ignorant of the law they violated or acted stupidly regarding the legal norms society had placed upon them. Others were impulsive and let emotions rule their actions. A portion of them was plain out mean. A sizable amount of them had mental or emotional problems that got them in trouble. He was convinced a few had been psychotic or antisocial to the point that they just didn't care about any law whatsoever. They were just your run-of-the-mill sociopaths.

After more thinking about the conversation with Maxine, Leo had begun to believe her attacker was in that last group of lawbreakers. The thought of a smart pyscho-rapist preying on vulnerable females in Macon, Georgia, made his blood pressure rise. Partly due to him having women in his life he wanted to protect, Leo felt a responsibility to do what he could to bring the guy to justice. He could only hope at this point it had been an isolated attack and was anxious to talk with Detective Captain Barbour to find out if that was true.

The ringing telephone on his cluttered desk brought Leo out of those thoughts and back into the day's activities. He picked it up and tried to place the familiar voice on the other end of the line.

"Is this the locally famous Little Leo?" asked the caller.

Leo's brain raced to process the identity. Not many folks called him by his early childhood name that usually meant it belonged to someone from the distant past.

"I don't know about famous or little," replied Leo.

There was a bark of laughter that sounded genuine which allowed the prosecutor to recognize an old friend. Although he hadn't seen or heard from him in a few years, Leo knew he was speaking with a classmate from law school, Levi James.

"Well, it's been awhile, but I seem to remember seeing your name in the paper and your face on TV. And, you at least appeared not to have added any poundage since law school, unlike my fat ass," drawled Levi.

"What you see is what you get. You just have to keep moving, old friend," Leo said with a laugh.

"No shit, Leo-Bob," retorted Levi.

Leo chuckled like a kid at the reference. The two of them had referred to each other by adding Bob to their names back in law school as a nod to some of the characters from the old *The Waltons* television series.

"Not all observations I make are profound, and some platitudes coming from my mouth are just that, Levi-Bob. What's going on in your high dollar neck of the woods?" asked Leo.

"Aww, life on the lake suits my fancy pretty good. Still fishin', huntin', and raisin' hounds. I'm dispensin' a little justice here and there."

Leo thought Levi's life-style served his personality perfectly. His house on Lake Oconee seemed as outdoorsy as he was. His recent elevation to the Superior Court bench in the circuit where he resided was recognition of a sharp legal mind as well as to the political gravitas obtained over the years since school. The speech patterns Levi often used belied his keen intellect and not many people would believe how well he knew people in high places-the kind of people who could ensure advancement.

"Well, I've been following your career change through the advance sheets," said Leo. "Didn't I see where the Georgia Supremes reversed you recently?"

Levi let out a stream of profanities referring to the justices of the Georgia Supreme Court in less than glowing terms. Leo had to suppress the urge to laugh at the interesting combination of curses coming through the telephone. He couldn't ever recall hearing so many scatological terms or imaginative uses of the F-word. His last sentence in the rant was an often-used reference that had caused Leo to Google the term before.

"They are screwed up as Hogan's Goat," Levi concluded.

"Sorry I hit a sore spot, Levi. Let's drop that topic of conversation. Was there a particular reason for the call this morning?"

There was a pause on the other end of the line and then an audible exhaling of air. When he continued, the slow drawl had all but disappeared as it often did when he got serious.

"Yeah, okay. I don't want to talk about those idiots in Atlanta. What I wanted to find out from the horse's mouth is if the rumors I've heard about you are true."

Leo was momentarily taken aback and unsure what his old friend was asking. The prosecutor had been thinking so much about Maxine's recent assault that other things going on in his life had been forgotten.

"Rumors? About me? What are you talking about, Levi?"

"That you're going to run for D.A."

It was Leo's turn to let out a sigh. He had been thinking about the possibility of running for the District Attorney's job for about a year and had even put out some feelers about his prospects. There were considerations, pros and cons, and other thoughts cluttering his brain as to whether to make such a commitment. Running for public office had not been anything to think about until recently, and if he was going to try, he was going to have to make up his mind in a few short weeks.

"To be completely honest, Levi, I haven't decided. I've been thinking about it, but I'm not convinced it's right for me," said Leo.

There was a snort before Levi responded once again with the southern accent, "Quit over thinkin', Leo. It ain't a bad position and you can parlay it on to the bench in a few years. I'll tell you, that should be your goal. It's the best damn job there is!"

"I think you've forgotten a thing or two about me, Judge James. First, I'm no politico like you. Second, I'm really not all that ambitious. And last, but not least, I like my life pretty much as it is. Being in the background, part of a team, living a slow and steady lifestyle, while avoiding stress by handling misdemeanors instead of felonies, are important to me," Leo replied and paused.

He continued, "If I decide to run, I've got to be sure it's not going to disrupt my life too much. I put myself through enough danger and added stress a couple of years ago the last time I prosecuted a felony case, and I sure as hell don't want my family exposed to any of that again. That being said, I'm intrigued with the possibility of making a greater difference in the community, and I think being D.A. might allow that."

"Hmmph, still the crusader. You ain't no super-hero, Leo. There's only so much you can do in whatever job you end up with when you're workin' for the gubment. You ought to know that by now. But yeah, you can help out your hometown I 'spect more than most folks. So, run, Leo-Bob. You got the experience, the name recognition and yeah, even the right motives to allow you to win. It's your choice."

Sounded almost like a campaign slogan, thought Leo. Before Leo could answer his friend, one of the office assistants appeared in his doorway. Vicki was a favorite of his and could always make him laugh even when he tried not to. She had her big eyes wide open and mouthed silently that someone was waiting to see him. Leo held up his index finger to signal for her to wait a moment, which caused her to pooch out her full lips and place a hand on a hip.

"Hey, Levi. I hate to break up this stimulating conversation, but I've got somebody waiting to see me. I appreciate your opinion and will take it under advisement, as my friends on the bench like to say," said Leo with a wink directed toward Vicki.

She rolled her eyes and started tapping her foot. The prosecutor laughed silently as his friend ended the call in typical fashion.

"Yeah, just remember what I said, Leo. If'in you wait too long, folks who woulda come to your goat roast will go to somebody else's. Don't let that happen. Call me when you decide, and I'll do what I can to help."

The dial tone was abrupt, and Leo shook his head as he placed the phone in the cradle. He didn't have time to finish processing the call as Vicki spoke in a mocked tone.

"You finally got time for the detective who's been waiting for you while you been joking and cutting up the last half hour?"

"There you go exaggerating again, Vic. I haven't been tied up that long, and what makes you think I was joking around anyway?"

"Cause I know you Lil Leo. I heard you using that twang whenever you be talking to one of your old friends from law school. It's pitiful. You sound like a dumb old redneck. You get to talking that, excuse my French, shit, and you forget how long you been flapping your gums," Vicki said with a smirk.

A tall but slouched figure showed behind the secretary causing Leo to shift his line of sight above her. Jimbo Barbour wore a crooked-toothed smile that was usually in place except for the times when he had to deal with the hard case criminals he encountered. His raised left eyebrow indicating he had heard the exchange between Leo and Vicki and found the conversation amusing.

"Good morning, Detective. Sorry I've kept you waiting. Somebody should've told me I had a distinguished guest," said Leo first looking at the man in the back and then at Vicki.

She began an exaggerated shake of her head and replied, "I know you didn't just go there. Excuse me; before I say something I'll be sorry for, I'm outta here." She squeezed by the looming man and continued to mutter as she made her way down the hall from the prosecutor's office.

"No worries. It gave me time to check on Facebook for new recipes," the man replied while holding up an older model phone. "I see you get about as much respect as I do around my office, counselor," he continued.

Leo grinned. "I love Vicki. We both started working here about the same time and picking at each other has been a favorite sport ever since. So, you found something new to cook for dinner tonight?"

The two men had known each other for many years and shared a passion for preparing food. They had exchanged menus and tips during their friendship and on occasion posted their creations on social media. Although Detective Barbour was older, Leo felt Jimbo retained a certain element of youth because of the banter that often flowed whenever they saw each other.

"Yeah, man. There's so much to choose from, it'll take me years to try 'em all. You ever tried buffalo cauliflower bites? I think I'm going to try this one as an appetizer or maybe as a side with some roasted chicken. I'm trying to be more healthy and I think I could eat a bunch of that without doing much harm," said Jimbo.

"Sounds like a plan, Jimbo. A lot more healthy than some of those desserts I've seen you posting. It's got to be better for your blood sugar. Come in and grab a seat. I've been waiting to hear from you," Leo responded.

The detective slipped his phone into the pocket of his rumpled jacket and sauntered into the office. He slumped into the chair nearest the desk across from the prosecutor. To Leo, it never seemed Jimbo was in a hurry to do anything, and he always looked as if he was in a perpetual state of amusement.

"So, you going to fill me in on what's going on with the Maxine Moore case, or are we just going to swap our menus for tonight?" asked Leo.

Jimbo's face reflected a not so subtle change to a serious look. His lips compressed into a downward line and his hazel-colored eyes became hooded. It reminded Leo that even though Barbour was a fun guy to talk with, he was foremost a somber cop when on the job.

"So much for foreplay, forgive the bad pun," the detective said with a frown.

He reached into a hidden inside jacket pocket and removed a tattered note pad. Shuffling through pages with a licked thumb and index finger kept him quiet for a few moments. When he finally found the page he was looking for, Jimbo raised his eyes and with an inscrutable gaze started talking again.

"Before I start, let me say this. I haven't worked a rape case in a long time, and I'm not sure I'm the best person to do this one. It took me awhile to develop any kind of rapport with the victim, and I'm still not sure how committed she is to helping. I think female detectives are generally better with these types of assaults," he said and then paused.

"That being said, I like and believe her. She made me want to help find the son-of-a-bitch who attacked her. It seems like she's had a rough time of it for the last few years, and something like this doesn't help too much."

"Yeah," Leo interrupted. "I can't imagine losing a kid like she did. Obviously her husband couldn't handle it. I guess that's why they got a divorce."

Jimbo seemed to process that statement with a slight shake of his head up and down before consulting again with his notebook. Concentration showed on his well-wrinkled forehead.

"The vic is a divorced and attractive forty-two year old female residing in northwest Macon," he recited before stopping.

"Oh hell, you know all the preliminaries, so let me skip to what you might not know. The perp was described as being around six feet tall, more or less, based on him being slightly taller than the vic's ex-husband who is around five-ten. Based upon similar observations she made, he's around a hundred and eighty-five pounds. She noted no body hair, as if he had been waxed or shaven. Since he wore some type of mask at all times, she could not see the color of his eyes. At some point during the incident, the vic was able to glimpse his mouth and reported no facial hair present. She stated his lips were more narrow than full and that one of his front teeth was slightly overlapped."

"Wait a minute, she saw his mouth even though he wore a mask?" asked Leo.

The detective cleared his throat and appeared embarrassed. "Um, yeah. She said he raised the covering from the bottom part of his face long enough to, using her words here, 'lick, nibble and suck' parts of her body during the attack. This was done for several minutes prior to penetration according to her."

"Oh," was all Leo could say.

"She reported that his voice was never raised above much more than a whisper, and she couldn't detect any accent or peculiarities of speech. He never harmed her physically during the entire encounter, and it seemed to her he took great precautions not to cause her injury. However, he had superior strength and easily maneuvered her into any position he chose. He told her several times he just wanted to please. She never felt it was safe for her to resist his actions," continued Jimbo.

"Have there been any other reported cases such as this one?" asked Leo.

"The short answer is I don't know. Like I said, I don't normally work on these types of cases, unless there's a homicide involved. I can say I don't see any kind of connection to anything I've investigated. Nobody currently in the sexual assault unit recognizes any similarities to pending unsolved cases either. I'm waiting to talk with a former detective about what information she might have, and I've got a few feelers out around the state to see if anybody else has seen anything like this one. As you know, women often don't report such attacks, so there's no telling," responded Jimbo.

The prosecutor's brain was processing what the detective had relayed when his telephone rang. Vicki's extension showed in the window letting Leo know the identity of the caller. He held up his index finger to Jimbo and answered.

"Yes?"

"Don't forget you've got a hearing in ten minutes."

"Oh yeah, thanks, Vic."

Leo cradled the receiver and looked at Detective Barbour. Jimbo was flipping through his notebook.

"I've got to go in the courtroom, but did you have anything else you can let me know?

"Just that we're waiting on lab results to see if we have any DNA, but I'm not too optimistic based on the precautions the perp took during the time he was in the victim's house. I'm also going to meet with the owner of the club later today and see if he's got any info on anyone who could be a suspect. I'm hoping there will be some video, but I don't know yet. Supposedly there are cameras, but you know how that goes. I'll keep you posted, Leo. But you know, this is really an unofficial visit, right. I'm only keeping you in the loop because you got me involved," said Barbour.

"I understand, and I appreciate it. Anything you can tell me about the investigation stays between us."

The two men stood and shook hands before the policeman left the room. Leo took his jacket off a wooden rack and got a file off his desk. He thought it was just a small token to remove one bit of the clutter in his life.

Get rid of a little and more takes its place.

CHAPTER SIX

Detective Captain Jimbo Barbour sat outside the club in his well-used Ford Crown Victoria waiting for the appointed time to go inside and meet the manager. In the stark glare of sunlight, the strip mall where *Promises* was located caused it not to reach the expectations of its name. He figured the place would even be a little on the spooky side after nightfall. He would have to classify the joint as sad and laughed to himself when he thought it might be better to amend the dated neon sign by placing *Broken* in front of the name.

An unlit Marlboro drooped from his lips. He had only quit lighting them a few days ago in the latest attempt to give them up altogether. If pressed, he would guess he'd quit at least once a year for the last forty-five he'd been smoking the damned things. It made him mad to think how much money had been spent and how much damage had been done to his lungs during that time. He hated the habit, but it seemed all it took was one more case to make him light up again. Stress relief had a price, and he knew the possibility that a new sicko was wandering around could send him into a nicotine fit.

A lot of years and a ton of cases had made for a career few others in the profession could compare with. Jimbo Barbour was a man's man who became a cop's cop. He had seen it all during his climb up the ranks. Starting as a bluecoat in the early seventies right after his honorable discharge from the Army and continuing until the current day, Jimbo lived every day, whether on the clock or not, solving whatever was thrown his way. It's what he did, and he couldn't imagine doing anything else. That was the main reason he was still working even though he could've quit years ago and started drawing a well earned pension.

The aging detective thought of himself as old school, but knew others on the force called him a dinosaur. He didn't care. Jimbo still preferred hitting the streets, interviewing witnesses while looking them in the eye and taking notes in cheap notebooks rather than spending his time staring at a computer screen. Not that he totally eschewed technology because it could be helpful from time to time, it just didn't hold the same punch to the gut he felt when catching someone contradicting a previous statement or better yet, getting a confession from a guilty perp. There was just not a substitute for the grunt work involved in policing, and he had to constantly remind the younger people toiling under his supervision of that fact.

The blood was coursing through his veins with renewed vigor at the thoughts of catching the asshole who had attacked Maxine Moore. After so much time spent behind his desk the last few months being more of an administrator than an investigator, Jimbo was antsy. Captain's pay was a lot better than when he first started as a rookie, but reading and correcting other's reports ran a poor second to actual policing. And lately, that along with attending never ending strategic meetings seemed to be all he was doing.

Jimbo smiled to himself as he thought how he had landed the newest case. It had taken Leo Berry the Third's intervention by calling and requesting his personal help with the victim. Otherwise, the incident may have gone unreported at worst, or assigned to a much younger detective outside his unit at best. It had still taken his major's speaking on his behalf with the Sheriff to give Jimbo the opportunity to investigate the case. Now, Captain Barbour would have to make progress in order to stay involved, and he was committed to make that happen even if it meant working nonstop.

The driver's door groaned when he got out of the car, which made him think of his creaking knee. It was the same joint that let him know of any change in the weather and reminded him he couldn't chase criminals like he did when he was younger. It also caused him to stand in place for a moment as he reached down and massaged the ache.

His gait was only slightly affected by the pain as he strolled across the distance to the front door of the club. Jimbo took some amount of pride in the tolerance he had when it came to such and still felt he could handle any discomfort better than men half his age. He never took anything stronger than what he could buy over-the-counter at Kroger or the bourbon and branch consumed in the evening. It was only part of the toughness constituting his personality.

Arriving at the front door, Jimbo pulled on the metal handle and was somewhat surprised when it opened. He entered the establishment and let his eyes adjust to the dimly lit scene. Over the years as a detective and a patron of more than a few bars, it never ceased to amaze him how differently such a business looked in the light of day as opposed to the more bustling atmosphere at night.

This place at least was not so dingy to make his allergies kick in. There was a certain cheapness about it that was shown in the furnishings and funky light fixtures, but it was at least clean enough that he didn't feel the need to look for sanitizer. He didn't see any trash anywhere and the chairs, tables, and barstools were all neatly arranged. A polished wooden bar in the center actually gleamed and formed a focal point of the space.

Jimbo eased in that direction as he continued to take in the general vibe of the club. His initial reaction was that it was geared toward more of an older crowd. At least it was not gaudy.

He noticed a nearby bandstand that contained a drum kit, two microphones and a keyboard. Further inspection showed a couple of guitar stands without the instruments.

A small dance floor was in front of the place where the entertainment would emanate from. It was some sort of polished wood, and Jimbo wondered if it was as slick as it looked. He laughed silently to himself as he thought about how his tired old ass would look out there busting some moves.

Jimbo ambled over to the bar and took a seat. He studied the liquor that was neatly arranged on the shelf behind the counter. The bourbons were well represented and he saw his favorite Maker's Mark in a prominent location. His tongue slid between his lips without thinking.

"Detective Barbour?"

Jimbo was momentarily nonplussed by the interruption of the guy approaching him. He was dressed casually in khakis and a starched blue buttoned-down cotton shirt and appeared more like a lawyer in his casual Friday duds than a club owner before business hours. There was a smirk on his face that made the older policeman feel like he had been caught doing something wrong by looking at the alcohol.

"Yeah, that's me," said Jimbo as he stood.

The two men shook hands and Jimbo had to admit to himself first impressions were favorable. He couldn't stand dead fish handshakes, and this man's was firm.

"Good to finally meet you. I'm Dom Vitale. I've been hearing about your exploits since I was a kid," the man said with a sly smile.

Jimbo studied the younger man's face before recognition set in. He broke into a broad grin before replying, "You've got to be kin to my old buddy, Sal."

Salvatore Vitale had been a friend for almost forty years before passing a few years ago. This younger version had the olive complexion and dark hair of the man Jimbo remembered with affection. They had shared much wine, home made Italian cuisine, and conversation back in the day, and now those memories came back.

"Yeah, Uncle Sal was one of a kind. He always said you were the one cop he trusted."

Jimbo laughed and shook his head. He recalled Sal's belief that most people couldn't be counted on unless their own interest was involved. Jimbo had earned that respect as a young officer by solving a burglary to Sal's business that ultimately led to the long friendship.

"I miss old Godfather *Polpetto*," said Jimbo referring to his term of endearment for the deceased man.

"You're probably the only person Uncle Sal would've let call him either a godfather or a meatball, and you got away with both. It's a tribute that stuck, though. Some of us in the family would refer to him with that nickname, but only behind his back," replied Vitale with a chuckle.

"Great memories of a good man," Jimbo said with another shake of his head. "I'd love to get together sometime and share a few when I'm not working and in such a rush. Today I'm afraid I need to find out if you were able to find any videos from the night I called about. I believe your employee mentioned to me over the phone you have a security system that records activity inside the club."

The younger man's expression turned serious as he replied, "Oh yeah, I've started looking at the footage, but I didn't see anything of interest happening that night. Pretty usual stuff. An argument or two was all I saw. I cued up one for you to see. Of course, you're welcome to see whatever we've got on tape. Let's go back to my office."

Jimbo followed Vitale to an area located on the far side of the club that he had not previously noticed. The entrance to the office blended into the space so as to be almost invisible as they went in. There was a large two-way mirror on the main wall that allowed management staff to observe the interior of the club without being seen by the patrons. Upon scanning the room, Jimbo nodded to offer his approval of the setup.

"Pretty sweet way to keep up with what's happening," said Jimbo.

"Thanks, I like having a window into the soul of my business," replied Vitale with a quick glance into the empty bar. "You might want to step over here to see the video screens."

Jimbo shuffled over a few feet to his right where he stood in front of three monitors. Not being particularly tech savvy, Jimbo thought the equipment appeared state of the art until Vitale spoke again.

"Sorry I don't have better stuff to show you the recordings. Planning on getting a new system later this year."

Jimbo didn't respond and waited as Vitale clicked some buttons. *No need to show my ignorance,* he thought with a smile.

For the next ten minutes the owner showed various shots and angles that could be accessed by the cameras located inside the club. Vitale carried on a commentary as he described the limitations of the system that had the effect of causing Jimbo to get impatient. Tolerance was not necessarily one of his virtues.

"Okay, I get the lighting is less than ideal and some of the customers can't be seen because of their clothing colors, but I want to see if you can find any white males in their thirties or forties a little above average height and weight who were present on last Saturday evening from about 9:30 until a little after midnight," Jimbo finally said.

"Yeah, okay. Sorry, I get carried away sometimes. I have made a few notes from my review of the tapes after I was first contacted and I've got them marked for you to take a look. Understand, I didn't know exactly what I was searching for," replied Vitale.

He then began fast-forwarding through the tape until pausing and capturing an image. It was fuzzy with muted light to one side of the frame. The man's face in the picture was nondescript made even more so from the glasses he had on, and he wore what appeared to be a dark colored sweater and matching pants without any distinguishing markings.

"A lot of our customers are regulars, but I don't know this guy. Records show he paid in cash. At least, I didn't recognize him when I went through the tapes of that night," Vitale commented.

Jimbo stared at the screen and tried to find any unique identifying characteristics. He noticed the haircut was stylish and full. It could even be a toupee, but no way of telling from the picture. There was no watch showing; however, on the right arm sticking slightly out of the man's sweater appeared a glint of metal. Bracelet?

"You got anymore footage of the guy?" asked Jimbo.

"A little, but this is the best shot I could find of his face. Here, let me show you."

Vitale proceeded to start and stop the machine another half-dozen times, but his statement proved to be true. Either the subject would be turned so that his face could not be seen clearly or the angle wouldn't allow a full viewing. The last shot did verify what Jimbo had seen earlier.

The man had lifted his right hand while sipping a drink from a cocktail glass. A bracelet resembling what the old detective remembered from his younger days as an ID bracelet clung to fabric of the sweater.

"Can you print copies of the tapes? I would like one of everything you've got from that night, if that's possible."

The younger man grinned and gave a thumb's up. "Anything I can do for a friend of Uncle Sal's would be my pleasure. I'm sure he'd approve. Probably smiling up in the Goombah section of Heaven as we speak."

Jimbo's returned smile conveyed the affection felt for his lost friend and the appreciation he now felt for the nephew. An old connection had made way for a new one.

Using the term of endearment Jimbo had heard Sal say to his kids, Jimbo replied, "Thanks, *Piccolo*. I believe you're right."

CHAPTER SEVEN

The dinner table contained scraps of the meal just consumed by Leo and his family. There was just enough meatloaf left for a couple of sandwiches, one of which the prosecutor thought would make the perfect lunch for tomorrow. The remaining green beans seasoned with chicken broth and diced ham awaited placement in a Tupperware container, as did a small amount of stewed potatoes loaded with black pepper. Leftovers were always saved and often found their way as snacks or supplements to other mealtimes.

Mindy had excused herself as soon as she had finished eating. She claimed she needed time to finish what she had called a copious amount of homework, but Leo and Dee suspected the young teen would be texting, messaging and using all the latest technology to catch up with her friends. Since she was in command of her grades and seemed to be socially well adjusted, her parents gave Mindy more latitude than they would have otherwise. Besides, they didn't hesitate to check up on their daughter every chance they got, and she knew it. That was enough of a threat for now to keep her honest.

"I talked to Levi today," Leo said as he speared one of the remaining potato chunks from the serving bowl and popped it into his mouth.

Dee raised an eyebrow and her dimples appeared along with a smile. She liked Leo's old law school classmate although she found some of his good ole country boy shtick a little too much.

"I bet that was a stimulating conversation. Did y'all play like you were on Walton's Mountain," she asked with a tint of sarcasm referring to the old TV series.

"Ha-ha, Wink made a funny," Leo replied addressing his wife with the pet name often used by him. "But, yeah, I guess we did," he finished.

They both laughed at the familiarity they shared. Humor had always been a major part of their relationship and either could always make the other giggle like a kid.

"He actually brought up a serious subject we need to discuss. You know what it is," said Leo.

The dialogue had actually begun on a trip to the Bahamas a few weeks before. A group of lawyers had approached Leo to ask him to run for District Attorney the day before the Berry family was going on a spring vacation. The timing was not great, and it caused Leo grief to finally talk with Dee on the last day they were enjoying themselves away from work issues. He had avoided bringing up the matter since.

Dee's smile turned upside down. She didn't seem pleased to have the topic of running for public office come up again. Leo knew her concerns from what she had voiced initially. Nothing about politics appealed to her in the first place, and the prospects of winning a contested election against an already established official were daunting.

"What about your job, Leo? Have you even talked to the Colonel about what he thinks? What if he won't let you have time off for campaigning? Do you think he'll let you stay if you lose?" she asked rapid fire.

She had a good point about his position as assistant solicitor-general and he knew it. His boss, Clay Johnson, was affectionately known as the Colonel. Leo respected the long-time elected misdemeanor prosecutor who liked Leo and gave him a great amount of leeway when it came to his job. Leo had, however, avoided talking to him about the prospect of running for D.A. because he was afraid of being perceived as disloyal, ungrateful, or something else equally negative.

Leo involuntarily dropped his head and stared at his empty dinner plate. He couldn't honestly answer his wife's line of questions, but he had resolved all doubts he had been going over in his head since beginning the thought process.

He raised his eyes and looked directly into the brown ones of the woman he had lived with for the last twenty years. They showed several emotions he recognized from those years together, but the one that shone through the most was love. There was not a doubt in his mind she would stand by whatever decision he made. If he committed to do this, Leo decided at that moment, he wouldn't let her down no matter what.

"Babe, I haven't talked to the Colonel, yet. I know I should have already, and I don't have a good excuse. I believe he'll support me, though. If not, I've got more than enough money left from what Papa left me to get us through," he said before pausing.

"I can't explain it other than to say I think it's what I should do. I've dreamed about it, and you know how I feel my dreams speak to me. At this moment in my life, in our lives, I'm as sure about the decision as any as I've ever made. I won't do it without your blessing, so what do you say?"

Leo reached across the table and placed his hand on Dee's. She appeared frozen in the moment and had a slight glaze on her face. The thought of making her distraught caused him instant regret. Just as he began to fret internally about what he'd said, the dimples he loved appeared again.

"Then we'll do it together," Dee said.

***

Leo lay still on his side of the bed with his thoughts jumping from one thing to another. The king bed's memory foam mattress would allow him to move around without waking his sleeping wife, but he tried to remain motionless in hope that slumber would overtake his way too active brain. He had always gotten by on less sleep than most people needed under the best of circumstances, and even less was necessary when there was a lot going on in his life. Leo would soon be taking on the monumental personal challenge of his first political campaign, and all the rest he could muster could only help him with that test.

Backers, people who would help him in the quest, had to be sought. He thought he better start by contacting as many of the local bar members as he could and try to secure their support. Many of them would probably not want to get involved because they would have to work with whomever was elected and wouldn't want to risk the ire of the winner if it was not Leo. The sitting D.A. was known to carry grudges and that alone could stifle backing by anyone other than the closest of Leo's lawyer friends.

Of course, he could count on his family, and the Berry name was fairly well known in the hometown. His father's heritage went back to the late 1800's and his mother's family had settled in Bibb County even earlier during that century. None of them had ever been involved in politics, but Leo didn't think that would hurt. There were a lot of folks lately feeling the need to throw all the bums out of whatever office they were holding. He thought the recent race for President was a case in point at least to some degree.

What do I know about running for office? The last time I ran for anything was in high school, and I got beat for senior class vice-president.

Leo smiled in the dark at the memory. He had been talked into the campaign by one of his friends, and a jock on the football team had won the election after invoking the spirit of the school's revered coach. It really hadn't mattered too much at the time to Leo because he had enough on his plate with other extra curricular activities.

His mind drifted back to those days, and Leo closed his eyes. They were good times and much simpler. He dreamed of them and then was led to his grandfather. The force belonging to Leo Berry, Sr. still held influence over the young prosecutor although he had been gone for almost three years. The wise old man's soul was strong and had never let him down, not even in death.

Papa, haven't seen you in awhile. How's Rusty?, referring to his grandfather's border collie Leo loved as a kid.

The apparition was real. There was a twinkle in those eyes that at first were without color but then became sky blue, as they had always been in life. Wrinkles appeared where a minute before had been a translucent yet smooth face. He puckered and whistled softly.

Leo listened intently and could hear a laughing pant in the mist behind his grandfather. There was a swirling of the air and the gentle huffing of a dog became clearer. The older man's face became as crystal clear as a high definition TV screen, and then his trusty pet was right beside him. His black and white coat looked brushed without any mats. The tongue hanging out of his grinning face looked as pink as cotton candy in the light of the dream.

He looks happy, Papa. I sure do miss you guys.

The old man looked down at his dog and then back at his grandson. For a moment his face seemed much younger, but changed when the stare moved.

We're both good, Leo. And, we miss you, too. We always keep up with you and the rest of the family.

Leo tossed in the bed and mumbled. If Dee had been awake, she would have known he was dreaming.

Papa, in case you haven't heard, I'm going to run for D.A. What do you think?

The hair on the older man changed from thinning silver-gray to thicker bushy brown and then back again. There was an enigmatic smile on his face that somehow remained the same.

Remember, son. Life is all about forks in the road and the choices you make when you come upon them. I have faith you'll decide the right one to take.

You're going to be fine.

CHAPTER EIGHT

Leo's morning had been the usual mishmash of shuffling paperwork and talking on the phone with people affected by the cases he handled. Keeping busy with the office routine had kept his mind from dwelling too much on all the preparation necessary for the upcoming campaign, but he had promised the Colonel when he informed his boss of the decision earlier in the morning that his job performance would not be compromised. He was more determined than ever to keep that vow.

He had been surprised by the Colonel's reaction, but not in a way he had originally anticipated. The moment had been filled with trepidation. Leo recalled the conversation that had taken place down the hall only a couple of hours before.

Colonel, I need a few minutes to talk with you about something.

The silver-haired man had looked up from the newspaper and his bushy brows arched upward forming a roofline across his lower forehead. There was a sparkle in his hazel eyes and a slight smile that caused Leo to wonder if the secret was already out.

Come on in and tell me what's on your mind.

Leo went into the office, pulled the closest of the wooden swivel chairs from the long conference table situated in front of

Clay Johnson's desk and plopped into the comfortable molded leather seat. There was a faint odor of lemon-scented polish emanating from the furniture that was probably nearly as old as the man in charge. He looked directly into the older man's gaze before clearing his throat and beginning.

Colonel, I think you know how much I appreciate what you've done for me. You more than anybody, started me down the path of what I love to do. I feel so fortunate to have had you as a mentor for over a decade. Now I want to take everything I've learned from working for you and try taking it to another level. I've decided to run for District Attorney.

Leo had paused and exhaled stronger than he intended. Perspiration formed at his hairline and in his palms as the Colonel continued to stare. Leo's discomfort escalated before Johnson responded.

Leo, I'd never hold you back from some career choice you make. But, would it make a difference if I told you I'm thinking about retiring?

His brain had raced as the new wrinkle in the best-laid plans had taken a turn. All of a sudden, there was an option for elected office not previously considered. Leo loved his workplace and the possibility of improving its operations appealed to him, but his boss had been a fixture in the job forever it seemed.

You're serious, Colonel? I didn't see that coming, especially this morning. I-I-I thought I was clear with my decision. But if you're saying your position is an option for me, I'd have to say I'd be interested. Thank you for letting me know.

They talked for a while longer as his boss told Leo of being tired after holding the office for the last forty years and that his health was failing as well. Since the election for both positions would be held at the same time and Leo had not announced his intentions publicly, it wouldn't require much in the way of thinking about the process of seeking the solicitor-general's position rather than district attorney.

Leo's mindset had shifted even further since the meeting with the Colonel and sifting the choices now presented. The more he thought about it, the more it made sense to seek the s-g's job. Prosecution of criminal cases was essentially the same to him, and he believed there was a better opportunity to make a difference in the community by remaining where he had been for the last several years. This was an opportunity Leo couldn't pass up.

Leo had ideas he wanted to implement that he would have power to do if he was in charge. He was sure by expanding alternative resolution of cases, streamlining operations and seeking more specialization of case prosecution, he could increase efficiency.

He could almost hear his deceased grandfather whispering in his ear. The beloved man, Big Leo, had always seemed to help him with life's choices as he grew up. Even though his Papa might be gone physically, the wise spirit of the man still appeared to Leo sometimes when needed.

Trust yourself, Leo. A fork in the road offers alternative ways to go, and whatever path you choose can be good if you make it so. You'll do fine either way. It's your choice.

The lawyer smiled to himself as the thought drifted through his brain. There really was no need to think about it further. Leo Berry the third was going to run for solicitor-general. And, he thought there was a good chance of winning the job. Maybe no one else would run against him when he announced his plans.

***

The workday was coming to an end as the clock read 5:25. Most of the staff had cut out as soon as the chimes sounded at five. Leo surveyed his desk and was pleased with the daily output. Piles of paper were in neater stacks than when the shift began, and the legal pad he had used for notes during the day was thumbed through exposing several ideas for the upcoming campaign. The last page staring back contained a list of people he had either already called and spoken with over the phone or had left messages for them to get back. He'd even decided the slogan would be, "Your choice."

He felt energized by the supporters already secured in a short period of time and was certain of gaining more in the days ahead. The first two friends he had talked with had readily agreed to be his campaign manager and treasurer. Russ Gunnels and Mark Stevenson hadn't shown any reluctance to accept the thankless jobs proving that friendships from school days were often times the best ones.

Leo had taken Russ's suggestion and a letter penned to each of the local bar members asking for their backing was ready for mailing. The prosecutor appreciated that his law school classmate was well respected by Macon lawyers and was confidant his name listed on the letterhead as the manager could only help in a contested election. His friend had also suggested that by contacting the bar as early as possible might have the effect of cutting off potential rivals.

Mark's position in the community as president of one of the local banks was also beyond reproach. He had been a friend of Leo's since high school and well respected for efforts to rehabilitate blighted areas of the city as well as for his support of the arts. With Mark's commitment to assist with Leo's campaign finances, Leo could breathe a sigh of relief in an area he found somewhat distasteful. Asking for money and keeping up with a checkbook didn't appeal to him at all, but the lawyer knew it was necessary to fund a countywide campaign.

The banker had also brought up ideas for raising contributions that appealed to Leo, one being a golf tournament. While the lawyer wasn't much of a player, he did enjoy the game and knew many guys who might sponsor such an event including his insurance agent. Leo had made a note to call How Lowbridge in the near future to see what he thought of the idea. That man loved a golf course more than just about anything other than a glass of merlot.

Leo was in deep thought and didn't see his colleague, Rob Scott, as he stepped into the younger prosecutor's office. When Leo felt another presence and looked up, the scowl on Rob's reddened face caused him to swallow involuntarily.

"You dirty asshole," Rob hissed through clenched teeth.

In the span of a few seconds before the conversation continued, Leo realized he should have let the senior assistant prosecutor know of his intentions before now. Not that it may have changed Rob's outlook of the situation, but there could have been more preparation for the brewing storm Leo could see coming.

"After spending all these years working here, you want to steal my chance. You wouldn't even have a job if it wasn't for me," continued Rob with a rising voice. "I ought to kick your ass, Berry."

Leo swallowed again at the anger shown. Rob was usually reserved in demeanor, and displays of anger were rarely seen.

"I should've let you know, Rob. It's been a pretty quick decision. Not anything I had planned when I came in this morning," Leo responded.

"You're so full of crap. I should've known you'd try to do something like this. You've been undercutting me for years. The Colonel's been grooming me for the position, not you. I don't get why you think you deserve the job anyway."

Rob's face had progressed to a darker shade of scarlet. He closed the space with two quick steps and now loomed over Leo's desk. There was a vein throbbing on the side of the older prosecutor's head that looked rather ominous to Leo.

"I'm truly sorry that you feel that way, and I can understand how you might be upset, Rob. I really feel like I messed up by not talking to you about my decision. It's an opportunity I can't pass up, and I think I've got a lot to offer. I guess I assumed we'd keep working together. I mean, if you want to run, too, we can still keep it going no matter who wins. There's no reason this can't be a friendly competition," said Leo pausing.

"I've got an idea, what do you say we go down to the Rookery? I'll buy you a beer, and we'll talk about it."

"That just proves how clueless you are, Berry. You really think I want to go anywhere with you, much less go drink a beer?" Rob shot back.

Rob backed a step away and looked back through the open door from Leo's workplace into the main office area. Leo had the impression his colleague was checking to see if anyone else was still there and had heard their exchange. Not knowing what was coming next, Leo stood and remained behind his desk.

"I don't know what in the hell makes you think you can win. You're nowhere near qualified as I am. You don't have my experience or community standing. You don't go to church, never served in the military, and you're way too liberal. I'll make sure the voters know the real Leo. I've earned this job, not you," continued Rob in a lower tone.

Leo was momentarily taken aback. He had never heard such an accusatory manner by someone he thought was a friend. They had always gotten along well together, and Leo had figured the friendship would continue even if there was a contested election between the two.

Trying to diffuse the tense situation, Leo smiled and responded, "Like Popeye, I yam what I yam."

Rob closed the distance to Leo and sneered. "Always a joke, Berry. That deprecating shit you try and pass as humor won't work on me. I don't think the voters will buy it either."

"What's going on?" asked a female voice from the doorway.

Standing in the location where Rob had been just the moment before was Paul Gregory, the chief probation officer for the court, along with Sandy Trimble, the other assistant solicitor-general. They were coworkers who shared a relationship outside the office.

"Ask Little Leo," Rob spat out as he spun on his heels and marched past Paul and Sandy.

The pair walked into the room with questioned looks on their faces. Leo sat down heavily and began stroking his close-cropped beard. It was a habit that he couldn't break and always appeared when he was troubled or in deep thought.

"This might be trickier than I thought," Leo said absently.

"So, I guess the gossip is true. Leo wants to be big boss," Sandy said to Paul.

"Good, now I don't have to void this check," he replied.

The well-built male accompanied by the diminutive female stepped to Leo's desk and placed a slip of paper before him. The prosecutor quit rubbing his face and glanced down. It was a personal check for two hundred and fifty dollars.

"I didn't know who to make it out to, so I left it blank. Just wanted you to know I will help any way I can. We need you to stay here, buddy," said Paul.

Leo felt something choking his ability to speak. The piece of paper made it all real in a new way he couldn't explain. It was his first campaign contribution. Emotions coursed through him as he circled the desk and grasped Paul's hand followed by an awkward man hug.

"Yeah, just remember you better win because I need to keep my job," interjected Sandy with raised eyebrows.

"Okay then. Let's play like Nike and 'Just Do It,'" said Leo with a grin.

"I just hope I don't split the office in two," he followed up with a frown.

CHAPTER NINE

The last two weeks had been blurred for candidate Leo. Having studied political science in college and having been involved in at least one other campaign for public office through helping a friend in his bid for a judgeship, the prosecutor had thought he had a grasp of what running might entail. It hadn't taken long at all for Leo to decide he had vastly underestimated the time such an effort took.

Meetings. Lots of them. Some had been fruitful with promises of support from friends. Some had been less so. One in particular had bothered him. It had occurred only two days after qualifying to run.

Qualifying to run. Now that was kind of a misnomer as far as Leo was concerned. Yeah, he had to meet residency and other requirements involving his legal experience, but really it just came down to paying some money. At least, that's how it felt to him when he had written the check amounting to three percent of the salary he would earn if he won the election. The guy who had taken his check said he hoped there would be multiple candidates so the party would score even more money. *What a jerk,* Leo had thought.

He had decided to qualify as a Democrat although he really thought of himself more as an independent. A couple of well-heeled Republicans had promised they could raise substantial funds to take care of his campaign needs if he chose their party, and it was appealing on that level. Local Democratic leaders made no such assurances, but the practical argument they made was that local voter turnout favored them. It had upset him to have to choose a party, but mainly because Leo felt affiliation should have nothing to do with the job he sought. It should be non-partisan, he thought.

Politics kept getting nastier on every level and the divisions caused conflicts that were difficult to work through. In the final analysis he had chosen the Dems because the community had historically been more associated with that party in countywide elections. He was hoping the opposition would think the same way and maybe the primary would determine the victor. Either way, some who would otherwise vote for him in the general election would be disenfranchised in the primary. Some folks were bound to be upset. It was a quandary that couldn't be avoided.

Then the meeting that still made him feel uncomfortable. Leo had been contacted by some of the local party leadership who promised to work with him in his quest for public office. All he had to do was to hire them as consultants. He had resisted the urge to run like hell from the restaurant where they had sat, and he had not given them an answer yet. There was just something unseemly about it, but he knew it would have to be addressed sooner rather than later. Leo wished that elements of the process didn't make him so queasy as he thought back.

***

We can't promise you'll win, but no candidate in a countywide race has done well without us, said the smooth-faced man who looked at least ten years younger than his age.

Leo sat across studying the faces of the three people sitting in a circular booth of the downtown country-style eatery. They were all folks popular in the black community. Since the Macon population was pretty evenly split, Leo knew he wanted and needed support from them in order to be elected.

You definitely need our help. Let's face it, Ronnie Brundage is gone get a lot of votes just 'cause how she looks. It don't matter who's more qualified, said the other male.

The candidate they were referring to didn't seem to be a serious threat to Leo. She was a relatively inexperienced lawyer only out of school a few years and had not shown much ability in the courtroom. Besides that, she rubbed most courthouse employees the wrong way by her use of condescending tones when speaking to them and by constantly referring to herself as Lawyer Brundage.

Yeah, and your buddy working with you is gonna take votes from you, too, added the third member of the entourage. She was the lone female with a big smile and bigger hair and seemed to love exaggerating the word buddy. Leo knew she didn't care for Rob whom Leo felt was his main competition.

Look, I respect what y'all are telling me, responded Leo. *But, ten thousand dollars is a lot of money and I just don't know what I would be getting for the expenditure.*

You'll get instant credibility, Leo. Our endorsements include others besides us. You'll get prime locations for any signs you want to display, and we'll even make sure they're in secure spots. Our folks will put them out for you. We'll run ads in our newsletter with our pictures right beside yours and right before early voting starts and the primary election is held. Our folks will light up social media like a Christmas tree. We'll also print sample ballots that show your name as the candidate being endorsed, and they'll be placed strategically, answered the younger man.

I'll need to run this by my committee. I can't commit that much money at the moment, Leo had replied.

Don't let this opportunity get away, Leo. We feel like you're the best candidate and just want to help Macon-Bibb get the best man for the job, added the woman with another big smile.

Leo had left shortly afterward with a sick stomach and a conflicted brain. He wanted the job badly, but was this the way to achieve it? Leo knew a contested election cost money, but he didn't even have that much in the account at the moment.

Although he didn't want to, something told him it would be necessary. Leo would have to step up efforts to raise money and might have to loan the campaign more of his personal funds. As distasteful as the meeting had been, a valuable lesson had been taught.

Nobody said this would be easy, he thought.

***

Leo was trying not to cause Dee any more emotional distress than she had expressed when he first made the decision, but could tell his efforts were not quite working in that regard. She already had a tired look around those brown eyes that Leo adored, and her dimpled smile had not been present as much. Any time he spent outside their home working on the campaign couldn't help but add to what she had to deal with alone in the household.

These deep thoughts permeated his brain while Leo sat in the faux leather chair of their small home office early on a Saturday morning. He stroked the stubble on his face and hoped it would all work out for the best. His philosophy of life dictated such.

Leo's cell phone vibrated in silent mode against the wooden desk breaking his train of thought. Tiki, the Jack Russell, raised his head from the carpeted floor and looked at his master as it buzzed for the second time.

You gonna answer that? Can't you see I'm trying to sleep here? He seemed to say with his expression.

Leo smiled down at the family pet and looked at the phone. It was Jimbo.

This can't be good, can it? He's never called me on a weekend.

Finally answering on the third vibration, Leo croaked, "Hello."

"There's been another one. If you've got time for a cup of coffee this morning, I'll fill you in. Waffle House on Riverside in thirty minutes?" asked Detective Barbour in somber tones.

"Damn. Okay, Jimbo. See you then," replied Leo disconnecting the call.

Tiki cocked his head with a questioned expression. Leo shook his own and frowned.

"I'll have to take you out later, sport. Duty calls."

The dog immediately laid his head back down on the carpet and closed his eyes. Resignation shown only made Leo feel more uncomfortable as he got up from his chair.

Oh well, at least I'll get a break from politics for a while, he thought.

CHAPTER TEN

Morgan Thomas stood in the shower and let the dual heads do their work. One above provided pulsating pleasure to his face and upper body. The waist-high nozzle delivered constant warm water soothing of his flaccid but satisfied member. The bathing was part of the ritual that he reveled in after a conquest.

When he removed himself from the steamy bath after a full twenty minutes of water therapy, Morgan's smooth skin was flushed pink from head to toe. As he dried off with an over-sized towel made of Egyptian cotton, he gazed at his physique in a mirrored wall. It revealed perfection.

No body hair was visible except for well-plucked eyebrows and fine eyelashes. He was lucky not to have much thanks to genetics, but what he had was shaved at least three or four times a week. The last time had just occurred before he had gone out the evening before. He despised stubble. The lack of hair only accentuated his sinewy form.

Man-child.

That's what he thought of whenever he admired himself. As he turned to another angle and flexed muscles in his buttocks, not an ounce of fat was noticeable. A faint smile appeared as he remembered thrusting the area just a few hours before.

Wasn't she lucky?

Morgan wrapped the towel around his waist and went into an elongated walk-in closet just off the bathroom. His OCD was apparent in the organization of clothing, shoes, and other accessories contained within. Custom made racks and shelving provided places for each, and all were separated into respective colors and styles. The most interesting feature of the closet was a ledge that contained several Styrofoam heads with wigs sitting on them.

He had started collecting them over ten years ago when he still had more than enough hair to comb. The brown crown was thinning back then though, and a chance trip to a store in Atlanta led to the first purchase. Not because he was vain about that kind of thing, it was because he felt like somebody else when he slipped into one. Since that first experience, the headpieces had become important for other reasons. Disguises for his shaved dome was his thinking.

There were also masks of various styles that he often used. Some were partial and only covered the upper half of his face. Some were tight-fitting material that fit like women's hosiery and further made it impossible to make out the features of his face. Some provided complete darkness for the objects of his affection. He would sometimes slip those over their eyes. All of the coverings had been tested over time and he was sure kept his identity secure from detection.

Glancing around the room, Morgan admired the orderliness of it all. The only item out of place was the supply bag that was used to carry supplies he needed when on a hunt. He had dropped it on the floor beneath the hair hats before his shower. Reaching into the bag, he pulled out one of his favorite coverings and placed it on the only open resting place. He then straightened the hair and pulled it snuggly on to the eyeless head shaped form that served as a private storage.

He grabbed a pair of gray sweat shorts off a shelf that contained several others of various colors, and a plain white tee shirt from another that was neatly folded. Picking up his bag with his free hand, Morgan then left the closet and went into an equally tidy bedroom adjacent to the bathroom suite.

After depositing the bag on the foot of the bed, Morgan watched himself in a full-length mirror located in the corner of the room as he unfastened the towel from his waist. The fascination he felt whenever looking at his naked body sometimes caused him to lose time, but now he didn't melt into the reflection. He slipped into the soft cotton clothing and then began to inventory the bag's contents.

It didn't register at first. Then a fact hit him hard as a brick as he shuffled through everything inside. The beginning of panic seeped into his brain, and it led to dumping the stash onto the bedspread.

Among the usual objects there was only one used glove instead of two. This caused instant reflection of the night before and the realization that he must have left it behind.

Damn it!

CHAPTER ELEVEN

Leo sat in a typical Waffle House booth sipping hot coffee. His butt and back felt comfortably molded in the seat as he scanned the restaurant. An eclectic cast of characters had joined him at the iconic eatery on an early spring morning in the south. It included a couple of Georgia Power workers seated at the short bar across from the grill dressed in recognizable uniforms completed by their hardhats. Other patrons in a corner stall appeared still dressed from the previous night on the town with at least one of them looking a little bleary-eyed.

That's right, soak up that alcohol, thought Leo.

He recognized a female realtor in one of the smaller cubicles enjoying a waffle dripping in syrup and sitting with whom he imagined to be a client. That person must've been especially hungry because there was so much food in front of her; there was barely enough room for it on the table top. It had to be one of those *All-Star* breakfasts. As that lady shoveled in a forkful of potatoes the restaurant was famous for, the sales associate smiled and gave a wave to Leo. He returned her smile and gave a slight shake of his head to indicate his acknowledgment of the food consumption, which brought an even broader grin.

Nearby the women, Leo also saw his automobile insurance agent, Howard Lowbridge, hunched over a copy of *The Telegraph* working on the daily crossword puzzle. His half-reading glasses were perched on the end of his nose as he scribbled words in the blocks. He never looked up when his server brought an order of dry wheat toast with two poached eggs on top. How, as friends and family knew him, only grunted thanks while he finished the task at hand. Since he was dressed in golf attire, Leo figured the agent had a tee time later that morning. It reminded him that he needed to check with his agent about an upcoming fundraiser golf tournament that had been planned.

The waitresses dressed in standard garb including paper hats scurried around the tables taking orders and then calling them to the cook using their jargon. The words made perfect sense to them, but it didn't necessarily to the customers.

"Pull one bacon. Pull two sausage. Drop three hashbrowns, one in a ring. Mark order scrambled plate, covered and chunked. Mark single OL, waffle. Mark order triple scrambled, hold grits."

Leo took another sip from his sturdy ceramic mug while continuing to look around the noisy rectangular facility. He had been coming to such places since he was a kid, and it amazed him the chain was so prolific now. It seemed there was one on every corner, and he knew of at least three others within a five-mile radius. Leo bet every one of them were full at this very moment.

He saw an unmarked Ford pull in front of the establishment. Jimbo got out and walked with a hitch across the parking lot. He came inside rubbing his head, and the old detective's face was inscrutable as he slumped into the seat across from Leo.

"I'm getting too old for this shit."

"Good morning to you as well, Jimbo," replied Leo.

"Well, if it ain't Detective Barbour," said the waitress as she stepped to their booth and set down a steaming cup of black coffee in front of the policeman. "You two want to get some food?"

"I forgot my antacid, Iris. I'll think about it when I finish my first cup," replied Jimbo.

The waitress broke out a toothy chortle and saluted the detective with the decanter in her right hand, "Yeah, man. This'll help your reflux alright. What don't kill ya makes ya stronger, ain't that what they say?"

"I guess so, I'm still kicking around this town and coming here regularly for your counsel and assorted medical advice."

This deadpanned response from Jimbo resulted in a cackle that caused a momentary hush from others inside the restaurant. Leo felt eyes on them, and he was a little embarrassed by the attention. Jimbo's crooked smirk proved he felt nothing like that.

"Ms. Iris, I would like a couple of soft scrambled eggs with cheese grits and a waffle. No meat or toast, please," Leo interjected when the laughter subsided.

She smiled sweetly at Leo and then called in his order. Iris walked away as Jimbo turned his attention to the prosecutor. The expression he bore remained unreadable.

"Maybe you should recommend your dentist to Iris," began Jimbo. After a second, he continued, "This is off the record, Leo. You're not on this case and I shouldn't even be telling you about this," said the detective.

Leo let out a soft chuckle, then gazed into Jimbo's greenish-gray eyes and tried to read the expression. What he saw caused mini-shivers unrelated to any needed dental work.

"There was an attack on another woman last night. We might have some evidence this time."

The detective took a sip and then glanced around the room. How made eye contact, and the two men nodded at each other. It was a familiar yet subtle salute that Leo felt while watching both.

"You know Howard?" asked Leo.

"We went to Lanier together. Back when the public schools were a lot better. Long time ago," replied Jimbo with a faint smile.

"Ancient history, before I was even born," said Leo laughing.

"Yeah, so was Nam."

"You served in Viet Nam?"

"As you said, before your time, Mr. Assistant Solicitor-General."

Leo paused and didn't want to seem insensitive. He had never served in the military but had a strong affinity to those who had. A lot of his respect was due to his late grandfather being a World War II hero.

"Hey, didn't mean to offend. I appreciate your service, Jimbo."

"No offense taken, Leo. How and I go back a ways is all. Similar backgrounds, you know."

"Okay, I get it. I like Howard, too. He's been my insurance agent for years and he's even helping a little with my campaign. Just tell me what you can about the new case," said Leo trying to get back to the subject.

Jimbo nodded and responded, "Call came in this morning before dawn. Female victim lives in an older home not too far from here. She's close in age to your wife's friend who was attacked a couple of months ago. Lot of similarities regarding the M.O. such as the guy followed into her house after she had gone out and then went to extremes cleansing the scene before he left. He made a mistake this time, though. He dropped one of the gloves he used. Fell under the corner of the bed," Jimbo recited before stopping to take a sip from his mug.

"How does the recovery of the glove help? I would think that's the reason he wears them. Keeps from leaving finger prints, right?"

"Sure, that's why he uses them. But, it's not always true that prints are prevented when they're worn. In this case, at least to the naked eye that hasn't been confirmed by the crime lab yet, it looks like there was a partial print on the inside of the found glove. I'm guessing here, but I'm betting he must've touched something that was greasy with some kind of residue before he put on the glove that transferred from his finger."

As Leo processed the information Jimbo provided, the waitress returned with his food. She handed it across the divide warning the plate might be hot. Leo's stomach grumbled in anticipation.

"You're still young enough not to need a purple pill or something before you eat that counselor?" Jimbo asked with his patented crooked smile.

"I'm getting there, Detective. Over forty doesn't seem so young to me, and my gut's not like it was when I was a teenager. Let's just say, I don't eat this way every day. So, when will you know if there's a match to any print?"

Jimbo's cat eyes locked onto the younger man's blue ones as he responded, "Hard to say. Crime lab's overworked and understaffed. We'll make a special request to speed things up, but it ain't like we're talking about a murder. They probably won't look at the case as a priority. I'm going to push it as a serial rape, but the fact of the matter at this point is this may be a second confirmed case. We got nothing to go on from the first complaint except for the mode of operation, M.O., you know."

Leo attacked the food on his plate as he listened to Jimbo. He had always been a fast eater and couldn't correct the routine no matter how hard he tried.

"Damn, buddy. You think I'm going to try and steal your breakfast?"

Leo smiled self-consciously and backed from his plate. He took a sip of water and swished the liquid in his mouth in an effort to dislodge grits that he knew had deposited between his teeth. He followed up by using the fingernail of his little finger.

"Sorry, bad habits die hard. Goes all the way back to childhood competition with my brothers at the dinner table. So, you're saying we very well might have a rapist on the loose who could attack again without warning, and we can't do anything about it? How about letting the press know so they can alert women in the community?"

"Well, I don't think I'd go that far, yet. We've got to be careful what information we make public. We don't want to cause a panic. We're still looking at possible connections to known past attacks. There's nothing confirmed at this point although there have been incidents over the years that were not thoroughly investigated. My gut tells me he's done this before. He's way too polished in his approach."

Leo cut a piece of the waffle with his fork and stuck it in his mouth. While chewing he asked, "You've been checking old reports and haven't found anything? I've got to imagine this guy has been doing this awhile also. What else do you think?"

"I think we're thinking alike, okay? I don't know whether there have been other vics who've not reported attacks for whatever reason, or if maybe the reports that have been made in the past weren't taken seriously because of lack of evidence. This guy is smart, but I'm still looking, Leo. I'll find him."

Jimbo slurped the last remaining drops of his beverage, set down the cup and then ran his hand through his thinning hair. He removed a couple of ones from his wallet and dropped them on the table.

"Speaking of which, I've got to get out of here. Places to go, people to see," he said as he slid out of his seat.

"I really appreciate the heads-up, Jimbo. I know you don't have to keep me informed like this. Go get the bastard," replied Leo.

The detective nodded and gave a half-smile before turning toward the door. Leo watched him leave and hoped what they said would happen sooner than later.

CHAPTER TWELVE

Detective Jimmy Barbour sat at the antiquated metallic structure as he had countless times before. It was more than an old beat up desk, though. It represented order. Somewhere he could come back to and figure reason out of chaos.

He wondered just how many cases he had cleared sitting in the worn leather chair where his tired ass rested. Thousands, probably.

Those didn't give him as much pleasure as they once did. There was always the next one to solve. And there were also the few he never had been able to shut the door on. He suspected at least a couple of those would plague him to his grave.

Jimbo wasn't thinking about those aggravations right now. The latest blip on the radar was what he was focused on. Some weirdo was out there in his city raping defenseless women.

When he was younger, the detective would pour over reports, talk to witnesses and use contacts on the streets to figure out what tact to take in order to get a just result. That kind of resolution only came by arresting a guilty offender.

Now that he was older, nothing had really changed about his tactics. Old-fashioned police work was what he believed in. His time was coming to a close, however. Retirement loomed on the horizon, and he both looked forward to the event while dreading it at the same time.

Nearly fifty years in his chosen line of work, and he felt the time spent was taking its toll on his mind and body. His second, and much younger wife, had been encouraging him to let it all go since before consolidation of the city and county governments occurred three years ago. That event had only made him feel more like a dinosaur by having to answer to an elected sheriff rather than to an appointed police chief, as one more level of office politics had been introduced into his life.

Politics. Just can't get away from that crapola no matter what you do.

The thought made him think of his younger friend, Leo and other family connections. He couldn't help look at the prosecutor kind of like a nephew who was little more than a kid, notwithstanding Berry was now in his forties and didn't share genetic links.

Jimbo had watched "Little Leo," as he was known in the Berry clan, grow up for the last twenty years and had helped him whenever possible. Part of that had been because of the kid's grandfather having asked Jimbo to do that when the grandson started a law practice. Back then, assistance consisted mainly to referring potential clients he encountered because of the law enforcement job. But, it also had included practical advice and inside information that had proven invaluable to the young lawyer's ability to develop skills allowing him to be successful first as a defense lawyer and now as a respected prosecutor.

It was from this history and from being around the judicial system for so long that caused him to hope the younger friend would win the election Leo was now embroiled in. He rarely had given a good shit about anything resembling supporting a candidate for an elective office, but it seemed a worthy effort this time. Jimbo had even committed to placing a few yard signs in spots he had access to showing support, something he had never done and would probably never do again.

There are only two things I want to do right now. Find the sick bastard who raped those women, and help Leo win.

Jimbo smiled. Retirement could wait for those two events. He had enough confidence both occurrences would happen sooner than later.

He opened the file folder before him and shuffled the contents. This latest attack bugged him even more than the previous one, if that was possible. First, there was the difference in how the victim had been stalked. A nightclub and a grocery store had been the last places the two victims had visited before their attacks. Absolutely nothing similar about the two places, he noted.

Jimbo had gone to the chain supermarket where victim number two had shopped just prior to her rape and gotten copies of the video surveillance tapes. He had already studied them three times. It was easy to find the diminutive good-looking blonde wearing red leggings and an over-sized sweater as she strolled through the produce department.

As the detective watched her travail to the meat counter, down the snack aisle, by the bread counter, and along the canned vegetables, he was unable to find a single male customer paying undue attention to her shopping. There was one older guy pushing a cart for his portly wife who made Jimbo chuckle as he checked out the younger woman's rear-end when she bent down to look at something on the bottom shelf of the cleaning section, but that was about it.

He decided to look one more time and tried to find anyone showing up in multiple scenes. His tired red-rimmed eyes scanned from side to side and only saw women of various shapes and sizes along with a couple of seemingly uninterested men contained within multiple frames near the victim. The store didn't seem particularly busy at that hour which helped the detective study the other patrons.

When the woman got to the self-checkout area and began scanning her items, no other customers were near the remaining stations. As she leisurely placed goods in hanging plastic bags, Jimbo watched as another larger female drably dressed in a loose fitting sweat suit and tennis shoes took position at an adjacent counter.

Jimbo froze the frame to better study the other customer. For some reason, the woman's appearance rang a bell in his brain. Her long dark trusses blocked most of her face so he couldn't get a full view.

Starting the video again, Jimbo watched intently while paying more attention to Ms. Dowdy, as he began to think of the other customer. She only had a few items in the cart she used. They were all cleaning items including a double roll of paper towels, a large orange sponge and a spray bottle of Lysol.

She fished out a folded wallet from a shabby cloth bag, extracted a couple of bills and stuck them into the machine. Ms.

Dowdy evidently didn't have a Kroger customer discount card, which struck Jimbo as odd. Nearly all frequent fliers used those especially when they appeared to need all the financial incentives that were available.

As she collected her purchases, and put the small plastic hand-held basket underneath the station, Ms. Dowdy's profile came better into view. She stole a glance toward the victim and Jimbo froze the frame.

The long hair was parted on the side, but no scalp could be seen. Bangs covered the forehead and the nondescript face didn't appear to have any makeup or lipstick. The gym top was zipped almost to the top, but Jimbo could see the throat revealing an Adam's apple not looking very female.

"It's a guy," said the detective out loud.

Jimbo studied long and hard trying to find anything resembling an ID bracelet on the man in drag, but couldn't see one. It was a letdown as he thought this might be a common suspect.

He started the video again and watched Ms. Dowdy exit the automatic sliding glass doors of the grocery store. A minute or two later, the victim went out the same way.

Jimbo switched screens to access the parking lot. He was able to spot the victim, but the other source of his interest couldn't be found. He watched as she unloaded her groceries into her vehicle and then drove off. Then in the distance a dark sedan parked near one unburning light followed a discrete distance behind.

Maybe a break, he thought.

CHAPTER THIRTEEN

Leo admired the surroundings while sitting in his two-year old ES model Lexus he called Pearl because of its shimmery exterior white shell. The car had been the only luxury he had allowed himself from the inheritance his grandfather left him. It fit in nicely at the country club where he was now parked.

The homes on the drive to the clubhouse were all at least two-story dwellings of brick, stone, and stucco with no vinyl siding in sight. The impeccably manicured lawns were weed-free which reminded the young prosecutor he needed to dig up the dandelions in his yard before they proliferated beyond control. The accompanying shrubbery and trees were symmetrically placed so that the houses were framed with wood and colors.

Leo thought you couldn't want a more beautiful spring morning in middle Georgia. There were a few puffy white clouds exploding against a light blue sky. Buds were popping everywhere and even the pines seemed a more vibrant green than normal. In another month the humidity would be stifling and make the body sticky by this time of the morning, but that was not true today. The only downside was the lime green pollen that would settle on the car by day's end.

Looking toward the driving range, Leo spotted golf carts arranged in a row around a circular concrete area. There appeared to be at least thirty or maybe even forty of the vehicles, some with clubs already in place on the backs of the battery operated transports.

The more, the merrier, thought Leo.

Lots of golfers meant a successful tournament and a few bucks added to the campaign account. The sponsors of the event had assured him that he could count on a few thousand dollars. Since everything about running the campaign cost a lot more than he ever thought, the expected money would certainly help.

Leo was not a very accomplished player of the sport. He liked participating, but had not played a lot of rounds. It was not because he didn't like golf. It was because he had chosen softball over other activities up until recently, and he was afraid his bat swing would be affected if golf took over. Also, hitting the little round ball cost more money, and whether true or not, it seemed somehow associated with a class of people he felt above his pay grade. At least, that's what he told himself until now.

He had recently decided that may not be the case and that the game might be something that could become more enticing in the future. Now that eyeglasses had become a necessity, softball had been relegated to one of those things that he "used to do." Hand/eye coordination was just too screwed up to maintain at the level Leo expected to compete, and he had barely escaped serious injury a couple of times.

Since sports had always been important, Leo had started by taking a few lessons from a local pro after his brother Eddie gave him a set of clubs. Now he felt at least not embarrassed to get in a round on occasion. He really hadn't found a group to play with on a regular basis, yet, but there were some guys wanting him to join them on Saturdays, and he was at least thinking about it.

Today, he was set to ride in a cart with his long-time insurance agent, Howard Lowbridge. Leo had never played golf with him, but had liked the guy for a number of years finding him professional and committed to his protection needs. He had been grateful when the older man had offered to help in Leo's bid for office, and was flattered when Howard asked to play in the tournament with him. It would be the first chance to get to know one another in a more relaxed setting.

'How', as his friends called him, was somewhat of an enigma to Leo. He had come from humble beginnings as an early resident of one of the local mill villages. He seemed polished, but Leo knew the guy had once ridden a Harley. He looked fit, but Leo remembered there was a time when the agent had weighed well over three hundred pounds. There had been several occasions when Leo saw him feverishly working on crossword puzzles, so he knew lots of words. Leo had also, however, heard him cuss like a sailor, which the lawyer had been taught, meant the opposite. As How would often say, "Profanity shows the limit of your vocabulary, but no better phrase describes disgust than '*damn it, man.* '"

Leo spotted his partner for the day getting out of a mammoth SUV and watched as the well-tanned shaved head ducked into the rear and retrieved his clubs. They looked worn and ancient compared to the ones Leo had in the trunk of his car.

As How began to lug them toward the carts, Leo popped the release so he could grab his and hurried across the lot in order to catch the Telly Savalas as *Kojak* lookalike. All he needed to make the look anymore similar was a lollypop stuck in his mouth.

"Howard, wait up."

Lowbridge turned around and gave a big grin. He set his bag down and waited on Leo to catch up.

"Counselor, you made it. Ready to make some money?" he asked as they shook hands.

Leo couldn't help but grin, too. The expression on Howard's face, the beautiful morning, and the fact he was away from every bit of stress that had recently consumed his soul made the lawyer feel all was well.

"You know it. I hope I don't embarrass you too much with how badly I play this game."

"Don't worry, it's all good. It's all about you today. Usually, it's about me," Lowbridge replied with a sly smile as they finished the handshake.

The two men walked to the carts and began looking for the one assigned to them. When they found it, How frowned as he looked at the scorecard.

"Damn it, man! We're starting on sixteen."

Leo was not familiar with the course and didn't know what that might mean. One thing though, he wasn't a good enough player to feel comfortable with a regular not being pleased with the starting point. A shotgun start meant they would be starting somewhere other than the first of eighteen holes, and How knew the course a hell of lot better than him.

"You're scaring me. Is that a hard hole?" asked Leo.

"Par three. Across the water. Usually about 110-120 yards. Practice a shot like that when we get to the range," How replied with a scowl.

It sounded like maybe an eight or nine iron shot to Leo. He already felt nervous based on his partner's reaction. Anything involving water in play made his palms sweat.

"Sorry, I didn't mean to sound negative, Leo. Today is about having some fun and raising some money for the cause. It's a four-man scramble anyway, and I'm sure somebody on our team will make it on the green."

"Who else is playing with us?"

"A couple of lawyers you know, Ollie Tucker and Buddy Faulk. They specifically asked me to try and get us together."

Leo smiled when he heard the names. Tucker and Faulk had practiced law in Macon for a lot longer than he, and they were good guys. He had handled cases with each of them on several occasions without incident. Leo couldn't say the same about all the other attorneys he knew.

"I'll gladly be the 'D' player with y'all. Thanks for helping put this together, Howard. After the stress of the last few weeks, this'll be a welcome diversion."

The scramble format of the tournament allowed A, B, C and D players in foursomes with A's being the lowest handicaps and D's the highest. They would all hit shots off the tees and then each of the players would be allowed to play the best shot of any of the four through the greens.

The two placed their clubs on the assigned cart. Leo thought it was a good sign that it was his and Dee's lucky number eleven.

"I'll drive," said How as he cinched the strap around his bag and then paused. Looking at Leo with an arched brow, he continued, "The course has had a little rain during the last week, and some holes may be cart path only or at least restricted to the ninety-degree rule. I don't know if there will be a marshal on the course, and my philosophy is that it's better to ask for forgiveness than permission. Just in case I need to take a shortcut."

Leo's eyebrows arched slightly as he thought about a car dealer he had ridden with a couple of rounds who would ride up to the green, over tee boxes, through all sorts of hazards while never missing a crevice much to the chagrin of the lawyer's back. He hoped How wasn't going to be that kind of operator.

"Don't look so concerned. I'll be careful because that's what I do. Besides, I've got good insurance," said How with a toothy grin. "You want to grab some breakfast before we hit a few? We've still got an hour before the tournament and there's a buffet set up in the clubhouse."

"I could eat," replied Leo.

They strolled to the front entrance while chatting about the upcoming primary. How asked why Leo was running as a Democrat and expressed worries that would hurt his chances of being elected. Leo explained that the job had been set up that way since the office was created in the nineteen-thirties, and that he truly felt the job should be non-partisan.

"I agree with that, but I've got to be honest, Leo. I relate more to Republicans, and a lot of my friends do, too. You probably saw my 'Make America Great Again' sticker on my car even though it's a little faded now. I want to help you as much as I can since you're a valued policy holder, and I think you're the best for the job, but I'll probably be voting in the other primary."

Leo had heard this line from more than a few people already and repeated what he had said before. It wouldn't change a lot of minds of those thinking that way, but it was what he believed.

"I respect your opinion, How. I'd never ask anyone to vote against his or her convictions. I'm trying not to get involved personally in the national or state races. I'll just say, local elections often mean more than folks realize. They're the ones most likely to impact you when it comes down to it. You're not going to call the President or the Governor when you have a theft in your business, or your kid gets in trouble for some stupid reason, or when you get a speeding ticket and want some help if possible," Leo said and paused.

"I chose to run as a Democrat for a couple of practical reasons. One, the voting citizens of Macon/Bibb historically turn out more in that primary, and two, very rarely has a Republican won an office county-wide. Both of my opponents are running as Dems, maybe for some of the same reasons. If I can win the primary without having to extend it to November, that would be ideal. Not trying to sound braggadocios, to quote my mother-in-law, but I expect to win. And when I do, I'm going to try and get our legislative delegation to fix it so the voters don't have to choose primaries for jobs such as what I'm running for. Political parties should have no voice in the judicial process, in my opinion. The law is the law. I'll prosecute cases without favor or affection to someone's political affiliations. The main thing I want to say today is, I'm very grateful for your support."

"Noble, and practical, I guess," said How holding the front door open for Leo. "I hope it works out for you."

They walked into an open room decorated decidedly from a male standpoint. A wide brick fireplace faced them and a circular bar containing swivel stools was to the right. There were at least twenty round wooden tables and accompanying chairs located in the large room.

On the opposite wall from the fireplace, there were long foldout tables bearing several aluminum food trays. Men, of all shapes and sizes, decked out in colorful shirts emblazoned with swooshes, pumas, and other animals, stood before the open steaming containers while loading plates with biscuits, eggs, grits, potatoes, bacon, sausage and fluffy homemade pancakes, a specialty of Ms. Florene, the club's cook.

"That's the thing about some of these old farts," deadpanned How. "Feed 'em some fat and cholesterol and they're happy to pay a hundred bucks a piece to play golf."

Leo followed like a puppy as How made his way through the crowd of men. He was adept as Don Rickles at making jokes and throwing out one-liners.

"Hey, hairlip," he threw at a white-haired guy with even a whiter colored moustache. "Where's your partner, Richard Cranium?"

"Close your mouth, you'll look smarter," he called to another.

"Wipe your mouth, you look like a porn star," he sneered to yet another guy.

"Damn, I thought those were out of bound stakes when I saw those white legs," he said to a skinny guy without a tan who was wearing dark colored shorts.

"Well, what do you know? If it's not assholes number one and two," he spoke to a couple of portly fellows talking to one another near the food. One of them gave him the finger. The other one blew How a kiss.

Different pronunciations of his name were used to address How. Some sounded like they were calling him Harrod. One guy dressed in green from head to toe referred to him by saying, "How now, brown cow."

All he spoke to acknowledged his remarks with equal insults. Leo couldn't help but be amused at the repartee. It sort of reminded him of some conversations he had heard when in the locker room at the now defunct Macon Health Club.

"Man, with friends like these, I'm glad I'm not your enemy," said Leo.

Lowbridge laughed and kept moving through the group. It was obvious he was enjoying himself. "What did I say? Was I thinking out loud again?"

"Who's your ringer this time, How-weird?" asked a guy with his shirt straining to stay tucked into his ill-fitting plaid pants. He was standing alongside a much thinner man that made the overweight guy look even bigger.

"Oh, if it ain't the professor. Wally, let me introduce you to Leo Berry. He's the candidate we're supporting today," said How. "Leo, this is Dr. Wally Davis. Don't let his appearance fool you, he's smarter than he looks. His claim to fame is that he went to school with Dr. Phil. That, and his unique putting style. His colleague is Flip Dent, but everybody calls him Scratchin."

Leo tried to keep his face from reddening as he shook the other two men's hands. "Glad to meet you, Dr. Davis and Mr. Dent."

"Don't let How-weird embarrass you too much today, counselor. When he gets into his Fireball, he'll probably loosen up a bit," replied Davis.

"Uh, huh," nodded Flip.

The prosecutor was at a loss for words and it showed. How, Flip and Wally were laughing heartily, and he wasn't sure what they were talking about.

"Medicinal purposes for essential tremors," was all How said about the subject.

The next hour went by quickly as Leo met several more of How's friends and fellow members of the club. All of the men were friendly toward him and seemed to share the same sort of humor. Leo also saw several friends from the local bar association and thanked them for their support by participating.

After breakfast, How and Leo went to the driving range and hit some balls. Leo felt marginally better after making some shots that approached what he was aiming for. He hoped he could replicate them during the round and not the chunks and blades that he had also made during practice.

When they got back to the gathering point, the club pro made a few announcements about the local rules while encouraging the participants to stay up with the group ahead of them. Leo had a hard time hearing the announcements that no one else seemed to care about. The carts debarked from the starting area with many of the group talking smack to one another.

"Hope you play well and come in second," was heard several times.

As they got to the sixteenth tee box, Leo saw why How had shown displeasure about starting with that hole. There was nothing but water between where they stood and the green. The pin was closer to the front edge, which made the shot even more precarious if you were going for it.

The other golf cart containing their two partners, Ollie and Buddy, had already arrived by the time Leo and How got there. Ollie was resplendent in a Mercer orange shirt and black shorts that accentuated his flowing silver hair and olive complexion. Buddy was more unkempt, but sported a lop-sided smirk that was infectious.

"The man of the hour, and Mr. Personality driving the cart, as usual," spoke Buddy with his customary lisp. He seemed to find everything funny and it showed.

"Everybody likes a little ass, but nobody likes a smart ass," replied How.

"Hey, Buddy, or should I call you Your Honor. Haven't seen you in awhile, since you were appointed as judge. Man, I really appreciate you guys letting this hacker play with you today, almost as much as helping me raise a little campaign money," said Leo as he reached for Buddy's hand.

"Call it our civic duty," said Ollie as he walked up. "We need you in the job. Just don't let How sling you out of the cart today."

Leo shook Ollie's hand after Buddy's. He was a guy Leo liked not only for his abilities in the courtroom, but as a lawyer with a quiet confidence. Someone who had been successful without advertising and making smarmy claims on television, Oliver Tucker was somebody the younger prosecutor admired as a role model for their chosen profession. He had also had an unfortunate run-in with somebody wanting to do harm, and Leo could relate to those circumstances. Neither referenced those events today.

The four separated, and How got out his range finder. His right hand shook slightly as he shot the distance to the flag. "One-O-Nine," he pronounced. "Uh, I might need some medicine."

Leo saw Ollie and Buddy both grab wedges as How first got a pint of Fireball out of his bag and then poured some in a Styrofoam cup. He took a swig and then took out a club that the lawyer wasn't sure what it was.

Leo was amazed at how quickly How's tremors abated and then mentally debated between his eight and nine irons before settling on the nine. He was sure he would need something longer than these regular golfers used.

"You're the guest and it's your honor," said Ollie to Leo.

The prosecutor was tenser than he was when he first addressed a jury. He took a few practice swings before addressing the ball he had placed a little higher than normal on a short wooden tee. He tried to keep repeating in his head, *Kiss it, Leo. Keep it slow stupid. K-I-S-S.*

As he took the club back and struck the Bridgestone golf ball, he breathed a sigh of relief as his usual fade caused the shot to make it over the water, but to the rough right of the green and in front of a bunker full of white sand. He was probably forty feet from the pin, but at least he was dry.

"Alright, Leo. Good start, youngster," said Ollie nodding to the prosecutor.

"No hill for a climber," chimed Buddy.

"L.B." added How in an exaggerated whisper. "Only shot you had."

Leo grinned and stooped to get the tee. He didn't ask what How meant as all the guys were laughing at the remark. He figured it meant his initials and maybe it would become clear why it was so funny at some point during the game.

The shots of the other three all landed on the green with Buddy's being the closest. From Leo's view, it looked to be less than three feet from the hole.

They congratulated each other and climbed into their carts for the ride around the lake and to the green. Ollie told Buddy to get the close-up marker and write his name on it as they all took off.

When they got there, it was confirmed Buddy had cut the other shots by a significant margin and the tape provided on the marker showed the ball only three feet and two inches away. His name with the distance was recorded on a small sheet of paper attached to a metal holder and then placed away from the green. If the shot held up during the tournament, Buddy would win a dozen golf balls as a prize. It was a little ironic that How was providing those rewards.

"Go ahead and make the putt, L.B.," said How to Buddy.

Buddy placed a marker to the side of the ball in case anyone else needed to play from that location and then did a jig when he made the short shot into the cup. His belly bounced as he laughed.

"Damn, I guess I am a L.B. to not only birdie the first hole, as well as maybe win some free golf balls from my pal, How. I trust you sprang for Pro V1s."

"Yeah, I did. Tax write-off under my advertising budget. Besides, I'd rather you get them than somebody I don't like. I had the balls personalized with my name to remind the winners. I almost had my picture put on 'em, if I thought I could get away with it, I would've."

"As if anybody could ever forget you," said Buddy still laughing.

"I hate to be dumb, but y'all have used that term L.B. a couple of times already and I don't know what you mean. I thought you were calling me by my initials," Leo said.

The guys snickered and How then responded, "Sorry, Leo. Just a term of endearment amongst us friends. It means lucky bastard."

"Okay, I hope I earn the initials today," Leo replied joining in the laugh.

***

The round was a total success in more ways than one. On every hole somebody else seemed to pick up the team. Even the worst player, Leo, made a couple of drives that were longer than the others and therefore used as the first shot in the scramble format. He also made a long putt for a birdie on number eighteen after Ollie was the only golfer to get on the green in regulation. All the players took turns shining even if luck paid a role on occasion. Fist bumps usually followed.

No amount of fortune was more evident than on their last hole of the day, however, another par four with water in play. How hit a draw off the tee that bounced on the cart path located on the left of the fairway. The bright yellow Calloway ball he had played throughout the round then took an unlikely trajectory to the right and landed in a patch of grass a mere three yards from the murky water.

A chorus of "L.B.'s" rang out when the ball was located safe and sound. A couple of the guys hit their shots in the water.

But Ollie then arched his second shot across the lake and after a hop, the ball hit the pin and squirted only a few inches away from the cup. The four grown men proceeded to pump their fists and then jump up and down like kids at the near eagle. Needless to say, another birdie followed that the group let Leo make to end the tournament for the team. All of them did the usual removal of hats and caps while shaking the other teammates' hands.

After totaling the score, How pronounced they were eight under for the round. Leo was happy and thought the result was pretty good. He could forget any crappy shots made at that point and dwell on the score.

"Eh, it's not bad, but I'll bet there are teams out here in the low to mid 50's, so don't get your hopes up too much, counselor," said How as they headed back to the clubhouse.

"This was really fun, How," said Leo as the cart returned to the parking lot. "I hope I can play with y'all again some time."

"You can count on it, Leo. We'll put up our clubs, then turn in our scores and see if we can figure out if the fund raiser did what it was set up to do."

The good news was doubled when the final results were tallied. Not only did Team How come in third place, Leo's campaign netted over five thousand dollars. And, Buddy's close-up won. Leo couldn't help but think the signs were all in his favor.

CHAPTER FOURTEEN

Dee and Mindy were riding from the public school where the daughter had just about finished junior high. The day was as nice as it got in Macon where temperatures and humidity often made residents feel like the crust between hell and earth had cracked. The air conditioning wasn't getting a workout like it often did in Dee's sporty new vehicle.

"Since you're almost fifteen, we're thinking about getting you a car. That way, you can learn to drive on the one that'll be yours. What do you think?" asked Dee.

"No kidding, for real?" Mindy asked with blue eyes widening.

"Yeah, part of it in all honesty, is that your dad and I are a little nervous about you learning on our cars. You know I don't even like to park mine near anything that could remotely cause a ding. Truth be told, I don't care for him driving it either."

Mindy let out an exaggerated giggle. Dee's protective attitude toward the possession she called Ruby was established. Among the family, it was a well-known secret that the pristine auto was really the baby of the house.

"I get it, Mom. Actually, the idea makes a lot of sense," she said pausing. "How much say-so do I have in the decision? Do I get to pick the car? I mean, I've been saving money for a long time and I don't want some P.O.S."

Dee stole a glance at the teen while she drove. "I'd be careful saying that to your dad. Where'd you learn that term anyway?"

Mindy rolled her eyes and responded, "I'm just talking to you, Mom. Besides, I've heard y'all use that acronym. You know I'm an honor student, right?"

Dee let a dimpled smile give away the fact Mindy tickled her. The daughter had always been smart, and as she had grown she seemed to always know a lot more than the parents suspected.

"Maybe we ought to restart the swear jar again," said Dee referring to the tradition the family had once used of putting money in a container any time one of them used a bad word.

"It would be kinda lame now, but I thought it was funny when I was little," replied Mindy.

They rode in silence for the next few minutes as Mindy scrolled through items on her phone. Dee concentrated on manipulating the vehicle in the heavy traffic. It seemed it had gotten as bad as metro Atlanta in some areas. *Not really,* she thought.

She was headed downtown in order to take care of a couple of errands since she was off work for the afternoon and Leo was so busy. She didn't know how he was able to do everything he had been doing lately. He hadn't been complaining, so Dee wasn't either, but she had seen the strain on his face for at least the last week. His caseload was heavy, and the campaign took every other spare moment of the day, evening, and night.

Dee was trying her best not show how she really felt about her husband's decision to run for office. Yeah, she supported his choice because of her deep love for everything that was him, and she knew he would never make up his mind about something so important without the deepest reflection. Dee didn't feel nearly as sure, though.

What if he loses? What will he do? Go back to private practice?

"Mom? Did you hear me?"

"Sorry, I was thinking about something. What did you say, sweetie?"

"Is it okay if I go to Amy's this Friday night?" Mindy asked still holding her phone in a position suggesting she was actively texting.

"Yeah, I think it'll be okay," she replied absently.

Mindy immediately began thumbing a response on her hand held computer device while Dee slipped back into her insecure thoughts. *We'll be okay. Leo wouldn't do anything to hurt the family.*

Dee drove up to the government building and scanned the area looking for a place to park her vehicle safely so that it would be protected. There was one fairly close, but it would mean having to parallel park. It made her sweat just to think about having to try such a maneuver.

Slowly, Dee pulled the car halfway behind a BMW and eyed the slot available. In the opposite space was a new-looking domestic car, and she made the decision to go for it.

It only took her a good ten minutes finally to get Ruby into the ample place and Mindy never even looked up from her phone. When she finally turned off the car, Dee looked in her daughter's direction.

"Do you want to come in with me?"

"If it's okay, I'll stay in the car."

Dee first gave her daughter a look that implied a degree of disapproval, but turned it into one of acknowledgement of the situation. She remembered being at that age when it wasn't cool to be with your parents. In the grand scheme of things, the phase didn't last long, and she knew her kid held values that would always bring her back in the family unit.

Before shutting the car door, Dee spoke to Mindy who was thumbing another message. "I'm leaving the motor running so you won't get too hot. Since the keys are still in the car, leave the doors locked. I won't be gone but a few minutes."

Mindy nodded but never looked up from her hand-held device. Any possible danger from such a situation was unfathomable.

***

Dee walked through the glass doors of the remodeled tax offices that had once been a bank. Everything looked clean and new unlike the former setting in the county courthouse, which had housed the unit before SPLOST funding allowed the makeover.

She pulled a ticket from a dispenser that indicated the order in which the first available clerk would help her and glanced up at the LED display to see how long she might have to wait. The lobby didn't appear to be overly crowded, but there were customers in front of each glass window where employees were located. There were maybe five or six such stations operating at the moment with a few more unoccupied.

It shouldn't take but a few minutes, she thought.

Now serving number 6811 at portal six flashed the display. Dee headed in that direction and walked up to the glass protected area. There was a man behind the counter who looked vaguely familiar.

"Well, if that's a face I haven't seen since high school. I'd remember those dimples anywhere. Dee Hewes, right?" asked the face behind the counter.

Dee couldn't help but flash her patented smile. It made some people think she was flirty, but it was just her natural look. She struggled to make a connection to the guy, but drew a blank.

"Yeah, that's right. Dee Berry, now. You look familiar, did we go to school together?"

The man nodded slightly and gave a smirk from the right corner of his mouth. His face was smooth and unlined. Dee thought it to be not unpleasant, but there was something that made her feel uneasy. He showed no facial hair other than faint outlines of eyebrows that almost looked doctored. His head was shaved smoother than a baby's butt.

He grinned, "Yeah, we did. We had a class or two together at Southwest. I sat behind you. I believe you always wore socks that matched your top back then."

Dee didn't know how to react. Part of her found it creepy, but another part was flattered this guy remembered her.

She glanced down at the nameplate and it was stamped Morgan Thomas in black letters on a gold background. "I'm sorry, but I don't recognize your name."

"It's okay. I wasn't popular like you. Truth be known, I had a little crush back then," the guy said smiling.

Dee shifted onto one foot and looked at the clerk. She tried to place his face into her memories. That one slightly overlapping front tooth in an otherwise perfect smile did the trick. It hit her like a ton of bricks when it registered. There was an incident that flooded back that had been long forgotten.

Back then, he'd worn glasses. They were weird and not hip like he wanted them to be. Some kind of tint that looked almost yellow. He had hair back then and it was a different color, too. A combination of blonde, brown and a tinge of black that made her think of a wild animal.

"Okay, ...Morgan. I think I remember you. How have you been?" she asked trying to appear more caring than she felt.

He gave a wink that made her want to shudder. "I'm doing great. Living the dream."

"Great. Me, too. Can you take care of this car tag renewal for me? I'm kinda in a hurry," she said uncomfortably as she handed the document through the slip.

He never took his eyes from her face as she slid the paper underneath the glass. She hadn't felt this uncomfortable in recent times as he took the form without looking down at it.

Finally, he averted his eyes to the computer screen in front of him and began a flutter of strokes. The man's fingers were nimble and they almost had a musical quality to the way they played across the keyboard. While Thomas was working, Dee remembered the awkward moment from school.

She was fifteen again. Probably about the same age as Mindy was now. The classroom scene before the teacher came in was always a little crazy. Kids were talking and laughing about stuff that didn't amount to dick. Not that she really knew anything about that even if she thought about such subjects. Dee only cared that she had done the homework assignment and that she wouldn't be called upon for any questions about *Lord of the Flies*. Such a depressing book.

When she hurried to the bathroom before the start of class, she had left her prized Coach pocketbook on her desk. Clearly a mistake. Just as she entered the classroom, there was that weirdo hanging close to her space again. He sat nearby her, and that was bad enough. But, here he was at the place where she would be sitting the next fifty minutes.

What the hell was he doing? He had his back to her and she couldn't see, but he looked like he was going through her pocketbook.

She walked hesitantly toward her seat, and he turned around. He gave a version of a smile that made her wince.

Her purse was open and she immediately felt violated. Dee felt her face flush before the words fell out of her mouth, "What are you doing?"

"Just waiting on you."

"Why?"

He offered a crooked grin and replied, "A proposition."

The young Morgan Thomas appraised Dee by looking her up and down. The gaze gave Dee shivers.

"How about we catch a movie Saturday night?"

She swallowed involuntarily before replying more loudly than she intended. "Uh, I'm busy."

His eyes narrowed slightly and she thought cruelty crept in his orbs. Then, his face softened a bit before he replied, "I understand."

He had walked away, and she grabbed her pocketbook. Dee furiously began going through the contents to see if anything was missing. Even though she couldn't detect a theft, she couldn't help but believe Morgan Thomas had been through everything it contained.

The memory evaporated as the older version of the long forgotten male made a statement. Dee felt herself shake her head as she said, "I'm sorry, what did you say?"

"You're good to go. Here's your receipt and new sticker," Thomas replied as he passed the papers underneath the glass where he sat.

Dee scratched out a personal check for the fee and passed it through the slot. She grabbed the documents and made a beeline toward the exit. If she never saw Morgan Thomas in this lifetime, it would be too soon.

Dee was still more than a little flustered as she hurried toward her car. Dee's turmoil became magnified as she approached and spied a scraggly figure standing near the passenger side where Mindy sat.

The man held a cardboard sign that hung to his left in a grimy hand. Dee could read the word HUNGRY written in all caps on the brown corrugated paper. Silver gray wisps of hair floated about his skeletal head and a similar colored beard adorned his chin.

Dee walked faster as the man became more animated and appeared to be in a conversation with her daughter. She couldn't hear what was being said, and concern was turning to panic as she saw the man place his other hand into the open window of the vehicle. It almost felt like a bad dream where she was trying hard to run, but somehow wasn't able, like being stuck in quicksand.

"Hey, hey! What are you doing?" she asked in a fear laden yet forceful voice as she finally reached the car.

The scarecrow turned toward Dee gripping several money bills in his right hand and raised the sign like an axe with his left. She stopped in her tracks unsure if he might strike her with the unlikely weapon.

"Good morning, pretty lady," he croaked through a mostly toothless grin.

Before she could respond, the creature turned away from her and spoke into the car once more before leaving the area in a pronounced limp. It sounded like he said, "Thankee, girlie," but Dee couldn't be sure about anything other than relief felt over his departure.

Sliding quickly into the driver's seat, Dee strapped herself in and locked the doors in the still running automobile. She looked at her daughter who returned the mother's gaze with a furrowed brow.

"You okay, Mom?"

Dee felt hot and not in a good way. Although the weather didn't quite call for her actions, she turned the air conditioner control down more before responding.

"What were you thinking talking with that stranger, Mindy? Don't you know how dangerous that is? And, just how much money did you give him?"

Mindy rolled her eyes and shook her head slightly from side to side while responding, "He's a homeless and hungry old man, Mom. I wanted to help is all. He didn't scare me, so I gave him a few bucks. Not a big deal."

Dee's psyche was still shaken from the encounter inside the tag office and could feel competing emotions bubbling up. Her daughter had always been a caring person, and she didn't want to change that loving part of her character. However, she worried Mindy was too naïve about the dangers of the world.

"Honey, I love that you care about people, but you have to be cautious with those you don't know. You never know when somebody might hurt you to get something you've got that they don't. Besides, he can get a free meal right down the street at the church if he's really hungry. I'd bet more money than you just gave away that he'll head right to the liquor store and spend it all."

Mindy shrugged her shoulders and replied, "Maybe so. But, like Grandma Shelley always says, 'Do what you can live with.' That's what I did, Mom. I can't help it when somebody you're trying to help might not live up to expectations."

The conversation ended as Dee began the drive back home. No doubt, the kid was growing up. She would tell Leo about the incident so he could weigh in later. She would also ask him if he knew that strange Morgan Thomas, too.

CHAPTER FIFTEEN

Leo sat at his desk awaiting the jury's verdict. The trial had lasted most of the day and was not very remarkable. Something he had done many times in his tenure as a prosecutor, presenting a case of DUI, required him to debunk standard defense tactics.

He had learned over the years of doing the job that a lot of stuff in trials was pretty predictable and certain offenses were more so than others. Leo remembered his own experiences of representing defendants before juries, and it had served him well now that he was on the opposite side.

The officer's not on trial, ladies and gentlemen, no matter how much the other lawyer tries to convince you otherwise. Officer Wolfe didn't single the defendant out to hassle him when he was weaving all over the road. The officer didn't deny the defendant his rights by asking him to perform standard field sobriety tests to see if he was able to safely drive his vehicle. The officer wasn't playing to the camera when he asked how much he'd had to drink, as you could see the defendant was swaying from side to side on the video. You could see for yourselves the defendant's ability to drive was impaired.

I submit to you that what the officer was doing was his job, protecting all of us from somebody who was a danger to himself and the public, too. We should thank him for that service. Who knows, he may have saved a life or two by stopping the defendant that night.

When the defendant made the decision to drink and drive, he showed a disregard for the law. The state trusts you all feel the same way and will return a verdict that speaks the truth. The defendant is guilty and we ask you to so find.

It was a variation of a closing argument Leo had given many times. There were other parts he often used that were included involving whether or not defendants refused testing or were over the legal limit of intoxication or were obviously less safe to operate their vehicles because of how they appeared, but no two cases were exactly the same. Once you had tried such a case, however, you could pretty much predict where the other side was going before you ever started.

While this trial was important to Leo, as they all were, his mind was jumping in several directions. The campaign consumed, and he had to admit, thrilled him more than he had thought it would when he made the decision to run. There was something about the race that brought out the competitiveness that had run deep in his soul since he could remember.

It seemed every day brought another challenge he had never faced before. One night he would be at a forum with his opponents and other candidates for various offices where they gave stump speeches to prospective voters. The next evening he would meet and strategize with supporters on the best way to get his message across. Some days he even went door to door in neighborhoods not deemed the safest to ask for votes.

In the current age, going that route was not done as much anymore. Social media was used a lot more as were other forms of advertising, and Leo was trying to dabble in all of it. But, his gut kept telling him personal contact was the best way to connect with people, so any free time he could muster was put to that use.

Tonight after work, Leo planned to go to his mother's house where he would get some good home cooking and then try to walk around awhile with her in the south Macon part of town where he had grown up. He was aware Mama had already visited over five hundred registered voters' homes nearby, and he wanted to see her in action. She was a force and a not so secret weapon in the campaign.

Leo glanced at his watch to see there were about thirty minutes left until the five o'clock chimes would ring on the big bell located one floor above in the courthouse. The prosecutor closed his eyes and leaned his head against the back of his chair. Trying to clear his head from everything running through it, he let his mind drift back to simpler times. When his brain did this, Leo often became teenaged kid again.

***

"You could be president of the senior class, man. Why don't you go for it, dude?"

Leo shrugged. He didn't really care about school politics like some of his friends seemed to.

"Really, you've got connections in every group. Eggheads, jocks, nerds, band mates, dopers, gays, you name it, Leo. They all dig you," said his friend, Darryl.

The two guys looked at one another and then started laughing. At first, it was more of a snicker, but then became loud guffaws that had both of them in tears as it finally subsided.

"Hey, I don't discriminate," replied Leo. "If I did, I'd kick out the redheads."

Darryl faked a scowl. His coarse auburn locks framed his face as it turned back into a big grin.

"No really, you could win, buddy," said Darryl.

"So, you'll be my campaign manager? And, just what do you want out of this deal, D?"

"Chief of staff, Mr. President. A chance to influence the head guy," replied Darryl with an exaggerated wink.

The two friends laughed again as they had many times over the course of their friendship that had begun as eighth graders. Now as they approached their senior years of high school, they had begun planning for college among other pursuits-mainly girls and how to get a better car.

"I don't think so, D. I've been V.P. for two years besides being in four other clubs and holding office in three of them. I want to take it easy our last year. I've got enough on my plate," said Leo.

"You need everything you can on your resume, man, if you're planning to go to law school one day," Darryl laughed.

Leo got a little tickled at the running joke that some of his closest friends constantly reminded him about after he announced early in junior high that he intended to become an attorney. They all had dreams for the future, but Leo's seemed too remote for the rest of the group to think of as being serious.

"Well, maybe I will run, but it's not about something I can list on a piece of paper. I'll do it only if I think I can make a difference. And, as for becoming a lawyer, all I've got to say is you just wait and see, buddy," said Leo with a hint of agitation.

"Whoa, man. Didn't mean to piss you off. I'm just kidding about the future. I believe in you and know one day a courtroom will be your domain just like a computer and an adding machine will be mine. We're destined, man. I can hear them saying something now. They're calling your name…"

***

"Leo. Mr. Berry. I didn't mean to disturb you," the elderly bailiff said.

The prosecutor blinked his eyes and was back in the present. Mini vacations in time, as he thought of dreams and memories of the past, occasionally invaded his thoughts. Leo found such memories not unpleasant and often illuminating.

"Oh, it's okay Mr. Beck. I guess I was daydreaming. Do we have a verdict?"

"Yes, sir. Only took twenty minutes, too. I'm thinking that's good for your side. By the way, I didn't get a chance to tell you before you left the courtroom, but you did a great job, Leo."

"Thanks, Victor," calling the distinguished former firefighter by his first name, as he had been called by his. While it was rarely done inside the courtroom, Leo liked the informality of addressing folks by their given monikers. It had taken him years to call older people in such a way without saying Mr., Mrs., Ms. or Miss. The titles had been ingrained at an early age.

"We'll see. You know how unpredictable juries can be," Leo said as he got out of his chair and grabbed his suit coat.

"Wait just a second. I've got something for you," replied Victor unmoving from the doorway of Leo's office.

The taller man with the short-cropped white hair and matching moustache took an envelope out of the inner jacket pocket and presented it to Leo. With a slight nod of his head, which the prosecutor took as a sign of respect, the bailiff slyly smiled.

"All of us who've worked with you wanted to give you a campaign donation. It's not much. You know, we're all on fixed incomes," he said with another smile.

Leo tried to stop the tear from his left eye rolling down his cheek, but was too late. He didn't look inside the envelope and put it inside his own pocket. Removing his hand from inside the coat, he immediately grasped Victor's larger one and they shook three times before unclasping.

"Thanks, I'm touched, Victor. Let's go hear what the jury has to say before I start blubbering."

The bailiff half hugged the prosecutor and patted him on the shoulder as they headed out of the room. Voices from the past still echoed as he whispered in Leo's ear, "What will be is meant to be."

CHAPTER SIXTEEN

Leo sat at the small bar looking out the pass-through from Mom's kitchen. The curtains on the back windows were open to let in the remaining sunshine of the evening, brightly illuminating the galley cooking area where an oversized aluminum pot sat on the electric stove. It emitted a low bubbling sound and escaping steam filled Leo's olfactory senses and made him even hungrier.

He had only eaten an apple at his desk during a recess of the trial earlier in the day, and the smell of his mother's homemade vegetable soup heightened the anticipation of one of his favorite meals. She always started the one pot feast with a beef roast as a base that had been cooked until fork-tender for several hours before adding fresh produce. Tomatoes, corn, potatoes, carrots, butterbeans, and okra were in the mix, and none of it came from a can. It was always delicious and satisfying, and he only wanted a cornbread muffin or a few saltine crackers to accompany the meal. Saliva formed at the corners of his mouth in anticipation.

Shelly Berry was an expert at southern cooking, and Leo never missed a chance to chow down on some when she offered. Although she downplayed her cooking, he had always thought

Mama could've earned a decent living if she had ever opened a restaurant.

"It's ready, but really hot sugah, so I'm going to dip us out a bowl and let it cool for a few minutes before we eat. We can catch up til it does," she said.

Leo watched as she ladled two helpings of the hearty soup into two rose flower printed containers. The one she prepared for him looked to be at least the size of a medium mixing bowl.

"Wow, is all that mine? Looks like it's for Jethro Bodine," said Leo, referring to the classic television character from *The Beverly Hillbillies.*

Shelly set their dinner on the bar where Leo occupied a wooden high-top stool, and the smell was enhanced at least double. She added spoons, paper towels and a sleeve of Keebler crackers.

"I don't think I can wait for it to cool. I'll blow on mine if I need to," replied Leo as he grabbed his silverware. "I haven't really eaten since breakfast."

His mother sat down next to him and watched as her oldest son pooched out his lips and let out his breath over the first bite. She shook her head and smiled as he shoveled it into his mouth.

"I can tell you're not eating right. How much weight have you lost since you started the campaign? I'm going to talk to Dee so she'll make sure you don't skip any meals," she said with a frown.

Leo gulped several spoonsful into his mouth only pausing slightly to blow between each before replying. He guessed a mother never quit being one even when the kid was in his mid-forties.

"Mama, you don't need to worry so much. Yeah, I've lost a few pounds and maybe I missed a lunch or two, but it's okay. And by the way, Dee stays on my butt almost as much as you do, so you don't need to bother her about it."

She didn't respond, but her body language spoke volumes. Picking up a utensil with her dominant left hand, she stirred the food in front of her. Shelly Berry had always been able to show displeasure without saying a word. Tentatively placing a small amount of food into her mouth, she chewed it more than seemed necessary to Leo.

He had found his rhythm and was almost halfway through the huge bowl before Shelly spoke again. The soup was so delicious and conversation interrupted his progress.

"I'm just trying to help. I don't want to see this election hurting you like that."

Leo quit eating and looked at his mom. She'd always worried about her boys, but he hadn't considered she might be overly concerned about the campaign. He reached out and patted her shoulder.

"Really, I'm fine. You know how we've always dreamed stuff that came true? It's already happened, and we're going to win. I'm positive," he said with assurance.

She allowed a half smile and replied, "No doubt."

They ate the rest of their meals in silence with only occasional grunts of approval from Leo. As he finished by raising the bowl to his lips and drinking the remainder of the liquid, Shelly's son smacked his mouth and then wiped with a paper towel.

"That was great, Mama. If you've got enough left over, I'll take some for lunch tomorrow."

"There's plenty enough to take for Dee and Mindy, too," she said as she got up and took their dishes to the sink. Shelly ran water from the faucet in both and then immediately began washing them. Although she had a dishwasher adjacent to the sink, it was rarely used.

Something about her attitude bothered Leo, but he couldn't tell what it was. He knew she was upset about more than his losing some body fat. She was pretty good hiding her feelings; however, Leo was adept at noticing the signs.

He went into the kitchen and watched as she poured at least half the remaining soup in a large Tupperware container. She then secured it tightly with a matching lid after allowing excess air to escape. The family had always called the procedure "burping," and Leo felt the same as gas escaped from his mouth.

"Mama, is something going on I need to know about?" Leo asked.

Since Daddy had died several years before, Leo felt the need to take some amount of responsibility for any of his family's issues. Part of it came from his training as a lawyer, but the majority had its origins in a conversation with his father when Leo was still in his teens.

Shelly placed the leftovers in a plastic disposable grocery bag and tied its handles in a knot before facing Leo and responding. Her hazel blue eyes were misty, and her voice quaked gently.

"It's nothing you need to see about right now. As I've said many times before, you've got to take care of yourself first, and let everybody else take care of their lives. 'Specially right now. You've got enough on your plate without feeling guilt over somebody else's problems. Your daddy was wrong to make you think you've got to look out for the rest of us every time something comes up with me or one of your brothers. The election is only a few weeks away, and then we'll deal with whatever we need to."

Leo's radar was on full alert as he studied his mom's face. There were a couple of creases on her forehead that appeared deeper than normal, and bags were under her eyes that were just noticed in the kitchen's light. Since she had always looked younger than her age, he realized whatever was bothering her added a few years to her otherwise youthfulness.

"Don't hide things from me, Mama. It'll only make it worse, and it's a sure-fire way to keep me from helping."

She turned and walked from the kitchen into her cozy den without responding. Plopping into her rocker recliner without cranking out the footrest, Shelly swung the seat in a gentle motion as Leo followed to the couch located nearest her chair.

"Alright, son," she started after a long pause. "But, I don't expect you to change anything you're doing on my account, okay?"

"I'm going to always do what's necessary or what I can to help you," he replied.

"I know," she sighed. "So, I guess I'll just have to tell you. First, Tommy's having marital troubles."

Pausing slightly, she let out the biggest bombshell, "And I've got a tumor in here," she said pointing to her lower abdomen.

Ignoring his youngest brother's problem for a moment, Leo addressed his mother's health issue. "Is it cancer?" he asked.

She bit on her lower lip and shook her head from side to side. "The doctor doesn't know for sure, but he said the chances are at least fifty-fifty."

Leo's brain was trying to process the information without showing outward alarm. He knew there was a history of colon cancer on his mother's side of the family with both her father and older brother having suffered. It had ultimately ended in their deaths.

He crossed the few steps separating them and hugged Shelly. Neither openly cried, but tears had formed in their eyes.

"I'm going to be fine. I've been through worse," she said.

"No doubt in my mind. You're the toughest woman on the planet," responded Leo.

They sat down together on the well-worn knobby blue cloth sofa and talked quietly about what had transpired over the last month. Leo had been kept blissfully ignorant while busy with the campaign and at the office. Shelly had dealt with her doubts and anguish in usual fashion by not confiding with anyone else after first noticing swelling and then seeing her physician.

"So, your internist referred you to a surgeon after getting the sonogram results? Is he the one saying it might be malignant?"

"Yes, he's a no nonsense kind of guy. He wants to get it out of there as soon as possible. I told him I'd let him know 'cause I had a lot going on right now. I figure I can wait four more weeks til you get elected."

Leo's mind was racing, but he would not allow his mother to wait that long to have surgery if there was a chance that cancer could be growing and/or spreading. He couldn't think of anything more important at the moment.

"Mama, I'm sorry, but you're going to see about this before the election. You need to call the rest of the family and let them know, too. This is a fight we'll have together."

She regarded Leo and then nodded decisively. He recognized the determination behind her eyes that he had seen many times in the past, but Leo couldn't help but let worry creep further into his thoughts.

CHAPTER SEVENTEEN

Morgan Thomas wheeled his sedan around the area careful not to drive at a pace that would cause alarm. During the midnight hour he had not encountered any other traffic, but he didn't want any homeowners who might still be awake and happen to notice his vehicle get suspicious of his activity.

After he had seen Dee Hewes, now Berry, earlier in the day, Morgan's thoughts had turned to memories of the once cute and now even prettier girl. That's how he thought of objects of his affection, *pretty girls*. He had begun thinking that way back in high school after being rejected by them so many times.

His computer terminal contained gates to personal information that the general public didn't realize. Morgan had used the easy access more than a few times to find out things like addresses, marital status and other stuff about such *pretty girls*. It was easy and what he had done after encountering Dee.

***

He had been with several over the course of the last couple of decades. The process of securing pleasure with those he classified as such had been honed through various methods and tactics over that time period to the point that Morgan had little fear when he chose the next pretty girl. Whenever some doubt crept into his psyche that a female didn't approve of his affections, he simply reminded himself that none had ever complained while he was with them, and he must be doing it right because he had never been stopped. He never gave a thought that one might reject his affections now.

Morgan smiled as he thought back to the first pretty girl. The occasion was really not planned at all. It happened at a college fraternity party where lots of freshmen students were drinking heavily. He had only sipped on some cheap beer that was flowing freely from a keg because he wanted to fit in. Morgan wasn't much of a drinker and rarely had more than one alcoholic beverage.

As the night had turned to early morning hours, his attention had turned to a thin blonde who had wandered from the house. She stumbled into a wooded section secluded from the back yard, and he followed more out of curiosity than for any other reason. For sure, he wasn't expecting she'd be the first of many to come.

She was cute and had nice legs although her top could've been filled out more. Morgan thought she might be looking for a place to upchuck, toss her cookies or otherwise throw up, to summarize the purpose of her semi-organized stagger toward the bushes.

However, when she got to the pine straw out of the lighted vicinity, she lay down and assumed a fetal position. Morgan waited a couple of minutes and followed. At that moment, he was not thinking about sex, but that would soon change.

He stood above her and took another sip of the tepid beer. She was vulnerable in the quiet darkness. There was music playing in the house up the way from their location, but the sounds of the party had died down. People had either gone back to their residences or had bedded down. Morgan imagined some had paired off, and he felt a stirring in his pants as a result.

He had never really come close to having sex with another person. Oh, he had thought about it many times to be sure. Everything he thought he knew about the act indicated that was normal as was pleasuring himself. No one else was needed for that, and he'd had lots of practice.

Now there was someone right here he could participate with that fun. She wouldn't mind, in fact, she would like it as much as he would. That was his first thought as he got down beside her on what was surprisingly soft ground.

Morgan cuddled with the girl and she didn't move. The erection in his pants found a new urgency, so he unbuckled his belt, unzipped and slid down the trousers and tighty-whitey underwear with purpose. Her short dress was easily displaced and her panties were no trouble either.

From what his father had told him when he turned sixteen, he knew he needed protection; however, he had none with him. It was something he would always be prepared for in the future. Not this first time, though.

He let out a repressed breath as he entered the pretty girl trying not to awaken her. She only moaned which motivated him to thrust once and then repeatedly.

She must've been enjoying it as much as him because she never tried to stop him. It was over much too soon, and the feeling of euphoria that overcame him gave him a joy he had never experienced.

Morgan knew then and there. This was a purpose in his heretofore pathetic life.

***

Morgan drove around the cul-de-sacs taking in the surroundings. There were several streetlights that would make it problematic to be with her. The one where Dee lived had one directly across from her house. Besides that, she had a husband and a kid. Who knows, she might have a dog, too. He knew extra precautions would be needed simply because she could recognize him.

He also knew about her husband. A lawyer. The guy was running for office. He worked in the court system. He had even killed another man that was deemed a justifiable homicide a few years ago. There was all kind of impediments to keep him from pursuing this pretty girl.

It only made Morgan more interested and would require more than the usual planning. He knew he was up for the challenge.

CHAPTER EIGHTEEN

Dee's breathing had slowed considerably from the few minutes before as she laid her head on Leo's right shoulder. Her ear slid down to Leo's chest as she listened for her husband's heartbeat as she often did when they were intimate. It was just one of the ways to make sure he was still with her, body and soul. After almost losing him to that slimy cop a while back, it had become almost an obsession to make sure he was alive and safe.

It had been her intention to tell Leo about the day she had just experienced. The two unnerving encounters were still fresh in her mind when he got home from his mother's house, but she could tell upon arrival that he had serious things going on behind his blue eyes. Dee didn't want to add another concern, so decided it could wait until later.

Leo had been tense from the time he got home. Dee saw it on his face. The lines on his forehead and around his mouth confirmed he was under even more stress than usual. She didn't need to add anything else to the equation.

He is a good man, and we're so lucky. She was prejudiced and knew it, but everyone said the same thing. It didn't matter what anybody might think otherwise, Leo Berry was the best man for the job, no matter what job it was.

"What are you thinking, babe," whispered Leo.

"I'm worried about you," she breathed back.

They were quiet for a while, before Leo said, "Mama's got a tumor in her belly."

Dee breathed in deeply and immediately understood the tension. Leo was dealing with something else besides everything she already realized. It wasn't fair, but it was an indelible part of his character to take on others' problems.

"I'm so sorry, baby. The timing sucks."

"I know, but there's never a good time to deal with something like this. I'm just hoping and praying it's not cancer. There's been enough of that in our family."

Dee thought about that for a minute remembering Leo's mother's father and brother had both suffered through bouts of colon cancer. She wondered if genetics was at work with Shelly.

"It'll be okay," she said as she stroked his arm. He seemed to settle without responding.

For the next few minutes the two of them remained silent and stuck in their own thoughts. Dee knew she worried more than she should, but it was part of her DNA. It was a portion due to being an only child and a slice being so in love with her husband.

Leo finally broke the silence and said, "I really don't know what I'd be like if I hadn't met you. I know it sounds corny as hell, but you make me a better man."

She felt better at that moment and tried to suppress tears. Her emotions were much more openly expressive than his had always been.

"I love you, Leo Berry. We'll get through this."

She heard him suck in a gulp of air without responding. He reached over and held her arm for a moment. It felt oddly reassuring.

"I'm wondering, should I drop out of this race?"

"What? Hell no, Leo. You're going to be the best S-G this county's ever had.

"I could go back to private practice. I would probably make a lot more money now. I've even dreamed about it, Baby. Just think, I wouldn't have to worry about kissing somebody's ass like one has to do in politics. I could be my own boss."

"You'll never have to kiss anybody's ass, Leo. You'll do what's right."

They settled into a rhythm and Leo was soon snoring. Dee spooned against his back as she fell asleep.

***

Leo felt good. The air was sterile and with every breath, he felt cleansed. Nothing else seemed important other than finding the source of everything. If he could, life's meaning would expose itself.

He had a wooden staff in his right hand and a pack on his back. Looking around, the bright blue sky had only one or two puffy clouds and mountains sat clustered in the distance unobscured. One stood higher than the rest with clean lines and slopes that appeared impossible to climb. The view made him seem older and wiser for some reason because that's where he would find the answers he sought.

As he hiked over and through the rough terrain, he thought about his life. There had been ups and downs. No matter. Everybody had to face that stuff. Overall, his existence had been full of positives that overshadowed the negatives. Still, questions filled his head.

If he were more religious, maybe he wouldn't be searching so hard. Faith would sustain him, or at least that's what some people had said to him. But those attempts to understand had never accomplished the desired results for Leo. Years attending church services, discussions with others who had spent their days in studious reflection, and reading the Bible cover to cover only caused more uncertainty.

The Source. Had to find it.

He checked his bearings again. The scene was not what he had first observed. Gnarly growths were on either side of him, and prickly thorns were everywhere.

Leo was not so sure of how he felt. He doubted everything. The range was farther in the distance now, and he had to squint to see the tops of the lower mountains.

What could he do?

He tried to decide if this was a dream. Sometimes in the middle of one, he would realize that's what was happening. Then he would usually wake up, occasionally in a sweat, and try to figure out what it meant.

His mouth was dry, so he squirmed to take off the backpack and get some water. After great effort it fell to the ground and caused a thud when it hit. Leo searched the contents only to find rocks of various shapes and sizes.

Water. I need water.

Panic was starting to build when coming toward him was a familiar figure led by a canine. The Border collie mix ran to Leo with his tongue out and a dog grin relaxing the stress that had been about to engulf the moment. Leo buried his face in the fur and felt joy at seeing the first dog he had ever loved.

Hey ya, Rusty. How ya doing?

I'm good. We were just looking for you.

Talking without speaking and with a dog's apparition to boot didn't seem impossible at the moment. It got even better when the figure Leo had first seen now loomed over him. His grandfather. His namesake, Big Leo. His mentor. A man who had been larger than life in his heyday, and yes, even a savior to some, was with him again despite having died some years before.

Papa. I know it's a dream, but I don't care.

The big man's smile grew wider. He had a youthfulness Leo had never known except in a few old photos.

Who said dreams ain't real? Dream it, say it, do it, and you can make anything come true, Leo.

The setting had returned to the previous clarity and Leo began to relax. Everywhere he gazed had beauty of its own and was a place you would want to spend eternity.

So, is this Heaven? Am I on the other side?

It is if you choose it to be.

I'm not sure what you mean, Papa. I'm pretty much not sure of anything dealing with religion, life after death, or why we even exist. Sometimes I feel close to understanding, and then the doubts creep back in. The rational part of my brain tells me I'm just questioning this stuff now because Mama's sick, but the other part says I need faith that I don't have.

The blue eyes of his grandfather appeared mirror-like as Leo watched intently. He realized, not for the first time, the resemblance therein. The notion that souls continue became sharper also. Leo had felt this in the past, and those memories flooded through his consciousness like water being released through a bursting dam. They came in past experiences: staring at the sun setting over the ocean, the death of his father, the marriage to Dee, the birth of Mindy, the near-deaths he had been through, and the passing of the man now standing before him.

You know, Leo. It's inside you and permeates everything. My advice is to not let your worries control your life. Everything works out eventually. Everybody has to learn on their own what works for them. Continue to do what you can to make things better, and don't let others' beliefs deter you. It'll be okay.

As Big Leo's last words inputted, the visions of his grandfather and beloved sidekick faded. Leo began sobbing.

***

"Baby, baby," Dee said as she gently shook Leo awake.

"Whuh? I was dreaming again," Leo rubbed his eyes and whispered in return. "I'm sorry."

"Don't say you're sorry for everything that happens, Leo. It's not your fault," she paused before continuing, "It'll be okay."

Leo nodded his assent in the early morning light. He was feeling better.

"You're right, Wink," he addressed Dee with her pet name. "Papa just told me the same thing."

CHAPTER NINETEEN

Detective Jimbo Barbour was frustrated. Despite feeling hopeful after becoming convinced he had glimpsed the serial rapist on the grocery store security tape, Jimbo had been unable to develop any other leads. He had spent a better part of two days trying to find where the suspect could've bought a wig locally, only to come to the conclusion that it was too easy to buy one on line.

There was too little needle in that big haystack.

Being a detective sucked sometimes. He would win, though. Jimbo didn't lose. At least, not often.

He kept going through the facts he knew hoping something would jump out at him. Because of lacking forensics in the cases, Jimbo was sure this guy knew something about science. He must at least like watching crime shows on television. It seemed like there were a lot of them on these days that Jimbo felt sure gave the freaks and criminal assholes ideas.

This guy wasn't leaving a lot of clues. Did he have some connection to law enforcement?

No, I don't believe so. The perp's interactions with the vics don't suggest that, he thought.

The partial print from the glove dropped at the second crime scene hadn't turned up anything, yet. It had been checked against the usual sources without success. It only meant the guy had never been arrested. Sooner or later, it could be used as evidence if there was an apprehension of a viable suspect.

His gut told him the man had an inside source. Jimbo kept trying to decide what that could be.

It's got to be something that gives him private info. Computers probably involved. Too much available to bad folks nowadays.

Jimbo rubbed his head. He felt close, but couldn't figure out the connections. He thought about other cases he'd been involved with. This one was different, but there were always similarities.

He'd solved many crimes in his time. He'd solve this one, too.

Jimbo struggled to focus. There had to be something he could do to find this sonofabitch. No way he couldn't figure this shit out.

As he tried to recall if there were facts he had missed, Jimbo remembered a case that plagued him in his early career as an investigator. It had bugged him then, even though he eventually solved the case.

The a-hole had felt invincible. He got bolder with each attack. He was all about dominating and controlling women. He attacked them not so much with ferocity, but with intensity of purpose. When he was finally caught, he acted as if the victims liked the encounters.

Yeah, same kinda guy. I need to find somebody who loves himself way too much and has access to information showing potential victims' exposure. Also, he's a master of disguise.

This one was smarter than most, but he'd busted way more than had ever gotten away with their misdeeds. It was what he told himself now while the irritations were mounting.

One thing for sure, if he didn't make progress soon, his bosses would be all over his ass. There were always other people in the department wanting to get ahead as well. He knew of at least a couple of younger investigators who would take great pride in undercutting and taking advantage of any opportunity to make him look bad.

Jimbo had even overheard one of them say, "That old T-Rex needs to go."

He got out of his vintage chair and the resulting creaking was audible in the jumbled room serving as his home office. Jimbo laughed silently at what could be his back or the old knee joints causing the sounds of age rather than the springs needing a spritz of WD-40.

Age is a sneaky bitch, he thought. *Maybe it is time for me to pack it in and call it a career.*

Hobbling around the room until the arthritis let up a little, Jimbo looked out his front window to see the first light of the morning creeping into his world. As he watched its slow development, a Honda compact travelled up the road to his house only stopping long enough to leave a newspaper in a designated black plastic sleeve beside his mailbox.

The Telegraph was one of the few papers around and a lot of people didn't take it anymore. If they did, the subscribers chose to read it on their computers. Real newspapers were information sources that seemed to be drying up like his sex life.

Nah, I'm still okay in that department. I'm like that Buffett song. It just takes a while.

Jimbo went out and got his paper. When he opened it up and saw the headline, the Captain spewed a few profanities. The article was tucked on the side, but clearly on the front page, and was titled, **RAPIST ON THE LOOSE.** No doubt, it was an attention grabber.

He quickly scanned the contents and cussed some more. Jimbo had to get to the office. He was fuming, but the Sheriff was going to be even unhappier.

CHAPTER TWENTY

Leo sat in his recliner drinking coffee while he reread the piece. It was being reported a rape had occurred in Macon the night before and there might have been others in the recent past. An unnamed source in the Sheriff's Office said an active investigation was ongoing. The article was short on details, but Leo knew the reverberations would be throughout the department and the community as well.

The last time he and his old friend had discussed progress, or the lack thereof in the case involving Maxine's attack, Leo was under the impression that Jimbo was personally handling the matter. Based on what he read, this was no longer true. Jimbo Barbour's name was not mentioned, and the unnamed source claimed a task force had been formed to investigate complaints of a serial rapist.

The latest victim was not revealed, as were none of the others. This was the norm for these kinds of attacks when such a report appeared in the media. The location of the three incidents was only listed as the North Macon area and that jibed with Leo's knowledge. The news was disturbing on a couple of fronts, and he made a mental note to try and get in touch with Jimbo when he got a moment.

He had planned a busy day ahead with the political race looming toward conclusion. Although it was normally a workday, Leo had asked to be off so he could do some things he had not found time to get accomplished. Since he had built up several weeks of vacation and he was otherwise caught up in the office, Leo would spend the day visiting supporters, putting out some signs and attending a forum with other candidates after dinner.

His mind was cluttered with not only the election stuff, but also with his mother's health and guilt feelings for what he felt was neglect of his family. Self-reproach had shadowed Leo throughout his adult life, and doubts lingered about his choice to seek the position. He was, however, too far into the process now, and his commitment was too strong to consider dropping out.

As if Tiki could read Leo's thoughts, the aging Jack Russell appeared at his master's feet. As Leo lowered the paper from his eyes and then folded it into the original shape, the dog jumped into the waiting lap. Its soulful attention was just what was needed for both, and Leo began rubbing and petting the coarse fur.

The canine had been a part of the family's life for years, and Leo knew Tiki's days would end sooner than later. He couldn't imagine that event now. Having been through that type of experience a couple of times in the past only made Leo love the animal that much more.

Its curled body relaxed in the hollow of Leo's lower body. Tiki's breathing slowed to a rhythm discerned only by the rise and fall of the pooch's slightly swollen belly. Leo stroked the distended underneath and watched the animal drift off to sleep.

The peacefulness of Tiki in such a position had a calming effect on Leo, too. Whatever might be ahead could be handled with the right amount of attention.

Mindy came padding into the room wiping sleep from her eyes. She sat cross-legged on the sofa and yawned. Dressed in her favorite vintage Indigo Girls concert tee shirt and baggy shorts, Leo realized his little girl was growing way too fast. It was just another concern to add into his brain's current overload.

"Diddy, I need some money."

She didn't call him that so much any more, and if pressed he would admit missing the term of affection Mindy had used from the time she could first speak. No doubt, his busy life the last few months made Leo feel as if he wasn't paying enough consideration at home.

Leo didn't stop the devotion shown to Tiki as he replied, "Many people do."

The teenager frowned and said, "Sarcasm doesn't help, as I've heard you say before."

Leo had used the same phrase on her and had to acknowledge the truth his daughter was now turning on him. He admired her ability to argue effectively and thought she could be another lawyer in the making.

"When you're right, you're right," said Leo with a smile, "How much do you need and what for?"

"Hmm, maybe fifty. Just the usual stuff for school and some of us are going to the movies tonight."

Leo shook his head as he thought of how the value of money had changed since he used to ask for a few bucks from his parents when he was her age. Mindy had never asked for much, so he knew he'd comply with her request. Besides, she was a good kid, and he trusted her.

"Well, I think I've got that much in my wallet. You know where I keep it, so get what you need. Just don't be giving away too much of my hard-earned pay to the homeless."

His daughter pursed her lips before responding, "Mom's already voiced her opinions about that. I was only doing what I thought was right under the circumstances, like you've always taught, Dad."

"You've got a good heart, baby. One of the reasons you're loved by yours truly. We're more worried about your interactions with strangers than your charitable efforts. There's a lot of danger in the world, you know."

"Okay, I get it, Dad. I'm careful. Speaking of which, Mom hinted y'all might get me a car when I turn fifteen. I think that's a great idea, in case you're wondering how I feel about it."

Leo had to laugh at the matter-of-fact way Mindy snuck that it into the conversation. If she didn't have a future as an attorney, she might become a psychologist.

"We'll talk about that a little more when the campaign is over, and if you keep showing us growing maturity," he added with an exaggerated wink.

Mindy jumped up and bounded to Leo. She was visibly excited at the prospect of having her own vehicle, and leaned over kissing her father on his cheek without waking Tiki. She was almost skipping while leaving the room in search of his wallet.

Less than a minute later she flashed two twenties at Leo as she headed to her room. A big grin was still on her face.

"I decided I could get by with less and show you I'm capable of fiscal responsibility. It's just a little bit of my growing maturity," she said with her own wink.

Tiki raised his graying head and eyed Leo as the master laughed. The dog let out a long yawn before going back to sleep.

CHAPTER TWENTY-ONE

Candidates for various offices up for grabs sat in metal folding chairs arranged in a line behind a makeshift podium. The auditorium of the community center currently held maybe fifty people, many of whom were family members or core supporters of a few of those seeking election.

Leo couldn't help believe the forum while in theory was a good way for the voting public to get to know the contenders, as a practical matter was a failure because of the general poor attendance. There were probably no more than a dozen uncommitted voters there, and based on other such events he had been a part of, maybe only a half of that number even had a passing interest in the position he sought.

What a waste of time, he thought.

His two opponents had chosen not to come or possibly had not been invited. Leo figured the former, as it was nearly impossible to make it to every such gathering during the campaign.

Leo's day had been long, and he reflected on what had occurred as the moderator made introductory remarks to the audience. She had a friendly manner and reminded him of his elementary school principal.

Most of the morning had been spent placing yard signs in different neighborhoods around town. He worked from a handwritten list that he had compiled over the last week. Requests for the two-sided plastic green advertisements were received via phone calls or chance encounters with supporters. Leo wanted to make sure he fulfilled promises to anyone wanting one even though he was unsure such postings were effective. He had to admit, the magnitude of having almost fifteen hundred of the items throughout the county was pretty impressive and he knew those running against him didn't have near as many.

He had less than forty left, and Leo wondered should he order some more. With less than two weeks until the primary and the campaign account almost zeroed out, he doubted whether he should.

Lunch had been at Ingleside Village Pizza, which served the best pie in Macon, and he limited himself to a single slice washed down with a diet soda. It had been difficult not to get a beer since nothing accompanied pizza better than a cold one, but Leo had more work to do before the day was done, and he didn't want to take a chance that anyone might see him imbibing and not approve. Word had already gotten back that somebody associated with one of his opponents represented Leo as an atheistic lazy drunk, and while not true, rumors could swirl at a moment's notice.

It was one of the things that griped him the most about choosing to run for office. Rumors, innuendos, and falsehoods had surfaced from almost the very beginning in an attempt to place Leo in a bad light. He thought of himself as a less-than-perfect man, but he had to admit it hurt to hear such negative comments especially when his family heard them, too. Those in his inner circle had told him not to worry about the lies being banded about, and he was doing his best not to. It was, however, especially difficult now that everybody was on social media posting their opinions on every subject whether fake or not.

Leo's mind shifted back to the present as a candidate for the commission gave her stump speech to the mostly bored-looking audience. He had heard every talking point so many times during the past few weeks that he could almost give any contestant's canned communication if asked. Since he was still down the line from giving his, Leo slipped back into distracted mind mode.

He had also taken some time to walk door to door in one neighborhood in an attempt to press the flesh of registered voters. In his mind, this was the epitome of campaigning. Yeah, you could run advertisements on television, over radio waves or in the newspaper, but nothing beat looking someone in the eye and asking for their vote. If the person residing there were not present, he would leave a brochure and hope for the best.

His mother had already walked the streets where Leo grew up and had reported great success with those she had come into contact with. He felt she was doing more good than anyone else could imagine. It was only one more act of love she had always shown to him and made him worry anew of her pending medical problem.

As he was pondering possibilities on that front, Leo heard his name as the emcee made a few introductory remarks about him. It was time for him to speak and answer any questions and he rose from his chair with what he hoped was an air of confidence. He strode to the microphone and smiled.

"Good evening, everybody. I appreciate the opportunity to talk to you for a few minutes and hopefully offer reasons to consider voting for me as solicitor-general.

"Let me first say some of you may not know what that office does for the citizens of Macon-Bibb. The name almost implies we're in charge of soliciting," Leo said and paused as a couple of people snickered.

"I think the job is really best described as the head prosecutor for the state court. Think of our district attorney as the chief prosecuting attorney for felony cases in superior court and then it may be a little easier to understand our responsibility is to do the same for misdemeanors.

"I've been working in the office as an assistant for over fifteen years now and understand every facet of the operation. I've evaluated and prosecuted thousands of these cases and personally tried over a hundred jury trials and probably at least ten times that many nonjury trials. And, I pledge to you that if you vote for me, I'll continue to be active in the courtroom."

Leo looked around the hall and it appeared he had most everyone's attention. Since that was a good sign, he decided to go on and not sit down yet.

"I firmly believe in the rule of law, but I also believe justice on occasion must be tempered with mercy. Good people make bad mistakes sometimes. And, we know young people especially don't realize that their actions can carry consequences that will follow them the rest of their lives. In those types of situations, there are ways I as a prosecutor can use discretion to assist those people so as to help them avoid tragic results."

An older black lady on the first row was studying Leo as he spoke, and he thought she looked familiar. He nodded respectfully in her direction before continuing.

"I want to assure you that when I'm elected, my door will be open to everyone. Before I close these remarks and try to answer any questions or address any concerns you might have, I'll quote the late Dr. Martin Luther King."

Injustice anywhere is a threat to justice everywhere.

"I agree with him. I will make it my priority and always seek equal justice for all. Thanks so much for your attendance tonight and your attention during my remarks. I'll be happy to answer any questions anyone might have, or if you'd rather speak to me personally, I'll stay around for a while after this program."

After surveying the audience and seeing no raised hands, Leo nodded and sat down to a smattering of applause. There were a few more candidates waiting their turn to speak, so he still had about thirty minutes of what he thought to be wasted time.

While half listening to the next few speakers, Leo felt weariness sink inside. The strain of work, his mother, and the consuming campaign were taking its toll and the lawyer knew it.

Maybe this choice wasn't the best one, he thought.

Leo had always thought life was all about choices that could have lasting effects, good or bad. That philosophy had first been instilled by lessons his grandfather had taught him and further reinforced by his parents. Therefore, as with this one, he had taken his time when choosing what path to take when deciding to run for office. Second-guessing wasn't productive and he would let this decision play out.

Everything will be fine, you'll see, his brain and heart told him in unison.

***

The program ended and several of the participants made hasty retreats from the hall. Leo stood and nodded to a couple of the other candidates before being approached by the distinguished woman who had earlier seemed to be regarding him.

She had a formal air about her person. Her dress was business attire chic that complimented her mocha skin and the creamy pearls around the neck. There were low-heeled pumps on her feet that made a distinct click on the hard floor.

"Mr. Berry, I'm Geneva Winfrey. No relation to Oprah," she said with a sly smile through perfectly white teeth.

Leo grinned and stuck out his hand, "Nice to meet you, Ms. Winfrey."

She gripped his hand firmly and replied, "You, too."

"I'm thinking I've met you before somewhere," Leo said.

The lady's smile now widened and there was a gleam in her eye that matched. She seemed pleased by his response and bowed her head.

"Actually, we've had two encounters, Mr. Berry. Once in a courtroom when you must've just started practicing law. The second time was only in passing, but it involved your daughter when she was maybe in the first grade."

Leo's brow furrowed. Courtroom experiences blurred after nearly twenty years spent in various ones, but he thought he should at least remember something that included Mindy.

The woman now laughed out loud at Leo, as he stood there perplexed. It only added to his frustration.

"I was on a jury panel many years ago, but didn't get selected. You were a young defense attorney then and representing someone charged with some sort of theft case. I suspected the prosecutor struck me because of the color of my skin. I remember you because of the way you were asking questions during voir dire which were obviously intended to determine bias against your client. I also remember you objecting when I was excused. I couldn't hear what you were saying, but I could see the animations at the bench. I was impressed by your passion.

"Fast forward several years later and I'm at Alexander II for an awards ceremony. Your daughter was being recognized with several awards including perfect attendance, highest grade in math and language skills and good citizenship. You and your wife were on the first row clapping like crazy every time her name was called to come on stage. There weren't many parents in attendance, so you two stood out. I remembered you then from the courtroom experience. I didn't get an opportunity to speak to you that day and regretted it."

Leo stood with his mouth open as he heard the stories he didn't really recollect. *Batson* challenges as she described, if not routine when a prosecutor struck a juror appearing to be based upon race, had been something Leo had been a part of many times in his life, so that memory of hers didn't ring a bell. The other remembrance was clearer, but he couldn't place her role there. Part of him was flattered, part of him was worried he couldn't recall.

"Wow, Ms. Winfrey. That's all I can say."

"Don't worry that you can't remember those times, Mr. Berry. That's part of your charm and why I am offering to help you in your campaign," she replied with a smirk.

"So, you're an educator. I love it. Ms. Winfrey, you've made my day. It's been a really long one, too. I'd be honored and greatly appreciate any assistance you can give me."

"Yes, I've spent over thirty-five years in various positions including as a teacher, guidance counselor, principal, and curriculum director. I'm thinking about running for a slot on the Board of Education next year when I finally retire. So, I might be able to learn something about an election by helping you, too."

The two of them continued the conversation for the next twenty minutes until they were the only people left besides the building custodian awaiting their departure. By the time they finished talking, Leo felt he had known Geneva, as she insisted he call her, for all his adult life. He knew she would be a strong ally.

As he drove home, he couldn't help but believe now that the forum had been well worth attending.

Told you so, Leo's inner self responded.

CHAPTER TWENTY-TWO

Morgan sat at his home computer randomly Googling subjects. Most of the ones he looked at involved sex in various forms. There were thousands of sites to check out. Any desire that could be had could be found on the Internet.

He was bored more than usual and wondered if he should go out. Sometimes he got lucky when that was the course taken and another pretty girl was found waiting to be plucked.

Most of the time lately, Morgan had grown even more irked by the local night scene. He was familiar with all the haunts and he knew that some of the regulars at each of those places would recognize him even if he were disguised in some fashion. There were only so many places to go in this hick town, and it was a chance he couldn't take with the recent attention in the press. He was a little pissed by that attention, but not really worried.

A part of him was ready to leave Maconga, which he thought was an apropos name of his hometown. On occasion, he had visited other urban areas of the state and figured there were endless possibilities for a man of his talents. It would be easy enough, and he had not ruled out that move in the future.

He glanced again at the screen and saw what others would classify as graphic pornography. The pictures and videos seemed mild to him. Morgan could do much better than these amateurs. He'd done so many times over and pleased many women. Females loved him. He had no doubt.

He laughed to himself as he thought maybe he should make his own videos. Morgan always took care to cover his identity, and no one would ever recognize him.

Morgan had often relived previous encounters. It was what sustained him in between those times. It seemed lately that those earlier meetings didn't hold the same charm they once did, however, and he needed more. Self-pleasure was a poor substitute for the real thing.

He slurped the final swallows of his diet cola and turned off the computer. The restlessness he felt was an itch that needed scratching. Absentmindedly, he felt himself. He was huge down there.

Walking to his closet, he paused briefly to gaze at his body in the mirror of his bathroom. Morgan admired his physique as he flexed. The smile he produced didn't look disturbing to him. Any woman would be pleased to be his partner.

Inside the double-sized enclosure where he kept his clothes and other items as well, he slid hangers one at a time. He loved costumes and had many. This night called for something different.

A particular type of woman had never consumed Morgan's desires, at least that's what he thought. Sometimes he liked outgoing girls, other times the quieter ones appealed to him. The most important trait was they had to be lonely. They needed him. He would oblige.

He kept looking for the perfect fit for the night. The problem was he didn't know what to expect. So many choices.

After going back and forth for at least ten minutes, Morgan settled on a retro look. The double knit shirt and pants were functional in the middle-Georgia climate, but they made him feel like a golf pro reject or worse, a refugee from the disco era.

Morgan smelled the clothing. It was clean and had a slight odor of Bounce as if tumbled a few days ago with a dryer sheet. He wanted to share the experience with somebody.

The only problem with sharing was he couldn't trust anyone. All his life and he'd never found a single person to confide in. He'd never had friends to speak of. At his age, it was unlikely he'd ever find someone, and it made him mad for only a moment. Self-sufficiency was A-OK.

Morgan slipped on some glossy patent leather loafers and chose the blonde toupee that gave a youthful look. It fit snugly on his shaven head. He then grabbed the bag where he kept his supplies and left the closet.

***

He pulled into the parking lot of *Promises* and stayed in an area that was not well lit. He felt the few cars here probably belonged to employees. They would more than likely still be here when Morgan decided to call it a night.

The nightclub was one Morgan had patronized on occasion, but had not visited in a few months. As he thought about it, the last time he had been there was the night when he hooked up with that Maxie chick. He felt a stirring below as her memory arose. She had been just what the doctor ordered that night. Maybe he'd get lucky again.

A sign hanging outside containing crooked lettering proclaimed it was "Throwback Night." Morgan supposed it meant patrons would be dressed in some sort of homage to past days. Or, he thought, the guests were meant to put away some alcohol in their guts in order to forget their troubles.

As he entered the place, it looked somewhat seedier than usual. That didn't matter that much as long as there were some pretty girls hanging out. The crowd was usually a little older than the ones springing up downtown and was made up of divorcees, middle-class blue collar working folks, and a few professionals who were either on the way up or on the path down to a new level. It was a good mix for Morgan, and the joint was crowded.

The fringes of the club were not as well lit, and he slipped to the farthest edge away from the stage and dance floor. A two high-top table with accompanying stools was the best for him and allowed for an unobstructed view of all sections. Someone had already borrowed one of the seats, which made it even better. He didn't favor someone approaching to ask if he was using the other one while conducting his surveillance. Morgan wanted to be as inconspicuous as possible. Also, he knew there was an emergency exit door nearby just in case there was a need to get out of the joint unnoticed.

After positioning himself with back to the wall, Morgan gave the place a measured study. The purpose was two-fold and equally important. First, he looked for potential targets. Second, any threats needed to be recognized.

A waitress dressed in Daisy Duke shorts sashayed to his spot within a couple of minutes and flashed an imperfect smile through ruby red gloss. Her hair was dyed red with roots beginning their creep to mousy brown. She had tiny golden butterflies pinned in her lobes, and Morgan noticed right away three more tattooed just above her ample left breast. The tube top she wore was at least one size too small.

"Hey, baby. What can I get ya," she asked in a nasally tone.

Morgan avoided direct eye contact even in the relative dark and responded, "Jack and Diet Coke."

"Sure, sweetie. Ya waiting on anybody else or are ya by yourself tonight?"

"Maybe," was all he said.

"Well, okay cutie. I'll get ya drink and be right back. Rosie's gonna take real good care of ya tonight," she said with a wink and another waxed smile.

Morgan watched as she shook her hips walking toward the bar. Her body was not bad and the heels on her feet tightened the legs leading to her firm ass. He had been with worse in the past and could probably make it happen for her if he got horny enough.

It would be the best she's ever had. That voice would drive me crazy, though, he thought.

That was the thing. He'd had sex with women other times when it was totally voluntary, but it was never as good to him. It was too much like work. It was much more pleasurable when a pretty girl played hard to get.

He continued observing people around the establishment and saw three or four potential women who might be worthy of his special attention. There was a single brunette with her back to him sitting by herself at a table near the dance floor, another single blonde at the main bar sipping on a martini and two females without male companionship whispering to each other as they did their own study of available men.

Morgan didn't notice any visible dangers lurking. There were several single guys probably looking for a version of what he sought, but for the most part they seemed pudgy and just lonely. The fit ones were with somebody already and paid him no mind.

"Here ya go, sugah. Jack and diet. Ya wanna start a tab?"

"Not right now, I'll settle up in case I leave early."

"Alrighty, but I hope you'll stay and keep me company for a while. That'll be six-fifty," she said bending to expose more cleavage than before.

He handed her a ten and told her to keep the change. Since Morgan rarely drank a whole one anywhere he went, he doubted he would need her services again.

A big grin and jiggle resulted as she responded, "Oh, baby. Thank ya. I'll check on ya in a little while."

She shook a little extra as she walked away and Morgan snickered. Some of the girls he came into contact with were so stupid. It would be so easy to bang this idiot. It made him want her less despite her fetching derrière.

Once again he began studying the subjects. He decided to exclude the couple of whispering women since they were probably travelling together. Too problematic.

That left two potential scores, but he couldn't tell if they were pretty girls, yet. Their faces were obscured and Morgan was unsure. It was still early and he had more time to observe.

He spent the next fifteen minutes watching the twirled-up straw-colored haired one swilling vodka at the bar. She was on her second one in the short time he'd been there watching. Anybody drinking hard liquor like that would be an easy mark for him.

The longer Morgan inspected her; his initial interest began to wane. He could tell even from the distance that separated them that she probably once was a looker. Now the face was showing some lines that Botox hadn't smoothed. The hair when let down from its swirl might help obscure the aging appearance, but it seemed overly peroxided and would more than likely be brittle and coarse to the touch. He had never been very interested in older women, and this one qualified.

Morgan took a sip of the cocktail that was still less than half consumed. As weak as it was, he had no buzz, and he was clear-headed. It made it easy to turn his attention to the last hope for the night, the brunette seated closer but with her back to him.

The crowd had thinned somewhat since Morgan's arrival nearly an hour before, and he moved to an adjacent table recently vacated. It gave him a better view of the girl, and he felt that old excitement start to build.

She had shoulder-length wavy tresses that complimented creamy complexion. The stylish outfit she wore accented her figure. He could imagine how enticing it would be to see that body without the covering.

Just as he began to formulate the beginnings of a plan, two unexpected things happened to change his mind. The butterflied waitress came over again, and Morgan noticed an older guy across the room studying him.

CHAPTER TWENTY-THREE

Jimbo had been feeling pretty much like crap since being reamed out by Sheriff Davison a few days before. He'd had enough of that from superiors before the departments were consolidated, and he was now too old to listen to berating from somebody younger than him. It only made the investigator want to quit the job more than usual.

As he rode around town in his aging cruiser, Jimbo recalled the lowlights of the confrontation with the law enforcement chief. He fumed internally at the memory.

How did a veteran like you screw up so badly, Barbour? You know better, Captain.

With all due respect, Sheriff, I don't think I have.

Oh yeah, you have. Number one, taking a call on a case you never should have. Two, not going through regular protocol. Three, not getting assistance. Four, letting the press get wind of an investigation. Should I go on?

No, sir. All I can say is I'm working on it.

Not any more, you're not. We have investigators to take care of routine cases. Your responsibility is to supervise the officers under your command. If you can't do that, I'll find someone else to do the job. Understand?

Since then, Jimbo had become consumed with the bastard causing all the trouble. And, he didn't mean the sheriff, Leo Berry, or the Telegraph. He would solve the case and find the raping mofo even if it was on his own time. Then he'd retire from this game. He was tired.

There were two places Jimbo knew victims had been selected from. One was the grocery store. The other was that nightclub, *Promises.* For the last couple of nights, Jimbo had taken turns patrolling both.

So far, it had been a bust. It was a long shot, but sometimes criminals returned to the scene of the crime. Jimbo needed a break, so he would keep it up if it meant working extra hours. The wife wasn't very happy, but she'd get over it.

His hip hurt when he got out of his car and headed toward the club. It got a little better by the time he entered and wondered if a stiff whiskey would help. He wasn't on the clock, so what would it hurt.

When he got inside, Jimbo did a quick look around and nothing caught his attention. Wanting to blend in and not bring notice to himself, he limped over to a sidebar. He didn't sit down at first, but ordered a Maker's Mark and water from a bartender resembling a nephew, acne and all, he saw once a year at the family Christmas gathering.

Jimbo took a sip and let the elixir slide down his throat. It was soothing on many levels. He strolled from the bar and walked to an area that allowed an unobstructed view.

Systematically he went from section to section and reviewed everyone there. Part of him didn't expect anything.

Why anyone committing an assault like had occurred would return to the scene was a mystery to Jimbo, but stranger things had happened. At any rate, there was no other option at this time in the investigation.

He propped his elbow on a shelf that jutted from a wall located close to the bar where he had gotten his drink. There were no seats located there and no other patrons nearby at that moment. It allowed him privacy and a good vantage point.

On the far side away from where he stood, Jimbo spied a single guy with a golden haired head. There was a familiarity from a video he'd seen before notwithstanding the different color of the man's mane. Jimbo's curiosity was piqued immediately, and he honed in on the man.

His radar was singing when a waitress walked over to the object of his consideration. She was all over the guy and obviously flirting with him. Jimbo watched raptly as the woman worked. The suspect seemed more than a little nervous.

It was obvious the woman liked the man. She was bending over him and her tits were practically in his mouth. She appeared to be on a mini trampoline as she bounced, and the tight top containing her huge boobs could barely contain those cantaloupes. The man didn't seem to notice as he stared back at Jimbo.

There was only a brief moment as the two men's eyes met. It was enough for Jimbo, and he felt the need to see the dude up close and personal. He headed in that direction.

The band started about the same time. It was a testament to disco as they started singing about shaking your booty. The dance floor between the two men was suddenly crowded with couples dancing and singing along. Jimbo couldn't see nearly as well.

Jimbo stumbled a bit as he tried to make it across the floor and almost fell before righting himself. When he finally got his balance again, the guy was gone. The investigator swung his gaze in every direction trying to find him but was unsuccessful.

Goddammit! He thought.

The place was jumping and everyone was feeling the moment except him. Jimbo only wanted to find the guy who he'd just seen minutes before. His gut told him it was the sorry asshole he needed to arrest.

He was torn. Should he head outside and try to find him or talk to the waitress. Jimbo decided on the latter tact.

When Jimbo finally made it to the area where he had seen the redheaded waitress flouncing for his suspect only moments before, neither was present. Glancing at the table, Jimbo hoped to find a glass he could confiscate and check for prints, but he could find no helpful evidence. In fact, it appeared to have been wiped down with a wet rag that left visible swirls on the surface.

Speeding up his hitched gait, Jimbo moved toward the main bar where he saw the server standing with her back to him. Her behind was in synch with the booming music as if the lyrics were being repeated for her exclusive benefit. Arriving but not wanting to startle her, Jimbo tapped lightly on an exposed shoulder.

She turned to the detective and the big smile that was plastered fell away. He saw disappointment written all over the made-up face.

"Can I help ya?"

"I hope so. I'm looking for the man you were talking to over there," replied Jimbo as he pointed to the table where he'd seen them.

The song wouldn't end, and it was difficult to carry on a conversation with all the noise. Jimbo nodded to an area away from the bar, and the two of them went there. It was only slightly less blaring, but Jimbo at least had her alone.

"Do you know the customer you were serving?" Again Jimbo used his head to indicate the table reference earlier.

"Are you a cop or something? Why you wanna know?"

The detective pulled out his badge and the waitress gave it a short glimpse. She rolled her eyes and blew a bubble with gum she had been working over since their meeting.

"Never seen him before that I remember. Didn't get his name 'cause he didn't say much. He's a good tipper is about all I know."

"Did you see where he went?"

"Nah. He hauled ass like he had a bee up it." She giggled and continued, "I thought he might wanna another Jack and diet, so I went to ask him. He said he had to go and then he booked before I really introduced myself, you know? I thought we might get to know each other a little better after my shift. I guess that didn't work out. Why ya looking for him?"

Jimbo avoided answering her by asking another question. "Did you notice anything about him that stood out?"

She appeared to contemplate before answering, "His hair was thick. Didn't have a part, you know?"

The nasally 'you know' phrase was starting to irritate Jimbo but he tried not to let it show. "Anything else you recall?"

"Not really." She paused. "Well, it ain't much but he kept a napkin around his drink the whole time. And, he sipped it through one of those tiny straws we use to stir with, you know?"

"Rosie, you're needed over here," hollered a bearded beefy bartender who had entered the space where the conversation was occurring. He didn't seem intimidated by the older guy when Jimbo attempted his steely gaze.

"I'll be right there, Biff. Sorry, detective, but gotta go."

She hurried from him swinging her butt in double time. Jimbo felt so close, yet still far away.

Damn it, man.

CHAPTER TWENTY-FOUR

Leo was feeling pressure building on several fronts. With just over two weeks left before the primary, the campaign required even more of his time. Barely keeping up with the heavy caseload at the office was not helping and here in the hospital waiting room was not the place he wanted to be.

His mother had wanted to postpone the hastily scheduled surgery until after the election, but Leo and his brothers insisted she do it as soon as it could be done. This was a family decision made the previous week after Mom had gone through a sonogram and other tests showing a soccer ball-sized growth in her abdomen.

Leo and his brothers had been in the doctor's office that day when he told their mother the chances the tumor was cancerous stood at least fifty percent. They now camped out in the cramped waiting room and were trying their best not to show concern, an endeavor at which they all were failing.

"What are we going to do if it's cancer?" asked Tommy, the youngest of the four boys.

"Let's don't worry about it until the doctor talks to us," Denny snapped back.

The two of them gave each other looks that were not the friendliest. Leo and Eddie glanced at one another and shook their heads. Their two younger brothers had always been siblings who would be close buddies one minute and at each other's throats the next.

"Hey, we'll cross whatever bridge as it comes. We've got to be strong for her. She's been a rock for each one of us at one time or another," said Leo.

Tommy and Denny were at least temporarily mollified and walked closer to Leo and Eddie's position. All four huddled together and shared a quiet moment, as their eyes grew moist before separating again into other parts of the room.

Leo, being the oldest, had emotions running throughout his nervous system while trying not to show them. When in any crisis involving a member of the family, he was always transported to a conversation with his father when he was only a teenager.

Leo, if something happens and I'm not there, it's up to you to take care of your mother and your brothers.

Those words from his departed daddy stuck with him now although they occurred twenty-five years before. He hadn't wanted that responsibility, but had accepted it then and he did now. The directive had been taken to heart more than once. Eddie broke the brief spell.

"It's been two hours," commented Eddie looking at his watch.

"I'm going to smoke a cigarette. Be back in a few," said Tommy wiping his eyes with his sleeve as he walked out of the room toward the elevators. Although all the boys had experimented and smoked when they were younger, Tommy was the only one of the Berry boys who had retained the nasty habit.

"He's a mess. I don't know if he can handle it if Mama doesn't come through this," Denny offered.

"If he could just find a woman who would stay with him for awhile, it might help," suggested Eddie referencing Tommy's current separation from wife number three, four if you counted the one he married twice.

Leo didn't comment but thought both brothers' assessments were essentially true. Tommy's relationship with their mother was close and had elements of codependency. At the same time, his relationships with other women never seemed to last and held way too much drama. Leo's preference was to stay out of trying to help with either and let it all play out unless specifically asked by Tommy. He had too much other stuff to think about than his youngest brother's struggles with the opposite sex.

For some reason, another memory cascaded back. The Berry boys were kids again. Tommy had gotten into a tussle with a neighborhood kid at the bus stop earlier in the day and had suffered no injuries except to a new shirt he wore.

Their father was working two jobs so was not at home to hear of the encounter. If he had been, Leo was sure he would've been dispatched to confront the bully. It was another of the father's drills to the oldest son that he had to protect his younger brothers.

Since Daddy was not there, Leo now remembered how their mother questioned Tommy about the torn shirt and then picked up the telephone. She called the offending child's mother, and the four boys listened as Mom showed her mama bear side. It was the only time in his life Leo could remember Mom threatening another person, but he could still hear her say, "I'll meet you in the street and beat your ass if your kid ever does that to mine again."

Tommy slid back inside the room smelling of Marlboros and the strong coffee he held in his darkly tanned hand. He flopped in one of the lime green chairs and uttered a profanity. Leo knew if the doctor didn't come in soon, the disposition was only going to get worse. Tommy had inherited enough of their father's trigger temper to ensure such an outcome.

As if summoned by thought, Dr. Martin Sanford walked into the area with weary eyes drooping. He wore blue scrubs that stretched across his protruding belly and a matching cap that perched on a balding head. Wisps of white hair could be seen trying to sneak out of the paper lid.

Tommy stood first and the other men followed suit. "How is she? Is it cancer?" Tommy blurted.

The surgeon's eyes fastened on Tommy and talked to him directly, but shifted his gaze to each of the others, too, as he spoke. "Your mother is fine and as strong as any patient her age I've ever treated. The tumor was contained although it had attached to an area that required more time in order to remove. The initial pathology shows it's benign."

Leo felt he could breathe again as he exhaled. He reached out his right hand to the doctor and gripped one that was larger but almost delicate in touch. They shook each other as Leo croaked his appreciation. His brothers performing in similar fashion followed him.

"Because of the length and location of the incision, she'll have to take it easy for several days, but otherwise she can resume her normal activities. She'll be in recovery for probably another hour, and we'll keep her overnight. Y'all can take her home in the morning. You boys see that your mother doesn't get too froggy until she heals," Dr. Sanford finished before leaving the room.

All that Leo could think at the moment was, *Whew, one bullet dodged. Now I need to dodge a few more.*

CHAPTER TWENTY-FIVE

The restlessness Leo felt was an itchiness inside and out of his body. While there were three or four dry spots on his skin that had sprung up seemingly overnight, impatience over the election exactly two weeks from now made him want to scratch his brain. Alone in his cramped office, Leo alternately rubbed his head and arms.

Since it was Tuesday, the prosecutor had already been up several hours, first to attend jail court and then followed by a visit to the hospital to make sure his mother was scheduled for release after her surgery the day before. Thankfully, his brothers were there and took care of getting her home. Now his grey matter seemed as scrambled as the egg sandwich he had consumed hastily between the two trips.

Reliving the court session, he thought of the usual homeless, mentally ill, addicts and repeat misdemeanor offenders seen on a regular basis and wondered if he could ever make a difference in their plight. It was a problem all over the country requiring more resources than local governments would or could address adequately, and Leo was but one part of the equation. It was, however, one he wanted to be a part of and try to assist in finding ways to combat. He kept telling himself that was one of the reasons for running the race.

One frequent flier, as they were known in law enforcement circles, stood out during the early morning proceedings. The latest arrest, his ninety-eighth over the course of the last dozen years, made Leon Wright a candidate to achieve the record for most detentions in the local jail, if he could only live another few years and maintain his current level of bad behavior.

Mr. Wright, you're charged with criminal trespass and soliciting at the Food Mart. Do you want a lawyer to represent you?

Hell naw, Mr. Berry. I know my rights and I don't need no state lawyer telling me what to do. I plead guilty and throw myself on the mercy of the court. I'm hoping the judge will give me time served so I can go home and check on my family. They been sick, you know. Not as sick as me.

The shriveled up man was no older than Leo, but looking at least twenty years older, pulled open the white jumpsuit and showed the colostomy bag that was attached on his side. The old bailiff standing closest to the defendant took two steps back fearing it would be flung at him. Wright had done that in the past to people in authority when things were not going his way.

Leo had not immediately replied, but had shaken his head at Wright to let him know the time served would be a lot less if he didn't show out in some fashion. After years of dealing with the man, Wright would usually not give too much grief to Leo. The prosecutor was not sure why other than once when he had first gone to work in the Solicitor's Office, Leo had run into him on the street and gave him a few dollars to buy a Nu-Way hotdog, or so that's what Wright said he was going to buy with the money he begged for.

How are your mother and brother? The judge asked. *I haven't seen them in court lately.*

Leo remembered them, too. They were also frequent fliers although had nowhere near the arrest totals of Leon. Mama June and Brother Melvin liked to drink at home and mainly got in trouble only when Leon partied with them rather than staying on the streets as was his usual custom. They had been charged several times with disorderly conduct on the occasions when they got together.

That's cause they moved to Laurens County, Judge. I don't get down there to see them too much since they left. You reckon I could get out? I'd appreciate it if you could also get me a bus ticket so I could go without trying to find a ride.

I don't think the folks down there would appreciate it very much if I sent you to Dublin although I suspect there are many in this room who would gladly buy a ticket for you to get out of Macon.

Several people in the audience laughed as the judge continued, *The Court recognizes you from many appearances before me and on the record notes you have had your rights explained to you earlier this morning and countless times before. Since you've indicated your desire to plead guilty, sign the papers Mr. Berry has, and I'll impose a sentence of thirty days in jail with credit time served. I'm sure the deputies will be glad to get you out of here today, Mr. Wright. Unfortunately, I'll be shocked if I don't see you in the near future.*

"Earth to Leo," came a voice from his doorway.

Leo glanced up to see Jimbo standing there. The older guy looked to be as tired as he felt himself, maybe even more so. The wrinkles were deeper in his face, and the eyes were faded to a lighter shade of bluish-green.

"Looking kinda beat, Detective."

"You ain't lookin' so well yourself, Little Leo," replied Jimbo.

"I've been meaning to call you, Jimbo."

"Same here."

Captain Barbour slid into the room and slouched into one of the vacant wooden chairs across from where Leo sat. His rumpled sports jacket slid open revealing a pooch above the leather belt where his badge was attached.

"You got a recipe to share or maybe an update on your investigation, if you're even on it anymore. I saw the article in the Telegraph a few days ago."

The cop's mouth moved south into a sour scowl before replying, "It sucks to be me sometimes. But you know what? It's like that line from that song, and I'm not gonna let it bother me tonight."

Leo recognized the partial lyric from the old southern rock song by The Atlanta Rhythm Section and smiled. Love for that particular music genre was something the two men shared despite the difference in their ages. Since Leo was a little kid during the height of its popularity, Jimbo had often talked about meeting many of the artists who called Macon home during that period. Leo thought it was cool that Ronnie Hammond, the late lead singer for ARS, was born and raised in Macon. Music was a part of the rich heritage of the city.

"Just avoid the whipping post, old man."

Leo's response and reference to The Allman Brothers seemed to lift Jimbo's mood and he grinned. "Been there and done that, too," Jimbo said.

"Campaign's about over," he continued while changing the subject, "So how's everything on the trail?"

"Ready for it to be over. You didn't answer my question though. Are you still working on finding the guy who raped Maxine?

"Yeah, just not officially. What I'm about to tell you is between us, okay?"

"Of course, Jimbo."

The investigator grimaced as he shifted in the less than comfortable old wooden chair. "I think this ancient body is rebelling this morning. You got anything for pain?"

Leo fished in the top drawer of his desk and came out with the Kroger brand of acetaminophen. He passed the container to Jimbo who popped the top and swallowed three with a sip of coffee from a Styrofoam cup.

"The sheriff has instructed me it's not my job to look for the shithead responsible. There's a unit assigned to the investigation. I've reached out to them and offered to do anything I can to help, but they've been lukewarm. I guess they think I'm just an old dinosaur and haven't included me, at least so far."

Jimbo took a deep breath and went on, "That being said, I've been reviewing some things trying to look outside the box. I hate that term, by the way."

"Yeah, me too," said Leo.

"Anyway, I've brought some videos I wanted you to look at. They might show our prime suspect. If you've got time and the equipment, that is."

"Yep, on both accounts. Please follow me to our state of the art media room, " replied Leo with a touch of sarcasm.

The two men walked through a maze to the rear of the suite of offices. Near a grimy microwave that even Ajax couldn't clean, located in a cramped area with two chairs accessed only by moving one of them, sat an aging television with a VCR/DVD underneath.

Jimbo arched his eye toward Leo as the prosecutor performed the necessary maneuvers to allow both of them to sit in front of the screen. The detective groaned as he flopped into an even more uncomfortable chair than the one he had just vacated.

"I know, I know. That's why the defense always says the state has the advantage. We have all the resources. Let's hope this thing still works," said Leo as he held out his hand for the DVD.

Leo pressed some buttons and slid in the disc. There were whirring sounds followed by a high-pitched whine before the picture indicated three files.

"I've made copies of three videos I got off security cameras. The first one is from the nightclub the same night your wife's friend was attacked. The second one is from a grocery store before another assault was made. Believe it or not, the third one is from the same club evening before last when I paid it an unofficial visit. Watch all three without my comments and tell me what you see."

Leo nodded and clicked on the first file titled *Promises* 1. He watched intently and easily made out Maxine seated at a bar. Leo didn't recognize the premises although he had heard of it and knew there had been one or two cases he had prosecuted as a result of the place over-serving patrons.

The quality of the recording was grainy, but he could tell without difficulty several things. First, the club was rather large. Second, there was a big crowd in the area being recorded. Third, his wife's friend looked sad and lonely. She was staring at her drink and not talking with anyone. It was impossible to tell how long she had been at the location since it was obvious from watching the time counter of the clip that it had been edited until this point.

He saw but could not hear the bartender address Maxine and then shortly thereafter she paid her tab. She didn't appear intoxicated as she left the area.

Without warning, the camera angle changed and Leo was now seeing a more shaded area near bathrooms that were more visible. Maxine walked into view headed toward the facilities. She paused and looked toward the darkened space. Leo could make out there was a man seated by himself, but couldn't make out features until Maxine suffered a fall that was not her fault.

When that happened, the man in the shadows stood and Leo got a better look at him.

Probably average height and build without remarkable features, he noted. The dark and curly hairstyle was on the longish side covering his ears. Leo still couldn't make out facial features.

At first, Leo thought the man was going to walk to Maxine and assist her. After taking a half step in her direction, however, he made an abrupt turn and then a quick exit out of camera range. Before he left, Leo could make out the man's face somewhat better although there were no distinguishing marks or qualities. The first video ended at that point.

Leo turned slightly and said, "So, I'm guessing at this point the guy in the last few scenes is your suspect. If he is, kind of eerie to think we're watching the guy who attacked her later that night."

"Like I said, reserve your comments 'til you've watched all of them," responded Jimbo.

The second file Leo clicked was labeled *Kroger.* Right away the superior quality of the picture was evident. He watched in silence as different cameras followed an attractive blonde who appeared to be mid-thirties. Leo supposed she must be a victim, but wasn't sure. He carefully studied her surroundings looking for a potential suspect, but never saw one.

When she was checking out, the camera settings must've been manipulated to focus on another female near the checkout station because it was zoomed toward her after a general shot of the scene. The apparent interest became evident, and Leo was able to discern the person in the video had male characteristics that probably wouldn't have been noticed otherwise. After a scene or two in the parking lot that wasn't particularly of note to Leo, the file stopped.

Leo glanced at Jimbo and then brought up the last item listed as *Promises 2.* Scenes from the club came up again with a different cast of characters and not any clearer. It provided a stark contrast to the pictures from the grocery store.

The initial camera angle showed the place was crowded and recorded activity provided almost too much to observe. Leo's eye scanned searching for a suspect or a victim, but was unsuccessful.

After a couple of minutes, Leo was beginning to think the tape was useless until another viewpoint, probably the same one from the first file, showed an area near the restrooms. In maybe the same seat as before, at a high-top table in the shadows, sat a single guy.

The prosecutor strained for at least fifteen minutes trying to get a clear look at the man. He watched as a flouncy waitress attended to him. He could tell the man was checking out different areas, but because of the camera angle couldn't find the sources of whatever might be of interest.

Leo was just about to tell Jimbo this was a waste of time when the suspect suddenly stood up. For the first time, a full profile appeared and the picture was frozen on the screen.

The man's hair was obviously different from the first video. However, there were enough similarities for Leo to think this was the same person. Leo couldn't help but exhale a swoosh of air when the realization hit him.

"Any idea who he is?" asked Leo as he put his face closer to the television.

"No," Jimbo grunted.

"Well, somebody's bound to recognize him when you release pictures."

The detective shook his head and said, "I don't know about that. He's obviously into disguises and I've shown them around at both locations, in the office and even to the victims without anybody saying they could identify him. I'm afraid if I issue copies to the media I'll spook him and never be able to find him. Hell, Leo, I almost had him this last time. I was the reason he bolted out the back door. He saw me and got lucky."

Leo reconsidered and couldn't fault Jimbo's reasoning. The photos weren't of the greatest quality and blasting such photos might also have the undesired effect of scaring the public as well as send the guy into hiding and destroying evidence such as his wigs. There were at least three that would help make a strong case if they could be found in his possession. It was a tricky choice under the circumstances.

"Yeah, I guess you're right. It just bothers me to think this predator is out there and somebody might be able to put a name on him if they saw this," Leo replied nodding toward the screen.

Jimbo's cellphone began to ring in muffled tones inside his jacket. He pulled it out and his lips pursed when he saw who was calling.

"Leo, I've got to take this and need to get out of here. Keep the tapes for now and maybe you'll get a chance to look at them again. Maybe you'll even have an epiphany," the detective said as he ambled out of the room.

The prosecutor removed the disc from the player and slipped it into his pocket. He'd put it up and try to watch it again later. Right now he had other work to do.

CHAPTER TWENTY-SIX

Morgan had called in sick for the last two days. Part of him really was. This ordeal was unlike anything he'd ever suffered.

He'd always felt in control. Now he felt he was losing it. That was new.

His conflicted brain told Morgan he needed a change in the routine. He was starting to make stupid mistakes. Maybe he'd become too complacent.

The other night in the club had been terribly close to being disastrous. How asinine can you be to go back to the same place again?

After reliving the experience multiple times, he thought everything had to be okay. Nobody knew who he was in that place. He'd changed his appearance from previous trips and the waitress was different. Morgan laughed to himself as he thought about her pitiful attempts to impress him.

The truly funny thing was she had no idea that women who tried to show him interest had the adverse effect. There was probably some kind of psychological term for it, but he only wanted those not seeming interested in him.

Does that make me crazy?

Morgan didn't care. He had functioned his entire adult life just like this, and he had no intention of changing now. The main question was whether or not he needed to move from Macon.

That timeworn cop probably didn't remember him, but Morgan had recognized the old fart. The geezer had been around the town for as long as Morgan could recall. He had to be close to seventy if not older. Some locals even called him a legend because of his ability to solve crimes others couldn't.

Morgan had met the guy many years ago in connection with a case the detective was working on. It was early during his days working in the tax office when Barbour was trying to check on a partial tag number. Although the details were a little fuzzy now, Morgan had been able to help provide information that eventually led to an arrest. He had actually liked solving the problem for the cop.

That had to be at least twenty years before, and Morgan thought he looked a lot different now. Back then he had hair with sideburns and a droopy moustache. No way would the guy make a connection to the slick-shaven current Morgan. He hated facial hair now and couldn't imagine ever allowing it again.

Still, through years of the activities and skills honed with experience, Morgan didn't think he'd ever come this close to being caught. He didn't keep any records of his conquests since beginning the chosen path in life, but Morgan could recollect every one. He knew without counting there had been more than thirty women out there in the world fortunate enough to experience his expertise.

Because of his modus operandi, Morgan felt secure very few of those *pretty girls* had made formal complaints to the authorities. If they had, there would have been more publicity. He thought more than likely; the girls had enjoyed his attention and secretly hoped he'd come back one day. It only reinforced his convictions that he was invincible if not invisible.

He sat in his car sipping on his favorite canned cola as the thoughts swirled. Driving around the metro area of central Georgia had long become one way to settle his mind on the rare occasions of experiencing doubt. The parking lot where the plain sedan sat contained several vehicles just like his and calmed him further after the morning trip.

Analysis of his situation was almost complete. Not that money was a concern, but an offer was on the table that made retirement a valid option. The local government was proposing an *early out* for some employees in an effort to reduce salaries and benefits for those unlucky enough to be hired later. Morgan was way too young to think about quitting work, but the extra credit being offered by the idiots in charge was too good to pass up. With the money and investments he already had in the bank, he would be set for the rest of his life without ever hitting another lick.

Just think about how much extra time I'll have finding new pretty girls to date.

He would need the additional time because it was clear to him now that he needed to leave this town. Before that, he needed to be with one more.

Preparations were being made. It would be his biggest challenge ever, but he was up to it.

CHAPTER TWENTY-SEVEN

Leo tried not to be nervous as he looked around the television set. On air reporters had interviewed him in the past, but this was different. The taping was scheduled to appear on the local station at least twice over the upcoming weekend and could possibly influence voters in next Tuesday's primary. A lot was at stake, and he knew a bad performance could spell disaster for the campaign.

His other opponents sat beside him and the show's moderator/interviewer shifted in a seat cattycornered to their left. The balding man with an epic comb-over was a former newspaper journalist who appeared more uncomfortable before the camera than the three people with much less experience. Randy Savitch was well respected, however, and known for asking tough questions.

Leo breathed in slowly and studied the two lawyers next to him. The female African-American defense lawyer candidate occupied the space between him and Rob Scott, his fellow assistant solicitor-general.

Ronnie Brundage had changed her hairstyle at least five times since the campaign had begun and the latest effort was probably the least flattering, thought Leo. It involved extensions that were unnatural in appearance due to their color, and they didn't seem to be attached properly. Her business suit attire would be more appropriate if the length of the skirt weren't as short and was perhaps one size larger. The color of her too-long fingernails and lipstick at least matched, he also noted. She kept clearing her throat, which made Leo want to slide over in case she had some kind of bug.

Rob was dressed conservatively in a dark gray suit, starched white shirt and nondescript matching tie. He was serious in demeanor with a pinched look on his handsome face. The last few months had taken a toll, as he was thinner and had a few more facial lines. Leo and he had continued to do their jobs in their mutual office as they had for many years, but the once friendly relationship was best described as strained now and it showed. He was sure Rob would find such a thought distasteful, but Leo couldn't help to feel a little sorry for his co-worker.

Leo tugged on the bottom of his navy sports coat to remove creases and adjusted the sleeves of his light blue cotton shirt. He then tightened the knot of the power tie that had been chosen by Dee and reminded himself to look directly into the camera when he spoke.

A young production assistant with a headset warned that the taping was about to start just before music blared a little too loudly signaling the show's beginning. Savitch introduced himself, and then the camera panned to the candidates as he did the same for them.

"We'll start by giving each candidate one minute to make an opening statement. Mr. Scott, by luck of the draw, you're first."

"Thank you. For over twenty years I've served as assistant solicitor in Bibb County. I serve my church as a deacon, and I've been a member of the congregation for over forty years. I'm an army veteran and currently hold the rank of Lt. Colonel in the Georgia National Guard. I've been married to the same woman for over thirty years, and we've got two grown children, and grandchildren, too.

"I'm the best man for the job because I'm the toughest on crime. I'm the most stable, and this is not a joke for me. Look at my experience and you'll agree," Rob finished earnestly although somewhat harshly, thought Leo.

"Okay, Mr. Scott. Ms. Brundage, you're next," said Savitch.

The female fidgeted in her seat before responding. "Uh, yes. I'm lawyer Brundage. For the last three years I've been defending citizens in court from over-zealous prosecutors like these two men. That's why I decided to run for solicitor-general. If I'm elected, I'm going to clean up the office and stop the abuse on innocent people. Uh, thank you," she ended abruptly with a bat of her eyes catching everyone else off guard, especially the moderator.

Now Savitch looked even more awkward. A nervous laugh precipitated him responding, "Oh, okay. We'll need to explore that further in a minute. Uh now, let's hear from the last candidate, Leo Berry."

Thinking on the fly that the two opponents had given him an opening he hadn't really thought of, Leo nodded at the camera and gave a slight smile.

"Thank you, Mr. Savitch. I appreciate the opportunity to be on this show and tell the voters of Macon-Bibb why I believe I'm the best candidate for Solicitor-General.

"For those of you who don't know what the job entails and why it's important, I'd like you to think about an office that is responsible for processing and prosecuting over ten thousand criminal cases a year. Cases involving a wide range of matters involving traffic, thefts, and domestic violence require not only experience evaluating and presenting them in court, but also need personal attention from the person in charge who will set policies to ensure equal justice for everyone affected.

"I want to be that person helping to make those crucial decisions because I love this community. On my mother's side, I'm a five generation descendant and on my father's side, four generations have lived right here. I went to public schools in Macon and didn't go off to college when I graduated high school. I stayed and got my undergraduate and law degrees at Mercer University.

"I've been a practicing attorney ever since. First, I had a general practice for several years and represented folks needing help. For over the last fifteen years, I've been working in the office as an assistant solicitor so that I've got a total of twenty years experience on both sides.

"Ultimately, a Solicitor-General needs not only experience, he also needs an even temperament and personality to deal with different people he comes into contact with. I hope each of the voters will come to the conclusion that I am the person to be elected to this position. Thank you."

"Well, okay then. We'll move right into the questions and start the first one by following up on something Ms. Brundage brought up in her opening," Savitch paused and continued.

"That sounded like a serious allegation you made against these two men. Can you explain what you meant by calling them over-zealous and why the office is in need of cleaning up?"

The woman tried clearing her throat and it sounded more like a croak when she responded. "I've had clients that were treated unfairly by Rob Scott and Leo Berry. Neither one of them would listen to me when I told them my clients were innocent. Both are more interested in getting convictions than in justice. I will say, Leo is a little better than Rob in that he's not quite as rude, but I've had clients go to jail when they shouldn't have because neither believed what I had to say. They always believe whatever the cops say. And everybody knows, police lie. That's why I'd fire both of them."

Savitch's face seemed to be caught between a smile and a frown. He finally said, "Those are pretty broad statements, Ms. Brundage. I think maybe…"

Rob interrupted and the camera shifted to his reddening face. "That's such bull sh--, crap! What you've just said would be slanderous if you weren't so incompetent. That's your major problem, you don't know what you're saying much less what you're doing. I don't know how you got through law school, much less how you passed the bar. I wouldn't be surprised if you're not disbarred in the near future. I feel sorry for your clients."

"Okay, okay," interjected Savitch in an obvious effort to settle tensions. "Maybe this would be a good time to take a break for our sponsors."

"Excuse me, Mr. Savitch, but could I have a moment to respond before the break?" asked Leo.

"Uh, yes. I think it's only fair since you've not had a chance to answer Ms. Brundage's, uh, charges."

"Thank you. I take what Ms. Brundage just said about me, and Mr. Scott, too, as personal attacks on our characters. I can say unequivocally those statements are false and total mischaracterizations of what we do everyday in our jobs.

"Without naming defendants, their charges and the results of prosecutions of their cases, I'm pretty sure I know to whom she's referring as her clients. While we handle thousands of cases every year, she and I have only had a couple together in the past year or so, and I remember both. Since those cases have been resolved and are public records, anyone interested in the outcomes could have access to the files and make their own determination.

"Every case coming through our office is evaluated individually to determine if the evidence is sufficient to proceed. When a defense lawyer raises questions about an evidentiary issue or offers their own evidence to clarify something in a case, we look at it carefully. It is not unusual for us to decline prosecution or possibly compromise the case in a plea bargain under such circumstances.

"Neither case I remember with Ms. Brundage falls in the category requiring compromise or dismissal. I stand by my decisions in those cases. Although I can't speak for Mr. Scott, I daresay he would say the same about cases he's had with Ms. Brundage. We share the same philosophy with respect to criminal prosecutions.

"One other comment I want to make about her statement concerning police officers. Yes, I have many friends in law enforcement, and I tend to believe what they say most of the time because of knowing them personally or from working with them professionally on a daily basis.

"I think a lot of people might remember, however, I've had issues with some officers. Not only have I prosecuted a few for abuses or crimes they've committed, but I also had one threaten my life a few years ago, and it didn't end well for that particular man.

"I remain committed to doing my job with equal justice to all, and that's what I plan to do for as long as I'm allowed," finished Leo as he stared directly into the camera.

The show went on taping for another twenty minutes after that, but it didn't need to. One candidate had taken the upper hand. Highlights of the interview appeared multiple times on different media sources.

CHAPTER TWENTY-EIGHT

Saturday mornings had always been special to Leo and his family. This one promised to be even more so because of the plans that had been made to spend the day together. It would be especially sweet for Leo since it was the first weekend since the campaign had started without anything scheduled other than personal time. At least that's what he told himself as he leafed through the newspaper in the quiet early morning.

Tiki, the once non-stop energetic Jack Russell, now was settled in Leo's lap as had become his custom whenever his master sat in the comfortable recliner. More so than not, the dog now could be found in the same chair curled up when Leo was not there. The Berry's pet seemed more lethargic with the passing of time, but the vet had recently assured the family it was due to old age and not to any other underlying medical condition.

Since his girls, as Leo thought of Dee and Mindy, still had at least another hour or two of sleep before breakfast, he planned to go out for a three-mile run and try to coax Tiki along when he was finished with the morning ritual of reading the paper while enjoying a couple of cups of coffee. There had been a time when Leo wouldn't even attempt to go outside without asking the four-legged friend to get his leash, but now Tiki didn't always want to tag alongside.

As Leo flipped to the opinion page he was surprised to catch his last name in one of the letters to the editors. In bold print the title was "Berry's the best choice." Only a couple of paragraphs, the letter penned by a respected local lawyer explained how the author knew all the candidates but what separated Leo from the other two was the combination of experience and temperament.

What made the letter of support even more special to Leo was that he had not solicited it, nor had anyone associated with his campaign. He didn't know if anyone even paid attention to such, as letters from supporters of various candidates had been flooding the page for the last several weeks, but it did warm his heart to see the kind words.

He would be glad to see the election end. In some ways it had been one of the most positive experiences Leo had ever gone through. There was no better feeling than to have someone come up to you and pledge his or her support and thank you for seeking the position. The process was far from being rewarding when someone showed no interest in what you were trying to do, or if even worse, when someone expressed disapproval.

Leo had always been the type person who sought consensus and compromise. It seemed politics no longer pursued the same. Polarized opinions had become so strong on many fronts not only on the national level, but also on state and local levels, too. While it hadn't been quite as bad in the current campaign, Leo had experienced some negative reactions from people for various reasons that had depressed him.

Partisan politics had been dividing the nation for too long, and Leo had no intentions to let that kind of thinking into his campaign. The job he had been doing and what he wanted to accomplish by winning would not allow such thoughts. So, when someone said they could not support him because he was running as a Democrat and they were all "libtards," Leo replied respectfully and always said he planned to run the office without favor or affection to political views.

Completing the newspaper scan without anything else grabbing his attention, Leo laid it aside and addressed Tiki. "Wanna go outside?"

The dog stretched in Leo's lap with all four legs going stiff to the side and his neck elongating until his mouth strained open. His pink tongue uncurled outside canines that were still sharp enough to do damage if needed. Tiki then turned his head to Leo and offered a doggie grin that indicated he was in agreement. He jumped out of the warm lap and shook off the remnants of his morning nap and headed toward the front door. Sitting on his haunches, he awaited Leo to join him.

After a quick trip by the hall bathroom and exchanging his bedroom slippers for running shoes, Leo fastened the retractable leash that would extend up to sixteen feet. He opened the door and followed Tiki outside into the dawning light.

The dog started slowly down the curved concrete walkway, then stopped and lifted its snoot in the air. He turned his head back and forth sniffing audibly. It caused Leo to stop and take in a couple of deep breaths, too. Japanese tea olives along the nearside of the house produced a pleasant fragrance and a slight breeze shared it with the neighborhood.

Shifting his gaze across the cul-de-sac, Leo studied the vacant red brick house sitting on a hill. The three separate circles making up the area where his home was located only contained thirteen houses on spacious lots, and the abandoned one diagonally from where Leo stood was the only one not containing a family. It had an unfortunate history of ownership from two nasty divorces and another mysterious departure that had resulted in three different foreclosures. The once beautiful dwelling was now showing signs of disrepair bordering on spooky. It made Leo sad, and had all the other neighbors gossiping.

After the latest takeover by the bank owning the mortgage a year ago, the house had seen little activity to indicate anyone was even contemplating moving in. At least two separate listings by realtors hadn't produced interest in the property other than infrequent suspicious actions by people looking around the place and not appearing as potential buyers. Leo guessed since there was no realty company's sign in the front, the house must still be in limbo.

Tiki strained against the leash and acted as if he wanted to walk across the street and up the winding driveway. He had not exhibited that behavior in a couple of years since one of the previous dog owners' departure. During those happier days, Leo had often let the Jack Russell off his tether and let him romp with a pair of matching Bichons that resided there.

Warily, Leo followed Tiki as the dog continued snuffling and proceeding with purpose up the incline leading to the former stomping grounds. Leo didn't know of any reason to be concerned at the present moment, but since the events of a few years before when his life had been threatened, he occasionally experienced flashbacks that made him gasp for air and reach for a sidearm that was not there.

Counseling hadn't completely resolved those feelings of anxiety that could hit without warning. He supposed being almost run over, being shot at and killing another human being were sufficient reasons causing such reactions.

Grown up weeds jutted knee-high from once manicured beds in front of the house and patchy grass shared space with dandelions all over the large sloped yard. It would take a team of lawn care workers at least a day to spruce up the area and that didn't include the backspaces containing a gahnite pool filled with scummy water.

Leo stopped at the top of the driveway and looked back across to his home. His grass had been mowed a couple of days before and the shrubs trimmed into pleasing shapes. The contrasting views made him gloomy and angry at the same time. Good times had been shared here with former neighbors and he wondered if someone would ever purchase the place and restore the place to its former glory.

Tiki resumed tugging away toward the gate separating the concrete from the rear of the house. Leo could tell the weathered door was cracked ajar as they approached. A sideways glance revealed piles of junk and cardboard boxes of various sizes cluttering the opened three-car garage. There also were several propane gas containers stacked near the doorway that led into the house making Leo suspect illegal drug manufacture. Since the place had been vacant for months, Leo was surprised to see all the clutter.

The dog only paused momentarily when he got to the gate and pulled reluctant Leo through. They walked down a few stone steps that had a matching pad leading to the once picturesque pool. It was worse than he had imagined because it had been plenty bad the last time he'd been here several months before when the last owners left.

Abundant creeping vines and unchecked weeds grew up through decking around the stagnant poolside. The odor coming from green water was putrid, and although Leo couldn't tell what kind it was, there was a small dead animal floating amongst other debris. The sights and smells caused a gag reflex and made him glad he hadn't eaten breakfast yet. Even Tiki shook his head as if trying to get rid of the stinch.

Leo started backing away, but only had taken a few steps when a voice cut through the stillness of the morning.

"What are you doing in my yard?"

Tiki's low growl showed his displeasure with the stick figure man standing about twenty feet from where Leo and the dog were located. The guy resembled a scarecrow, thought Leo. He was dressed in a stained and faded blue chambray shirt and nasty frayed jeans. The unlaced work boots adorning his oversized feet were scuffed and way past their prime. A grimy cap sporting a Bass Pro Shop logo sat on the back of his head.

Leo slowly advanced a few paces with Tiki who continued his grumbling through a snarled face. He checked the lock on the dog's leash before offering a tentative right hand to the stranger while muttering under his breath for Tiki to be quiet.

"Good morning. I didn't realize someone had bought the place. I'm Leo Berry from across the street and this is my boy, Tiki."

The stranger's right hand came from behind his back holding a claw hammer that caused Leo to stop in his tracks. Tiki's growl became fiercer.

"I've seen you over there. Wife and daughter, too, I guess. Didn't know your name," he said with the tool still hanging nonchalantly by is side.

For a few uncomfortable seconds that seemed like an eternity, Leo's new neighbor twirled the hammer then switched it to his left hand. Then he ambled forward and held out a closed fist.

"Fist bump, my hand's too dirty to shake. Name's Jake Smith," he said with an enigmatic smile.

Leo grinned and met the gesture with his own closed hand. "Nice to meet you, Jake."

Jake then stooped and reached tentatively with his hand held down to let Tiki smell. The dog gave a short sniff and seemed satisfied for the moment. He stopped the earlier protesting and now rested on his rear beside Leo. He still watched the two men with his head cocked, but no longer appeared ready to launch an attack.

"Not so sure about your companion, Mr. Berry. Thought he was about to take off a finger or something."

"Oh, he's protective, but not dangerous, at least most of the time," Leo said with a laugh. "And please call me Leo."

"Okay, Leo. I understand. Just lost my shepherd, Butch, a few months ago. Looking to get a new pal after I get this place into shape. Liable to take awhile the mess it's in," replied Jake with a grimace.

Leo shook his head up and down. "I couldn't help but notice you had a lot of stuff in the garage."

Now Jake laughed a deep and throaty one before responding, "You mean a lot of shit. Believe me, that's not all of it either. Helper's gone in my pickup right now to take a load to the dump. Got to get it outta the way before I can start doing some repairs. Think there were some squatters living here and maybe cooking some meth or something."

Now Leo shook his head from side to side. He glanced around the back of the house again taking in all the work it would take to clean up the area.

"I'd say you've got your work cut out for you alright, Jake. I've been real busy the last few months, so I must admit I haven't been paying close enough attention to what's been going on over here. Anybody coming and going who were maybe doing something they shouldn't have, I must've not noticed. I'm sorry for that because I believe I'm a better neighbor than that. Everybody around here is."

"Good to know. Well, I'd like to spend more time getting to know you and Tiki, but I need to get back to work. Lots to do,"

Jake said as he turned to head toward the house. "You're welcome to stay awhile if you like, and I imagine I can find something for you to do to help."

"No, I'd like to give you a hand, but I've got other plans for the day that hopefully doesn't include physical labor," said Leo with a smile.

As the two men went up the few steps leading to the garage and Leo started down the long driveway, Jake turned from inside the garage and said, "Something else I might should mention. Probably nothing, but I've noticed a car in the cul-de-sac the last three times I was here that didn't seem right."

Leo's radar blipped on and he stopped walking. "What makes you say that?" he asked.

"Um, different times of the day and night either when I was coming or going, I saw somebody in a dark sedan, Ford, I think, riding slow around the circle. Couldn't get a clear view of the driver, but I think it was a guy with long hair. At least, the one time I got a peek when I passed right by. It struck me odd 'cause he didn't wave when I threw up my hand. Since I've only been over here off and on for a couple of weeks now, I'm not sure if he's legit or not. Just seemed a little strange. Like I said, probably nothing," said Jake.

"Doesn't sound like anybody I know, but I'll mention it to some of the other neighbors. Probably just somebody interested in your house. We've got a pretty good neighborhood watch and one or two really nosy ones," replied Leo and paused. "I'll let them know to leave you a copy of contacts in your mailbox in case you notice anything else."

"Okay, thanks," shrugged Jake as he headed into the house.

Leo continued his trip and registered the meeting with the new resident. *Too soon to know how he'll fit in, but seems nice enough,* he thought.

CHAPTER TWENTY-NINE

Time seemed to be speeding up for some reason, and Leo didn't understand why. At different intervals, life sped up or slowed down, depending on the circumstances. Right now, it was in hyper-drive.

Yesterday was a blur and when he thought about it, the last few months had been pretty much the same. After getting a little scared and meeting the new neighbor across the street, he had spent a good portion of the day with his family.

First, Leo, Dee and Mindy had eaten a breakfast of banana walnut pancakes, eggs and bacon he had cooked while they debated politics. It was one of the few places the lawyer felt he could offer opinions on the subject without fear of isolating someone with differing views. Leo relished the family times around meals and realized they had not done enough of those recently due to the campaign, work and school obligations of his core three unit.

Mindy was quite astute for her age and while somewhat more to the left than Leo and Dee, pretty much agreed with them on what was going on at the national level. They all thought there were no good choices, but one was more dangerous than the other. Leo believed both sides thought that way toward the other's candidate. The main belief they shared concerned the divisiveness of the country that seemed to be getting worse rather than better and the current contenders didn't appear to be helping the mood. They all agreed the art of compromise was missing.

After the morning meal, they had piled into Leo's car and drove to his mother's house. His brothers and their families came, too. It became a family gathering not quite to the scale of Thanksgiving or Christmas, but close nevertheless in scope of the activities.

Shelly's pool and deck were immaculately prepared for the group, and Leo could only whistle at the difference in the water's clarity as opposed to that he had witnessed earlier at the house across the street. Mom took great pride in maintaining the area behind her modest home, and it showed. Colorful flowers and other potted plants adorned the brick fence around the deck, and the outdoor furniture was spotless from his mother's earlier cleaning.

Everyone, but especially the kids who ranged in age from a few years to the teens, splashed away for hours. One of the fun mainstays was to make sure everyone was toppled off floats or was bombarded by others performing cannon ball dives. Sunscreen had to be applied continuously in the middle Georgia sun, but everyone knew it was necessary to ensure against the dreadful sunburns they had all experienced before.

As they always seemed to do when the clan congregated, the Berry brothers shared stories of growing up while everyone laughed to help burn some of the calories of the huge meal that had been consumed. The matriarch was now back in form and had made sure everyone was overfed.

Now in her mid-sixties and having lived through the loss of her husband, Leo's dad and namesake, as well as enduring other personal tragedies and health concerns, Shelly seemed to relish the family get-togethers more than ever. She grinned constantly and was heard laughing throughout the day. As he sat at his home office desk, Leo thought it had been great to see her so happy yesterday and hoped there were many such days ahead.

He was up again before dawn and had slept less than five hours. As he did on occasion, Leo sat at the desk in the home office area. Nothing was stirring, not even Tiki who must be in Mindy's room, he thought.

The Apple computer screen was not bright, but added enough of a view to allow him to surf. He was not sleepy and the stillness of the house caused his mind to wander as he checked out the usual sites. Among his favorites were local news and various sports sources.

After the family fun, Leo remembered how he and Dee had retired early and enjoyed intimacy in the quiet solitude of their bedroom. It was something that they seemed to need from the recent stresses. Sounds of their lovemaking had been lost in the white noise of the ceiling fan. Afterwards, Dee was soon slumbering on her side away from Leo, and he had cuddled against her treasuring the time until awakening with a start.

For some unfathomable reason, Leo was feeling unsettled. He knew that he shouldn't be. In his heart of hearts, Leo had resolved earlier doubts about his decision to run for office mainly because the chances of winning were looking good. Taking on the role of Solicitor-General would mean a lot of work because of what he wanted to accomplish and maybe that was a part of his uneasiness.

It couldn't be due to his family situation either. Everything was stable at the moment. His mother had proven to be as resilient and independent as always by bouncing back very soon after her surgery. His brothers and their families were doing well also even though Tommy's life bounced around from happy to sad in conjunction with the latest woman.

Leo was a little worried about Mindy's looming fifteenth birthday, which meant she would soon be behind the wheel of a car. But she'd always been a good kid and able to master anything in front of her, so he felt certain that training would go well, too.

His thoughts were interrupted when he noticed some illumination peek through the slightly opened blinds facing him. The low beam parking lights of a vehicle circled the cul-de-sac at a tortoise pace. Alarms sounded in Leo's mind at the suspicious behavior. A glance at the clock on the computer screen showed 3:08 a.m.

He got up from the swivel chair and walked to the front entrance of the house. He then peered through slits of the wooden shutters that ran lengthwise next to the door. Due to the street lamp directly across the circle, Leo could make out the dark sedan's form that stopped close to his mailbox.

It was impossible to tell who was driving or if there were multiple occupants. Because so many cars looked similar nowadays, Leo couldn't even discern the make much less the year of the car.

On a stand next to the entrance where he stood was an asp baton. It had been a gift from his friend, Jimbo, after Leo complained about a coyote roaming the neighborhood sometime ago. He only carried it on occasion when out with Tiki during dark hours. The heavy metal stick that telescoped two feet from the handle could cause major hurt to anything within range. Without thinking, Leo grabbed the familiar weapon along with a mini-mag flashlight and started out the door as quietly as he could.

***

Increasingly, Morgan thought he could be losing precious control. It was an emotion creeping into his being he didn't like. Maybe emotion was the wrong word since feelings like love and hate didn't really exist with him, and that was what he believed that term described.

No, losing control was something else. For most of his adult life he had been in charge of what he wanted to do. His superior intelligence allowed such behavior. Feeling threatened was something not known in a long time, and it made him go back to days when an inferiority complex ruled.

High school. How he despised everything about the time and place. Insecurity ruled. The cool kids wouldn't have anything to do with him. The few who did were nerds, geeks, or a combo platter of social misfits. And forget about girls.

Especially the cute ones. He remembered how they would practically run away if he tried to talk to one of them.

He hadn't really thought about those days in forever until he saw Dee some weeks back, and now the period appeared in his dreams and permeated his waking thoughts, too. She had rejected him back then, but she didn't know any better.

His all-consuming reflections about the girl were a problem Morgan couldn't seem to shake. They were making him do things that were stupid. Why else would he persist in riding around the neighborhood where she lived with her do-goody husband and brace-mouthed brat?

Sure, he believed in conducting the necessary research when planning to hook up with a *pretty girl,* but he'd never even thought about one with all the trappings this one presented. He'd surveyed several others before just to make sure there weren't any potential people or other problems to interrupt what he was planning. He'd never tried to set up a meeting with one with so many issues he couldn't regulate.

Nosey neighbors, only one way in and out of the community, street lighting, dogs...Not to mention family members. And, she could possibly recognize me, too. It wouldn't matter what kind of disguise I wore. I've never been with a girl who knew me beforehand. I shouldn't take a chance like that. All of the uncertainties should deter me, he thought.

But, he had also noted Dee was alone at the house a good bit. The husband and daughter were gone a lot. He might have to cut the time with her a little shorter than usual because they could show up unannounced, but he could plan for such contingencies. And, he could keep his head covered in some fashion, just like now. She only needed to see and feel his superb body like he'd done with other dates.

Morgan broke into a lascivious grin. Thoughts of her beneath him aroused him as he circled slowly around the street where she lived. She had to be in her bed at the very moment. He stopped the car just past the mailbox, but kept it in gear. All he could think about was her.

He slipped his right hand under the elastic of the black sweatpants he wore and began stroking his now throbbing penis. The looseness of the garment allowed free movements that became more urgent. Just as he was about to explode in ecstasy, there was a tapping at his window that caused him to remove his hand and grab the pistol stuck between the seat and console.

***

Leo walked down the driveway toward the car parked with the engine still running located not far away. He couldn't identify the operator, but could now tell it was a black Ford Fusion sedan. He glanced at the tag that was obscured with some sort of muddy colored plastic cover. He could make out the letters HT and the number 9. It looked like a government license plate. The tint of the windows didn't allow him to see the occupant other than it appeared to be a man with a wide-brimmed hat on his head.

His brain told him to be careful. With a flick of his wrist downward, the baton slid to its full length with a metallic click.

Leo continued around the back of the vehicle to the driver's side and positioned himself slightly behind the door.

He raised the rod and lightly tapped the window three times. The head inside turned quickly to the left, then right and then was still. Leo felt tension throughout his body that caused him to grip the baton tighter.

After what seemed like minutes, but in reality was only seconds, the window slid downward until it was about halfway open. Leo took a step forward and even in the muted light saw blonde curls cascading from underneath an Indiana Jones style hat. It registered weird on more than one level.

The head didn't turn completely toward Leo, but there was enough of one that fair skin was shown. The lack of any quick movements from the occupant did little to ease the nervousness that was now coursing in him.

"What's going on?" Leo asked.

There was a pause before the response came, "I'm sorry if I startled you this morning. I know it's early. "

"Why are you parked in front of my house?"

"Didn't know it was yours. I was checking out the vacant one across the street."

Leo's suspiciousness was growing by leaps and bounds. In his mind there was no good reason for such an activity at this time of the morning.

"At 3:00 a.m.? Why would you be doing that?"

"I'm sure it seems crazy, but I've been looking at the place for awhile. I've been thinking about making an offer on it. I work a late shift and rode by after I got off. Sorry, I didn't mean any harm. I can show you some ID, if you want."

Leo now felt conflicted. As nutty as the explanation seemed, for the guy to offer his identification dispelled some distrusts.

"That'd ease my mind some," Leo said after a moment's hesitation.

There was some fumbling around in the car, as the driver appeared to open the console. It made him even more nervous, so Leo flicked on the small flashlight he held in his left hand and shined it in the open window. He could see the other man's face better now as a driver's license was handed through. Leo's initial impression was that the guy probably was about the same age as him, but when he looked at the provided identification, it showed the man was almost ten years younger. The face was unremarkable with no distinguishing features except for longish blonde hair and darker stubble on the face. The name on the license was Richard Jones and listed Summit Avenue as his address. Leo recognized the area across the Ocmulgee River in east Macon.

After studying the picture and the other information for a few seconds, Leo handed it back through the window and briefly aimed the light at the occupant. The driver accepted the license, but averted his face from illumination.

"That's a bright light you've got there, sir."

Leo turned the device to face the light onto the street beside the vehicle and replied, "Yeah, sorry. It comes in handy sometimes, Mr. Jones. Look, I didn't mean to hassle you, but I'm sure you understand your actions appear pretty suspicious. For the record, the house across the street has been sold and is no longer on the market."

"Ah, that's disappointing, but good to know. I'll have to cross it off my list. Once again, I'm sorry for causing any concern. I guess I'll have to keep looking elsewhere for my next house."

The car pulled from the spot leaving Leo feeling perplexed and shaken. He hadn't felt so close to a potential danger since the dealings with dirty cops a few years ago. Even though there had been no visible threats from the man driving away, he couldn't help believe there was something that just wasn't right. He would call Jimbo later and have him check the guy out.

***

Shit! Morgan thought as his right hand closed around the grips of the small .380 he always kept concealed in the car. Morgan hadn't seen Berry come up behind him and a fleeting worry that the idiot had seen what he was doing before had immediate effects. The hard-on was gone, but his superior brain engaged.

As the conversation went on and Morgan slipped into his falsely apologetic persona, he kept his face at angles away from Berry knowing the hat and wig would also further blur his face from detection. He never wore the same such disguises more than once when on the prowl, and he always had multiple aids as protection if confronted.

Since the gun was only a last resort, he had pushed it further into the crevice, but still handy if needed. He didn't even glance at it when he handed over the fake identification to Mr. Goody Two Shoes. Morgan felt sure even that goddamned light wouldn't be able to detect the weapon in its convenient storage place.

The confrontation had only lasted a couple of minutes and now as Morgan struggled not to put the medal to the floorboard while driving away, he realized sweat was running down his brow, under his armpits and probably in the crack of his ass. It had been the closest to getting caught he had ever experienced.

He'd have to make sure he changed the license plate again and destroy the fake ID he'd handed over to Berry. No problem, since he kept several on hand in his garage. Even though the plastic cover helped in the concealment of the letters and numbers, Morgan rarely affixed the plate assigned to his vehicle when doing research. The job that bored him to death at least helped with having a supply of false plates he routinely used and then disposed of before they could be traced back to him.

This encounter had been too close, though. He had some serious decisions to make and he would, soon.

CHAPTER THIRTY

Monday before the election had finally arrived. Many people were relieved it was almost over. The candidates looked forward to a breather from long hours, rubber chicken meals in between giving standard stump speeches, and listening to complaints and suggestions from those who would be casting ballots. Because of early voting, many had already done their civic duty and there were predictions of record turnouts.

The public was also ready for it to be over, as well. A barrage of television and radio ads warned of impending doom if they didn't get out the vote for various people who would prevent the other side from destroying their way of life.

Social media sites were even worse. Information was available for all to see and choose to believe. There had never been as much of it. Some was obvious in its falseness, but other was not. It required informed voters to use multiple sources in order to verify claims or their veracity. Many didn't even make an attempt to try and find out if a claim was true or not. They simply believed their favorite sources of news without question.

Caught in the middle of national and state campaigns that had nothing to do with Leo's efforts to seek office on the local level, he felt especially glad to see it come to an end. He thought it was the most poisonous cycle he'd witnessed, and it had caused him to rethink his decision more than once over the course of the last few months.

Choices. People made many every day. Some, like what to have for lunch, didn't affect one's life past that moment in time. Others, like deciding to run for an elected office, could have lasting effects. Leo could only hope if his soul had somehow been changed, it was for the better and not for worse. Right now, it was hard to gauge.

As his mind wandered, Leo thought about some of the more important choices he had made. Of course, choosing to get married to Dee had been huge. That had led to happiness that couldn't have been imagined had he stayed single.

Another, spending so much time, effort and money becoming an attorney, had lasted since he started on the path at least since college, but probably starting earlier than that. Certainly it began before his and Dee's life together had even been contemplated.

Now, all of the courses taken so long ago, the study groups that met into the early morning hours, hours practicing opening statements and closing arguments before mirrors and family members, preparing for and taking the bar exam, and twenty years of practicing law had led to this moment. The fork in the road had been chosen to seek election. It would've been much easier not to do so.

He alternately rubbed his tired eyes and stroked the close-cut stubble on his face. There was weariness evident in his face when he looked at himself, but he knew it would pass soon enough. All of the hard work was going to pay off, Leo was absolutely sure of it. Confidence in the face of doubt had always gotten him through most challenges.

Sitting in his office chair early in the morning and getting a head start on the day before anyone else had arrived was not an unusual occurrence. Leo had done it many times over the years of working before starting his career as a prosecutor, and it had continued even though no overtime pay figured in the equation.

When embarking in the profession right out of law school, a valued mentor had suggested to Leo that he could be ahead of the vast majority of other lawyers simply by getting his start an hour before anybody else. Since the young grad came from a strong work ethic believing family, it wasn't a stretch to see the value in such an approach.

So, he was at his desk and doing the usual stuff, and nobody else was there to interrupt progress except maybe his own jumbled mind. Focusing on the last in a stack of incident reports, Leo decided the Stat 5, law enforcement's term for such, was lacking sufficient information to determine if a charge should be filed. He placed it aside in a small pile to give his investigator for further inquiry.

The necessity for additional research triggered Leo's mind of the need to contact Jimbo. The two hadn't talked in awhile and the prosecutor wanted to pick the detective's brain about the recent unsettling encounter outside his home. Leo knew the policeman would more than likely be awake and working, too.

He scrolled through the contacts on his cell phone and hit the call button. Jimbo's voice sounded scratchy when he answered on the third ring.

"Mornin', counselor. You're up early."

"So are you, Captain. Can you talk or should I call back later?"

"Well, you know, crime never sleeps and the early cop gets the worm. I'm paraphrasing, or something like that. Yeah, I can talk. What's up?"

"I wanted to see if you could check somebody out for me. There was a late night, or maybe I should classify him as an early morning visitor, parked in my neighborhood over the weekend. He told me he was looking into buying a house. I saw his driver's license giving his name as Richard Jones living on Summit Avenue. Drives a dark Ford sedan. Didn't get a clear look at the license plate, but part of it was HT9. Something wasn't right about it."

Jimbo scribbled on his notepad and replied, "Surely you didn't buy a story like home hunting after midnight. Is that house across the street from you still vacant? I bet the guy was looking for an easy mark."

"No, no and probably," said Leo and paused. "Why do you think I'm calling my favorite detective? I knew if anyone could find out, it'd be you."

"Flattery and a dollar will get you a cup of coffee somewhere, Leo. I'll see what I can find out about your mystery man when I get a minute. You know I'm still busy trying to find the other asshole on your list. I want to retire, but you keep sucking me into your personal vortex."

"Hey, man. I'm sorry about only calling when I need a favor. I'll try to be better when I'm elected. Hopefully, I can do it without a runoff. So, how is that other investigation going? At least I haven't seen anything in the paper lately."

"Uhh, no more victims we know of. I don't know what to say. I keep thinking I'm close to finding him and that I'm missing something. Maybe I need a little break. I'll check into your prowler. Hey, I need to run. Talk to you later."

The call ended abruptly and Leo laid his phone down on the desk. Just as well, he had more to do.

CHAPTER THIRTY-ONE

Dee awoke and glanced toward the clock on the stand next to her side of the bed. It revealed 9:38 and caused a momentary panic. She loved sleeping later into the morning, but this was a workday and she would be way late.

Then she remembered her decision to take a few days off because of Leo's election coming up tomorrow. Her head relaxed back onto the satin covered pillow, and Dee adjusted the ear bud so the droning of talk radio would help sinking back into slumber. It was a behavior Leo couldn't understand, but it worked well for her.

Soon she was dreaming of carefree times when she was a schoolgirl. Dee and her friends giggled and gossiped about cute guys and the latest hairstyles. It seemed that none of them were satisfied with their own locks, and all wondered if they should change them in some fashion. Dee complained that she wished for a more natural look without so much hairspray. Her friends told her she was pretty just the way she was.

They laughed nervously about sex and how far some of their friends had gone, but denied to each other that any of them had been further than some petting. Dee and Bonnie Burnett, her current bestie, feigned ignorance about anything to do with the subject, and listened with rapt attention as some of the others talked about one not in attendance named Dixie.

One of the girls claimed she had heard the naughty one say in a very public hangout, McDonald's, that it "was hot in Dixie tonight." Of course, they all believed she had said it because they all knew the chick was just that. She had dated every cool guy in the class and the rumor was there were more standing in line to be next. The two friends stepped away and talked in private.

BB, have you and Mike come close, yet?

Well, you know he wants to. Truth is, sometimes I want to, too. I'm scared, though. What would I do if I got pregnant in high school, for God's sake? I don't trust any birth control.

I can't imagine! Of course, I don't have a boyfriend now, but I'd be the same. I don't know who'd kill me first, Mama or Daddy.

How about Leo Berry? I heard he's interested in dating you. Friend of a friend told me.

Girl, you've got to be kidding. He's a grade ahead and doesn't know me. Besides, he seems like a nerd or something. He needs to lose those horn rims, too.

Me thinks you're protesting too much. I've seen him checking you out. He's smart and I bet he's got a future. Put him in some contact lenses and change his haircut, he'll be all right. Think about it. You could fix him up just fine.

Okay, I will think about it, if he gets up the nerve to ask me out. Let me ask you something else. Do you know Morgan Thomas?

That weirdo? You don't like him, do you?

No! He's a scary creep to me. I caught him going through my pocket purse the other day. Something about his eyes gave me the Willy Wonka's. I'm just wondering if I should tell somebody.

Did he take anything? If he did, hell yeah!

I couldn't find anything missing. That's why I'm asking you.

Well, if you didn't see a crime, I'd let it go. Might make it worse.

Dee woke up again, and this time the clock revealed it was 10:31. She needed to get busy, and jumped out of bed.

***

One of the tasks Dee had on the list of things to do was to straighten out the closet adjacent to the bathroom that she and Leo shared. Multiple pairs of shoes littered the floor on her side of the good-sized room while clothing was jammed so tight that it was almost impossible to remove a blouse, assuming she could find the one needed to compliment the rest of the chosen outfit for the day.

While she worked, a small portable television played in the background, and she listened to bits and pieces as Dr. Phil gave some poor soul hell about her failures as a mother. Dee was not a huge fan of the show, but he did make her laugh on occasion. It mainly helped her declutter her mind as she went about the same process in the closet.

By the time Dee finished reorganizing the area by taking three armfuls of clothes across the house to the guest bedroom's closet, the noon edition of WMAZ's news program had begun. She heard a follow-up story claiming no new leads had been developed in the recent spate of sexual assaults occurring in the community.

The news bothered Dee since Maxie had been one of the victims, and she knew how hard her friend had struggled since the attack. They had spoken a few times, and Maxie had relayed how terrified she felt to go anywhere. The report made Dee think she needed to do more for her and resolved to call Maxie again soon.

Dee frowned as she backed out of the closet when she noticed that one of Leo's jacket pockets was crumpled and slightly gapped open. He was usually pretty meticulous about his work suits, but he'd been so busy lately. When she reached over to straighten it, the firmness of a plastic DVD cover caught her attention and she pulled out the object from the pocket.

Now she smiled. Over the years Leo had worked as an assistant prosecutor, he had often brought videos home of various cases he was working on. It was not unusual for him to watch the tapes that would be used as evidence in some trial and ask her for an opinion as to whether she thought they would be helpful to a jury hearing the case. For the most part she loved watching them, especially when certain officers were involved in arrests for DUI.

Since she was ready for a little break before beginning another chore, Dee decided she would fix her a sandwich and watch the disc. Leo wouldn't mind and it might be entertaining, too. She felt he'd been distracted by the campaign and had forgotten he'd brought it home.

As Dee walked into the kitchen and set the disc nearby, Tiki ambled from the front of the house toward the side of the stainless steel refrigerator where his bowl of water and a separate container of dry food were located. He lapped up almost half the liquid before sniffing at the kibble. It appeared he was not interested as the pet snorted without taking a bite.

"What's up, Tiki? Mama's boy hungry?"

The dog licked his chops as if to affirm Dee's question and watched her as she took deli turkey from the fridge. After inspecting the freshness date and opening the package, she rolled up a slice and took a bite. He watched patiently as Dee chewed, swallowed and bit again. When she gave him the last third, Tiki gobbled it down.

Dee couldn't help but laugh at the reaction. She knew it wasn't good to give the old boy such food, but he was a part of the family and they all snuck him a treat from time to time.

Knowing that cheese was his favorite, Dee unwrapped a slice of cheddar and tore it into strips. She then laid it strategically in the bowl of dry food along with another half piece of turkey. He soon commenced eating vociferously as crunching the hard items was accomplished.

Dee assembled a sandwich using a slice of rye bread cut in half with the deli meat and cheese slathered with a mixture of mustard, mayo and horseradish sauce. She then got a couple of mini dill pickles from a refrigerated jar and a few jalapeno-flavored chips from a bag in a cabinet over the counter top where she worked. With her lunch ready on a paper plate, Dee took a seat at the round wooden table in the kitchen and opened her laptop that she often kept in that location.

As she munched on the food, the disc was loaded into the side of the Apple computer and the menu appeared on screen. She had no idea what the three files represented and almost removed the disc before going further. However, she was just nosy enough to click on the first one named *Promises 1* and then made out Maxie's image sitting at a bar.

Transfixed to the screen, her lunch was momentarily forgotten. She realized the tape had to contain images of a suspect. It was too weird to think, but the more she watched, the more she thought the pictures favored Morgan Thomas.

It couldn't be him, could it? No, you're letting your imagination run away.

Dee was conflicted, but needed to at least let Leo know her suspicions. She decided she would tonight.

CHAPTER THIRTY-TWO

Jimbo parked his aging county car in the parking lot of the tax commissioner's office. He wondered if he should've taken an Aleve or something because his arthritis was flaring. It reminded him when he got out of the automobile.

His limp got only slightly better by the time he entered the offices. The elderly security guard, who was probably less than five years younger than he, nodded at the detective when he headed toward the main entrance.

Damn, that guy needs to retire for good. The unspoken words in Jimbo's head made him give a half-smile as he passed by.

After talking with Leo earlier, he had gotten the idea to check tags directly at the office that routinely dealt with such rather than on his terminal. It had worked before on other cases, and although he couldn't remember the name of the man who had helped him in the past, Jimbo knew he would recall his face as soon as he saw him again.

A big-bosomed woman wearing a tight crimson top greeted him at the doorway, "Can I help you?"

"I hope so. I'm Captain James Barbour," Jimbo said as he flashed his badge while trying not to stare at her ample headlights.

"I'm looking for a guy who has helped me with investigations in the past. Can't remember his name. Very good with computers."

The female frowned and then responded, "We only have a couple of men working in the office. Both are competent using computers. I hate to say it this way, but was the guy over-weight?"

"Average size, or maybe a little taller," Jimbo replied.

"Okay, you must mean Morgan. Sorry to say, he's out sick today. Can somebody else help you?"

Jimbo was feeling somewhat frustrated, but hoped someone else could check out the info Leo had provided. All he could think about was the real case he should be working on and not doing personal favors for a friend. It wasn't a good use of his valuable time.

"Anybody who can look into some license plates will be okay," he said.

After telling Jimbo to follow her, the woman sashayed to an area that was segregated from where the general public gathered to pay various taxes. A plumpish girl who appeared barely young enough to hold a job sat in a cubicle inputting information with the deftness of a concert pianist. Her chubby fingers moved with precision and didn't stop when she looked up to acknowledge his presence.

"Sophie, this is Captain Barbour. He needs some help with something he's working on. Please see what you can do," said the curvy woman as she turned and left the two alone in the less than roomy office.

Without awaiting invitation, Jimbo sat down on a hard plastic chair across from the employee and pulled out his notebook. Sophie raised an eyebrow at his actions without comment.

"I'm trying to find the owner of a Ford Fusion with a partial plate containing the letters H and T and the number nine. Supposedly registered to a Richard Jones," Jimbo grunted.

"It's nice to meet you, too, Captain. Please make yourself comfortable," said Sophie with only a twinge of sarcasm.

The wrinkled creases on Jimbo's face turned into a smile that forced the girl to reciprocate. She now reminded him of a cherub; maybe it was her round smooth face. Something told him the angelic exterior hid a serious and thoughtful mind.

"Sorry, I guess I left my manners somewhere else. I was hoping the guy who has helped me before with such requests would be here. I think the other lady said his name's Morgan. Let's start over again, and I'll try to act more like a gentleman. Might be hard for me," Jimbo replied with a toothy grin.

Sophie's lips pursed, "Goody-goody, I get to play second fiddle to Rug Man."

The sarcasm was much more pronounced and dripped off her tongue than before, and Jimbo winced at her description as she began a series of strokes on her keyboard. Sophie's eyes darted from side to side as she read what appeared on the screen that couldn't be seen by the detective. After several minutes Sophie spoke in his direction, but she maintained her gaze onto the flat panel.

"Hmm, I don't see any cars as you described that's registered with that combination on the local data base. Of course, you don't give me much to go on. If I broaden the search to outside Bibb County, there might be some. It'll take much longer to do that, however. Are you sure of the make and the owner's name?"

"Not really, but that's all I got."

"Well, as I'm sure you know, and even Morgan would tell you if he'd bothered to come to work, license plates are stolen, or put on the wrong vehicle, or otherwise misused all the time," she said frowning.

"Yep, thought it might be a long shot," Jimbo said while his mind started creeping elsewhere.

"Don't mind me asking, but I take it you don't care for your co-worker, Morgan. Just wondering, why?"

Sophie hesitated but a moment before replying, "Something's wrong with him. Maybe it's just me, but a man in a toupee doesn't work these days. I know plenty of guys with receding hairlines and they look a lot better by buzzing or even shaving their heads. It's like he wants to be somebody he's not. Also, he's got this better than you attitude. Always acts like he's smarter than everybody else. And, he's always leering at women. He thinks nobody notices, but I do. The rumor around here is he's retiring, and I say good riddance."

Jimbo's natural tendency to be suspicious and his experience finding clues where you often least expected to come across helpful nuggets of information caused him to ponder the young woman's characterization of this Morgan dude. Surely this couldn't be the rapist he was looking for.

"Just curious, do you know what kind of car Morgan drives?"

"Not sure about his personal ride, but he gets to drive one of the county cars most of the time. That's another sore spot for me. I don't know why he should. Saves him a ton of money."

"So, a cheap Ford?"

"Yeah, a mid-size is the best the government does for us, or a smaller one if you're only less fortunate."

"Ford Fusion for Morgan?"

Sophie looked directly into Jimbo's eyes. The look on her face seemed hopeful that Morgan was being investigated for something.

"I do believe so, Captain."

"And he can take it home after work hours?"

"Uh huh," she shook her head up and down.

Jimbo wasn't thinking about Leo's unwanted interloper now. It didn't cross his mind that Morgan might be cruising the prosecutor's neighborhood. What had entered into his thinking was that someone who drove a generic sedan, wore a hairpiece, and had access to personal information worked here. That fit the profile of a scheming predator, and somebody he might need to check out.

CHAPTER THIRTY-THREE

Morgan's collections of disguises were no longer in their usual place. He had spent most of the morning gathering them into a thirty-gallon garbage bag, and now it sat in the middle of his bedroom floor. Before tying it, Morgan also added the things he carried with him on his dates. All of the items had been carefully collected over years of honing his craft. The thought of destroying the contents sickened him and caused inner turmoil. The only one not in the soon to be discarded sack was the conservative wig he wore to work.

He was pacing around the room as his mind raced. The confidence normally felt in his abilities to escape detection had been shaken as never before. The rational part of his brain told the other part that anything he had ever used while seeking and conquering pretty girls needed to be demolished. The other section of his soul that was more devious and still hungered for the next woman needed those items for protection and satisfying personal wants.

"Don't you understand? If this stuff is found in my possession, it could send me to prison," Morgan said out loud.

You're panicking over nothing, Morgie. The police have no clue who you are because you're the best.

The other part of him only spoke to Morgan and no one else could've heard even if present in the room. He was irritated to be called by a childhood nickname that bordered on deriding him as effeminate.

"Maybe, but I can't afford to take any chances. I've never had this kind of publicity, so at least one of the girls has been talking to the authorities. If somebody like Barbour connects the dots, it would be bad."

Ah, Barbour. I bet he doesn't even know your name and he's worked with you before, remember? Sat in the same room while you did your computer magic. Give yourself a break. He's nowhere smarter than you. You're not going to be suspected because of the disguises. If you get rid of them, you'll have to stop dating the pretty girls. You don't want to do that, Morgie.

"Stop calling me that. Barbour isn't as stupid as you think. Besides, even a blind hog can find slop, and I've gotten sloppy lately. My plans are to find fresh pastures. I'll get out of this town and start over. Any of this can be replaced when I do."

And just give up Dee? She's the one, you know? All the others have been mere substitutes.

Morgan quit pacing. He'd never been told that before. It made a certain amount of sense. Stepping over the bag, he untied the plastic and rummaged inside. He chose a dark headdress that hadn't been worn in at least a couple of years. Fitting it snuggly on his head, he looked in the full-length mirror across the room. Surely he could afford to save one, just in case an opportunity arose.

In the meantime, he would continue his plan to *Get outta Dodge*. Morgan didn't need to stay in Macon any longer.

CHAPTER THIRTY-FOUR

After working his regular job all morning long, Leo went into his boss's office as it neared the lunch hour. Since the campaign had begun, the man Leo looked up to as a mentor had been rarely seen. Part of it was due to a flare-up of non-Hodgkin's lymphoma, but Leo suspected a good portion of the reasoning was to stay out of the election process and the office drama. It had to be upsetting to have his prized assistants opposing one another in their efforts to succeed him.

The Colonel was leaned back in his weathered leather chair with one foot propped on a desk even older-looking than his nearly eighty-year-old self. The senior lawyer who had been the head prosecutor for four decades looked distracted and didn't seem to notice the younger attorney hoping to take over at year's end.

"Colonel, you got a minute?"

The gentleman turned his head and the trademark white bushy eyebrows raised slightly. A thin smile appeared on the unlined face, which belied his age.

"Come on in, Leo. I've got a few left."

Leo walked into the office he'd been in countless times before. For some reason, this moment was different from any other. It almost felt like a changing of the guard.

"I've been wanting to talk to you about the election. That is, if you don't mind."

The enigmatic smile didn't change. The man was unreadable, but motioned Leo into the chair closest to him.

"I hate this campaign has split the office like it has," Leo said as he sat down.

"Me, too."

Leo had not thought much about how the race would cause the problems it had when the decision was first made. He knew there were some who supported Rob, but that fact didn't bother him at that moment in time. The younger prosecutor had thought, somewhat naively, that it would all work out and everyone would be happy in the end. Now he wasn't as sure.

Leo studied the man's face across from him. It had a tired appearance. There was no doubt in Leo's mind that the contested election was a cause of concern.

"How are you feeling, Colonel?"

"Weary. About ready to go to the house and call it a day. The law has been good to me, but it's not the same anymore. Time for somebody else to take the reins. That looks like it's probably going to be you, Leo," he replied with the same inscrutable smile remaining in place.

Now Leo smiled. "I hope so, Colonel. I'm a firm believer that if it's meant to be, it will. I'm just glad it's almost over."

"I've got to say, you've run a good campaign, Leo. Your grandfather would be proud. Any chance you and Rob can work things out after it's over?"

Leo frowned as the conversation took a turn to his fellow assistant and opponent. The past few months had proven to be difficult to say the least. Some of the other employees in the office felt like they were walking on eggshells and the tension had been high whenever the candidates were together in the same room. No matter how hard Leo had tried to lighten the mood, Rob refused to let it happen.

"I'd like to think so, Colonel. I really think we work well together, but I don't know. Rob's so mad at me, and I don't see his anger going away any time soon, if ever."

The older man nodded and replied, "You're probably right. I'm hoping you can, though. You two are like my sons."

Leo contemplated the situation as he had several times since making the decision to run. He really wanted what the Colonel wanted; he just didn't believe it would happen. He knew that Rob felt betrayed by Leo and forgiveness seemed unfathomable for now.

"I'll try," was all he could manage in response.

The two men sat in silence for a minute or two. Emotions were swimming in the room, and Leo was trying to keep his in check.

"I'll always remember what you've done for me, Colonel. I'm going to do my best to keep your traditions."

The older man's eyes crinkled and he said, "Find your own, Leo. Just remember where you came from, and you'll do fine. Nothing ever stays the same."

With some effort, he swung his leg from the resting place on the desk. The well-worn leather chair let out a creak indicating its need for oil as the Colonel stamped his foot.

"Blood circulation problems," he said shaking his head and then looking up, focusing narrow eyes into Leo's.

"Whatever happens tomorrow, I'm going to be getting out of the way," he said pausing and then continued. "You know I supported Rob publicly, and I don't think it helped him."

Leo thought about that fact, but had already decided it didn't bother him that much. Rob had worked for the Colonel longer and while it had hurt at first when the long-time leader endorsed his opponent, Leo still felt close to the man who had hired him in the present role.

"You don't need to explain that, Colonel. I'll always be grateful for what you've done for me. I've learned so much from you, and I'm sure I'll call on you from time to time asking for advice. Of course, that assumes I win."

The man's eyes moistened and he nodded without speaking again. The coiffed white haired head looked around the office as if taking it all in for the final time.

Leo got up from the seat and walked over to his boss. He patted the elder man's shoulder.

"I'm going to take the rest of the day off, and most of tomorrow, too, if you don't mind. My work is caught up, and I don't have any more scheduled appointments. Tomorrow's going to be a long day with the election. I've got the jail cases in the morning, and I'll drop in for a little while afterwards. I'll see you later, Colonel," Leo finished softly before leaving the space.

Rob's office next door was shut, and Leo was about to knock on it when he overheard the other assistant's voice through the thin walls. Leo only stood there long enough to hear that Rob was in a private conversation.

"No, I'm not worried. It's in God's hands. I'm taking it one day at a time," spoke Rob to someone.

Leo immediately departed the area when he heard him speak and stopped long enough to pick up the briefcase holding the cases he had prepared for the jail court session scheduled in the morning. As he looked inside the bag to make sure it contained everything needed, a soft rap followed by the clearing of a throat got Leo's attention.

"Just wanted to wish you good luck tomorrow."

Standing in the doorway were several members of the staff. The only ones not present were Rob, one of the secretaries, and the Colonel. The gesture brought an immediate emotional response from Leo. He could feel tears welling in his eyes and fought hard not to let them form.

He knew many of his coworkers had worked toward the goal of getting him elected. Leo had talked to all of them individually when he first made the decision to run and had told them they should feel free to support whomever they chose, but not to be pressured in any way. Since then some of them had been more vocal than others, but he had been buoyed by all their efforts.

"Thanks, everybody. Y'all are the best," he croaked.

Leo got the frog from his throat and then continued while trying to make eye contact with each of them.

"Some of y'all might know already, but we're going to have a little party tomorrow evening at Michael's across the street beginning around seven o'clock. All of you are welcome to come, but no pressure," he finished with a grin.

Dorothy, the senior secretary of the bunch, stood in front of the rest. She wore her usual colorful and stylish clothing and acted as the spokesperson. When the announcement of Leo's decision to run had been first made, she had met with him and promised full support. Leo couldn't think of anyone who had contributed more assistance to the campaign except maybe his mother.

"Oh, you know we'll be there. We wouldn't miss it," she said while everyone else bobbed their heads.

A few of them left in order to cover the phones that had begun to ring. A couple of the others headed to lunch. Dorothy stayed behind and an anxious look took over her face.

"Do you really think we'll win?"

Leo liked the way she used plural rather than singular when referring to the campaign. He knew it took a team rather than an individual approach.

"I'm convinced, Dorothy. Quit worrying. It'll be fine."

"Well, maybe you need to call a few people this afternoon. I've made you a list," she said handing him a yellow sheet of legal paper.

Leo glanced over the handwritten list and had to smile. Everyone thereon had been contacted by him at some point and most had already committed their support. He recognized one community activist who had told Leo in the last week that Dorothy had contacted him at least twice before. He and Leo had laughed at her tenacious efforts.

"I'm taking the rest of the day and most of tomorrow off, too. I'll contact as many folks as I can. You know I appreciate everything you've done, Dorothy. I promise, everything's going to work out."

Leo walked over a few steps and hugged his fierce older lady assistant. She returned the gesture with a big squeeze and slaps on the back before hurrying out of his office. Her trademark, "Bye, bye heah," rang out as she did.

Just as he was about to leave, Sandy stepped inside the door. Leo admired her probably more than she knew.

"Give me the jail stuff. You don't need to worry about that in the morning. I hear there's an election for the next boss," she said with raised eyebrows.

Leo smiled and responded, "You think you could stand me telling you what to do?"

"We'll see," she said as she took the case containing the files and left the room.

He gathered his stuff and looked around again. It had been a comfortable spot to work in for a long time and held lots of memories. One way or the other, however, he knew he'd be moving out of here soon. Tomorrow would serve as a new beginning.

CHAPTER THIRTY-FIVE

Jimbo drove past the house owned by Morgan Thomas. The detective had spent the last few hours finding out every bit of information available on the guy. It wasn't much, and at this point, only amounted to little more than a gut feeling Thomas was dirty in some way. Those kinds of feelings were often proven correct in the final analysis while working a case, and Jimbo intended to check him out further.

Jimbo had talked earlier in the day to his contact in the Human Resources Department to see if Thomas had any on going personnel issues or past complaints. There were none in his file, but it was confirmed Thomas had filed papers to start the early retirement process made possible by recent efforts of the local government to save money.

The detective had picked up the same forms a few weeks ago, but still hadn't made the final decision to follow through. Now, Jimbo felt an urgency to look more into this guy before he might take steps to slip away.

Discussions with the department head and some of the other employees Thomas worked around aroused an antenna in Jimbo's brain. By all accounts the man was smart, but standoffish. He rarely interacted with any of them, and one or two thought he was weird in some way they couldn't really identify.

It was easy enough to find the residence after checking the property records. The house was in an older section of town that had once been a choice spot for Macon homeowners. The area was still maintained better than a lot of others, but outlying real estate was looking somewhat seedy. Jimbo bet many of the neighbors living in the vicinity were like him, aging and getting a little crusty around the edges.

From other listed information, it appeared Thomas had inherited the property some years back that led Jimbo to believe it was where the guy had grown up. That fact in itself didn't necessarily mean a thing, but in the detective's experience he couldn't remember very many people who had not moved at least once in their lifetime.

Here was a man who had probably never lived anywhere else for well over forty years except maybe for college; had more than likely never married; and who not much was known about. All of this added together only heightened Jimbo's suspicions about the loner currently under everybody's radar.

Jimbo parked the cruiser down the street and left the engine running. He had a vantage point allowing him to observe the front of the house and a partial view of one side. There was an aluminum double garage door located on that same wall and was pulled down shut. There were windows on both sides that might provide a glimpse inside, but Jimbo couldn't tell unless he was to walk closer. Several large hardwoods and ample pine trees also obscured sightlines. A green trashcan was close to the curb in front, and he wondered if he should look inside it.

Then he remembered there were some binoculars in the glove box that he once used on stakeouts. It had been ages since he had used them. As a captain, he now left those operations to younger officers, but there had been times when he had sat in a car and watched a myriad of illegal activities take place while peering through the same magnifying glasses.

Jimbo rummaged through the compartment that contained a stained coffee cup, a mileage log that hadn't been recorded in many years, discarded reports and other assorted paperwork. In the rear was a scratched and worn case holding the eyeglasses.

He removed them and blew dust off the lenses before wiping the remaining residue clean with the sleeve of his shirt. It became obvious the front windows were inaccessible as closed blinds obstructed any view. Shifting to the two windows on the closest side of the house, Jimbo was rewarded with at least a partial vision inside one room.

There was no movement detected in what appeared to be a bathroom area. Jimbo could make out a huge mirror running the length of what he could see of the space. Nothing was noteworthy except for one reflection that could barely be seen on one corner of a vanity. It was an empty Styrofoam head. Even from the distance and less than clear vantage point, the vacant eyes were haunting.

It normally had to hold a toupee. Why else would a guy have something like that?

Jimbo focused through slits in the shades trying to find something else out of the ordinary, but was unable to distinguish anything. It was disappointing and didn't provide any clues.

He wondered if Thomas was home. There was nobody present that Jimbo could discern, but that proved nothing. He thought about going to the front door to find out, but quickly ruled out the option deciding instead to watch for a while longer.

An older lady walking at a pace reserved for a younger person could be seen heading in Jimbo's direction. As she got closer, the detective noticed a firm and fit body dressed in knee-length white cotton shorts, a pink tee shirt decorated with cherry blossoms, and shoes that contained elements of all the colors she wore. The woman held a cell phone in her left hand and sported stylish sunglasses.

Jimbo slid the binoculars onto the floorboard in an effort not to arouse suspicion as she approached his vehicle. When it was obvious she was coming toward him, he lowered the window on his side of the car, but left the engine running because of the heat and humidity.

"Can I help you?" she asked through glossy lips.

"Maybe, I'm Captain Barbour with the Sheriff's Department," Jimbo replied trying to use an air of official authority.

The lady examined him through the dark lenses on her attractive and tanned face. Jimbo had the feeling she was sizing him up and was not intimidated in the slightest by his pronouncement.

"I think I've seen your face in the paper and on TV before, now that I've got a good look at you. Are you working on another high profile case? Maybe the rapes?"

Jimbo was disarmed by her questions, but not so much as to let it show. He knew any response could be tricky.

"More like grunt work. Just some background stuff. Sorry I didn't get your name," he said.

"Because I didn't give it," she half-smiled revealing even white teeth, before finishing.

"I'm Molly Anderson, president of neighborhood watch around here. Some call me the head snoop. Are you interested in Morgan Thomas for some reason?"

Jimbo's uneasiness increased as he almost felt a role reversal had occurred. This woman was not a dummy.

"Well, Ms. Anderson, it's nice to meet you. I really appreciate that you're active in the neighborhood watch program. You'd be surprised how much folks like you help us do our jobs. Tips come into the department often that solve a lot of crime," he said while sticking his hand out of the window.

Her grip was strong even though his hand dwarfed hers. The previous version of her expression now turned into a full grin.

"Pleased to meet you, too, Captain. Didn't hear you answer my question, though," she replied as they let go of each other's hands.

"Let's just say I'm doing some preliminary checks, okay? Since I'm sure you're well acquainted with everyone living here, do you mind if I ask a few questions?"

Molly pondered for only a second before answering, "What do you want to know?"

"I'm betting you're a good observer of people and just wondering what your impressions are of this neighbor," Jimbo said while nodding his head toward the Thomas residence.

"You're pretty slick, detective. I'll give you that and tell you why. First, I notice you sitting in an unmarked car. Next, you pull out binoculars spying on a house of someone who has lived here all his life. Finally, you refuse to give any valid reason for such activity, but still want to pick my brain. By the way, I saw him leave about twenty minutes ago," she paused.

Jimbo couldn't help but grimace. His poker face had now cracked completely due to this woman's observations. That made him even surer she could offer some information on Thomas.

"So, can you help me Ms. Anderson?"

She pursed her lips before replying, "I'll try for two reasons. I do support law enforcement, and I'm no fan of Morgan Thomas. Mind if I get out of the heat, and we ride to the park down the street?"

Jimbo reached across the front seat and opened the door to the passenger side. The woman walked around the automobile and climbed in. She buckled the seat belt before he put the vehicle in gear and drove away from the area.

The government maintained recreation park was less than a mile from the neighborhood. It had recently been spruced up with landscaping and new playground equipment. Several children were running around and climbing various structures with a couple of parents nearby watching them. A pair of older teens was tossing a Frisbee. A shady area with benches had a few folks engaged in conversations.

Jimbo parked under heavy foliage provided by hardwoods in a designated space that allowed a view of all the activity. He left the engine running along with the air conditioner and looked over at his passenger. She removed her sunglasses revealing hazel eyes decorated with just a hint of shadow beneath.

"My husband and I bought our house right about the time Morgan Thomas was born. Until Fred died three years ago, we lived there together and always knew everybody near us. When we were younger, there used to be parties and gatherings at various homes. Everybody's kids played together. It was just a great place to live."

A single tear formed at the corner of her left eye, and Molly dabbed it with her index finger. Jimbo wished he had a tissue to offer her and was uncharacteristically at a loss for words.

"I grew up like that, too," he finally said during the lull in their conversation.

"Anyway, getting back to why I think I found you outside the Thomas house, I've had an uneasy feeling about the guy for a long time. He was strange as a kid, and he's a lot stranger now.

"He comes and goes at all times of the day and night. I don't think he has a single friend. At least, I've never seen him with one, male or female. I guess you'd say he's a bit of a recluse."

"Any particular reason you find him strange?" Jimbo asked as he found himself admiring Molly's appearance. They had to be about the same age, but she was holding up much better than he felt he was.

"Ummm, I've never seen him do anything harmful. Before his parents died, that was tragic, by the way, he would at least attend the block parties with them. He was polite, I would say, although he never engaged in any deep discussions with me.

"One thing that always unnerved me more than a little bit was the way he stared at females. He was furtive about it. There were a couple of cute girls, my daughter was one of them, and I would see him spying at them from behind a tree or a bush. He wouldn't attempt to talk to them, but he would watch them from a distance.

"I asked Sherry one time when she was maybe thirteen, she's my daughter living up in Atlanta now, what she thought of Morgan. Sherry said he was smart and thought a lot of himself. I didn't see that side of him, and maybe that's because he was always so reserved around me and the other adults.

"I asked her whether she knew about him paying her special attention and she laughed about it. I remember vividly her saying that Morgan lacked social skills. I guess I passed off the behavior the same way after that."

"What happened to his parents?"

"Car accident," Molly replied shaking her head.

"It happened when he was in college. I think he was in his last year at Georgia College. A semi ran into them and both were killed instantly. They were a nice couple. Religious. I heard Morgan got a lot of money from the settlement. Ollie Tucker represented him. Do you know Ollie? I'd bet you do. He's a good lawyer. Nice looking, too. He represented me when Fred passed away," she said with a distant gaze out the windshield.

"Yeah, I know Ollie. Like us, he's been around Macon his whole life. Some of us never make it out of here," he said pausing. "So, Morgan Thomas stayed, too, and has lived in the same house since birth," Jimbo questioned.

Molly nodded and turned toward Jimbo. There was a wistful gaze in her eyes as her hand rested on his. For a passing moment there was a spark that made the detective wish he wasn't married, and then it blew away like a dandelion in the wind.

"I should get you back home. I really appreciate the information, Ms. Anderson," he said taking his hand away and putting the car in drive.

She smiled and placed her hand in her lap. They made the short trip back silently.

As he pulled up to her driveway, she said, "Could I interest you in a cup of coffee, Captain?"

"I better be getting back to work, maybe another time. Do you mind one more question?" Jimbo asked.

"Alright."

"Have you seen Morgan Thomas wear more than one toupee?"

She didn't hesitate. "He's got several styles."

Molly got out of the car and swayed inside her home. Jimbo was left with his thoughts.

CHAPTER THIRTY-SIX

Leo had been making last minute stops all afternoon long since leaving the office early. The purpose was to shore up last minute efforts to get the vote out tomorrow. His car had been an instrumental part of the campaign since the beginning, and he had put an extra two thousand miles on the odometer as a result. If needed, he was willing to offer rides to the polls that might add a few more.

After checking with some of the people who provided such service, Leo discovered it wouldn't be necessary for him to do that. Volunteers told him others might even view him as trying to buy their votes no matter if that wasn't his intent.

The radio was tuned to a local channel, and Leo listened as one of his familiar political ads came on. Although he wasn't sure how much the locals even paid attention to such, they were reasonably inexpensive to run, and Leo had enlisted some popular individuals to show their support for him in the short thirty-second spots.

There were several different versions of the same theme. *The job was an important one. It required not only experience, but an even temperament as well. Leo Berry was the best choice because he had both.*

The people enlisted to read on air had recognizable voices whether they were lawyers who were already doing advertisements for their practices; resident celebrities with their own followings; and popular leaders in the community. The advertisements were designed to be quick and to keep Leo's name mentioned as much as possible.

His favorite was the one Sam Adams delivered. They had become close friends after working on a case together a few years before. Even though the two of them had been on opposite sides at the time, a mutual respect had developed and Leo admired the professionalism Sam had shown in the difficult case. It didn't hurt either that the well spoken young lawyer had the polish and looks of a youthful Denzel. Sam's ad had created a huge boost in support coming from the African American community, and Leo was grateful.

The campaign team liked the concept and had suggested a similar approach for television. Because funding those were a lot more expensive, not nearly as many had been purchased for that medium. Leo had received positive feedback after showing them and felt they had been effective.

There was a building excitement in his blood because it was almost over. Months of work were going to bear fruition tomorrow. It didn't even register that he would have to do more if he didn't get a majority of the vote. Leo refused to think a runoff might be needed.

News reports had shown a significant number of voters had already cast their ballots, and it looked like a big final turnout was possible. Many folks had already posted through social media sites that they had voted for him. The last few cycles over at least a ten-year period had been mixed because a lot of people seemed to be disgusted with the choices they had to make in recent races, but the local contests were driving new interest. Leo liked that fact and was hoping for a mandate.

Just as the radio started playing an old classic Jackson Browne song, Leo was alerted to an incoming phone call from the vibration in his pocket and through the ringing Bluetooth link on the screen in the center of the dashboard. A quick glance showed it was Jimbo.

The light traffic and Leo's desire to talk with the detective helped his decision to punch the green phone icon accepting the call. His friend's too loud voice signaled Jimbo was also in his vehicle.

"Hey, Jimbo. What's up?"

"Leo, I'm out checking a few things. Do you know Morgan Thomas?"

"Uh, I think I know the name. I'm related to some Thomases, but I can't place him at the moment."

"Really? I didn't know that. This guy works for the tax office, so I thought you might know him from there."

"Maybe if I saw him. The name is familiar for some reason. Maybe I'm thinking so because of my cousins, Mickie and Pete Thomas."

"Okay, he's close in age to you and grew up here in Macon."

"I'll take your word for it, Jimbo. I don't remember him right now. Why are you asking me?"

"I think he might be the guy who assaulted your wife's friend and committed some other rapes. I've got a bad feeling about him. Just hoping since you both worked for the county and are about the same age, you could have some insights about him."

"Damn, Jimbo. If you're sure he's the guy, get a search warrant. Tie his ass up," Leo said with his voice rising.

"I would if I could. I'm somewhat restricted at the moment by the lack of that little thing called probable cause. Other than that tiny bit of a partial print on the rubber glove left at one scene, there's really no tangible evidence to speak of. I don't have a match to the suspect because believe it or not, he's never been fingerprinted. The guy's slick, Leo."

"So are you, my friend. You'll get him, if he's the man."

There was a pause and Leo thought for a moment the call had been disconnected. Then, "Leo, got to go. I'll talk to you later."

Crap, I should've asked him whether he'd found out anything about the man outside the house the other night. I guess he's preoccupied with the new suspect. I'll ask him next time I talk to him, thought Leo.

Part of him was glad Jimbo was working hard and had found someone he believed was the one responsible for the committed assaults. He knew his friend would continue his investigation until it was completed successfully. He was distracted by the upcoming day and had to devote all his time there for right now, however.

Leo still needed to make more stops before going home. No time to let up now.

It sure will be nice when there is more time to spend with Dee and Mindy, he thought.

CHAPTER THIRTY-SEVEN

Leo sat alone at the round wooden table in the kitchen of his home while eating his warmed over late dinner. It had been a long but fruitful day. Meetings with some of his staunchest allies had only increased the positive feelings he had about the outcome of the election.

Among the people he'd met with were several supporters who were planning to be out in force during prime drive times tomorrow with signs in hand urging voters to cast ballots for him. Leo and Dee were planning to do the same on a corner of Riverside Drive not far from downtown and their house. The plastic placards were already packed in his car and read in all caps, YOUR CHOICE on the top line, and BERRY FOR S-G underneath. There were also some others they were going to stick in the ground nearby that read VOTE TODAY!!

Mindy shuffled barefoot into the room dressed in an over-sized UGA jersey that hung almost to her knees as Leo crammed the last bite of homemade chicken salad into his mouth. She hesitated for a moment before sitting in an adjacent chair to her dad.

"Daddy, you look tired. You're okay, right?"

Since his mouth was full of food, he shook his head up and down without trying to speak. His exaggerated chewing and raised eyebrows caused Mindy to snicker and relax her concerned appearance.

After washing down the remainder with iced tea, Leo replied, "I'm great, Dino. Can't wait for tomorrow."

"Good, me too. I never thought I'd say this, but I'm ready for us to get back to normal. You haven't given me a driving lesson in a month."

"Yeah, I'm sorry about that and how everything around here has pretty much been put on hold for the last few months. I'll make it up to you very soon. Have you decided how you want to spend Election Day?"

There had been some discussion a few days prior about the topic. Grandma Shelly was going to be preparing food for the planned party after the polls closed, and Mindy had indicated she might volunteer to help her. Waving signs in the summer heat didn't really appeal to her, and she had thought the idea too cheesy.

"I think I'm going to help Grandma. I want to learn a few of her secrets in the kitchen. We'll all be together tomorrow night anyway, right?"

"Sure thing. I know she'll appreciate the help, but more than that, she'll like it that you'll be spending time with her. That's really sweet of you, Dino. You're a special kid. Excuse me, young woman," Leo said with a half-smile.

"Okay, then. Glad that's settled. I think I'll head to my room. I'm going to Face time Amy before sleep. Love you, Daddy," she said while reaching over to kiss Leo's cheek.

Leo continued to sit while trying to decompress. His racing mind was as ready to rest as his tired body. He closed his eyes and took a few long breaths through his nostrils and then exhaled slowly through his mouth. He had used this technique a lot lately, and it seemed to work as a way to help shut things down.

His routines had been disrupted to the point that he wondered if he could find them again when the campaign was finally concluded. Daily runs and the light weight workouts that normally followed had been a part of his life for close to twenty years, but he hadn't been able to find time to accomplish many since making the choice to go after the job of solicitor-general. Although Leo had lost about ten pounds during the campaign's duration, he didn't think it had been done in a particularly healthy way.

Leo didn't notice Dee's presence as she came into the kitchen until she began kneading his shoulders. Along with the deep breathing exercises, the massage caused a longing for the comfort of their bed. Maybe a session of languid lovemaking was a few minutes away. That would be a fitting end to the day.

"Babes, I hate to stop this right now, but I need to tell you something," Dee spoke into his ear just above a whisper.

Leo opened his droopy eyes not wanting to lose the moment. "Can it wait, this is feeling good to me," he moaned.

Dee increased the pressure and used her thumbs to loosen the knots in his neck and just above the shoulder blades. Leo felt slobber form in the corner of his mouth and had to suck it in before dripping onto his empty plate. He pushed the plate away from him and rested his heavy head on crossed arms. Dee used her hands up and down his spine causing Leo to forget everything that was wrong in the world. She continued in this fashion for a good minute until patting his back and spoke again.

"It's really important, Babes."

Leo lifted his head and replied, "Okay."

He sat up in the chair, and his glazed eyes tried to focus. *I'm so tired,* he thought.

Dee sat down at the table and reached over to pull her laptop between where she and her husband were. She angled the screen so that he could get the better view. She had paused a shot of a man in the nightclub prior to the attack on Maxine.

"I found a video in your coat pocket earlier today. I thought it was one of those you usually bring home for me to look at. When I watched it, I saw it wasn't the normal DUI arrests you usually bring home. I guessed it was something to do with the rapes."

Leo studied his wife's face. As worn out as he was, it was apparent she was distraught. He tried to process what she was talking about.

"I'm sorry, Wink. This is about a tape?" he asked as he tried to clear the fog.

"Yeah, you had it in one of your pockets. I figured you forgot about it. I viewed it today. I think I might know the guy who's obviously the target."

Leo's brain struggled to remember. Then he did. Jimbo had given him a copy that contained videos of a suspect. He'd forgotten to watch it during all the hubbub of the campaign.

"So, you think you know the guy?"

"Leo, he could be someone I went to high school with. I'm not positive, but I think it's Morgan Thomas."

Leo was waking up now. Part of him wanted to crawl in the bed and get some sleep. The other part was screaming that this was important, and he would have to wait.

"I've heard his name before. I probably should know him, but I don't. You do?"

"I saw him recently at the tax office. He's a weird man, Leo. When I saw the tape, I immediately thought of Morgan. It's not a clear picture, but I really think it's him."

Leo remembered his earlier conversation with Jimbo. Two people he trusted were thinking this Morgan Thomas was the rapist. He gave a great deal of credence to each of their opinions.

"He didn't threaten you, did he?"

"No, nothing like that. I recalled him from school, and he made me feel uncomfortable when I saw him again. Then I saw the video, and I thought it looked like him. Maybe it's just a coincidence."

Leo thought about it for a moment and then replied, "There are no coincidences. At least, that's what I'm thinking right now. You're right to be concerned, but we need to be careful not to jump to conclusions. Misidentifications can cause lots of problems. I need to call Jimbo."

He pulled his constant companion I-Phone from his pants pocket and located the detective's number. Sleep would have to wait for now.

CHAPTER THIRTY-EIGHT

Morgan drove his car back into the neighborhood slowly while checking up and down the streets near his home. It was late, almost midnight, because the last time he'd driven the same route earlier today he'd seen that detective again. He was with that busybody woman Morgan couldn't stand and who lived down the street, Molly Anderson. They had to be talking about him. He knew it and had driven out of the area before they could see him.

The vulnerability he was feeling had never been experienced before. It made him mad as hell and a little scared, though part of him didn't want to admit it. Possible outlooks of his future that Morgan had felt during the last few weeks were not a good thing in his brain. His conflicts had provided him with uncharacteristic headaches all day long, and he still had a dull throbbing that over the counter remedies didn't affect.

The house he had lived in all his life was dark now except for a faint glow peeking from the blinds on the side of the house nearest his bathroom. It was near where the unmarked police cruiser had been parked containing Barbour and Anderson. He wondered to himself whether the detective could see anything inside and then quickly dismissed the idea. Morgan had gotten rid of everything resembling proof.

Pressing the garage opener button, Morgan's eyes darted over the illuminated space as he drove forward. He didn't notice anything out of place except for the government car that often stayed in the currently vacant spot next to where he parked his personal vehicle. He had turned it in to the county a few days ago after a thorough cleaning. Too bad he would no longer have use of a free car since he made the decision to retire.

With another jab of his finger, he dropped the aluminum double door even before turning off the vehicle's engine. Morgan felt the need to hurry even though overt danger didn't appear to be nearby.

Upon entering the residence, he made a quick inspection to ensure nothing was out of place. Morgan was not used to paranoia, but self-doubts had all but consumed him most of the day.

He retraced in his mind for the umpteenth time what he had done. It shook his fragile psyche to remember.

***

After gathering all the stuff that had been used numerous times over the years of seeking worthy pretty girls, Morgan had taken the black plastic bag to a remote location thirty miles east of Macon and two counties removed. It was a place that was a dumping zone for citizens without garbage service. Two huge metal containers resembling construction debris removal receptacles sat in the area with piles of garbage already near the tops.

The place stank of rotten food and all sorts of other unpleasant odors that were unrecognizable. It was a combination of smells that permeated the senses and clung to the nose hairs.

No one in their right mind would want to spend a moment there if they didn't have to other than the crows that picked at more delectable morsels. Signs posted claimed that unlawful dumping was prohibited and that pickup was scheduled for Wednesdays.

Morgan was familiar with the site having disposed of items there on a couple of other occasions. The past visits had proven successful and gave him a sense of comfort now.

He almost gagged when he dropped the bag into a corner of the dumpster that was slightly less full of refuse. What appeared to be a deer's hoof stuck out of one of the other heaps and flies were swarming all around it.

Placing his hand over his mouth and holding his breath, Morgan hurried back to his vehicle. He didn't hesitate before cranking the engine and driving away.

Just as he got to the frontage road exit that led back to the interstate, a redneck in a dually loaded with what looked like a month's worth of garbage almost ran into Morgan's much smaller sedan while making the turn onto the travelled road. Morgan had to slam on his brakes before skidding to a stop.

The truck smeared with red Georgia clay around the wheels and dusty residue everywhere else remained in its place with the diesel motor rattling. Morgan's heartbeat had sped to the point of bursting and near panic developed as the driver's window slid down on the monster towering above him.

"What the hell, man? You taking your side down the middle?" yelled the bearded man with a crimson face. His scream could be heard through Morgan's rolled up window and his jacked up air conditioner.

For the first time since leaving the dump, Morgan realized he was well over the centerline of the road. He wasn't sure what to do next since he couldn't get by. He just knew he had to get out of there.

Reluctantly, Morgan let his window down with his left hand while his right reached toward the gun stowed beside him. Confrontation was not a part of his nature, but his choices were limited.

"Sorry, I'm lost. I guess I got off at the wrong exit. Trying to get back to Macon," Morgan said attempting to look clueless. The handle felt reassuring to his grip when it was found.

The man stared hard at him. It seemed longer than it probably was, but finally the guy spoke again. Morgan couldn't help but think the guy had a weapon in the truck that was bigger than his own.

"Hang a right, then left. Ain't nothing out here," he said before spitting a glob of brown liquid out his window.

"Thanks," Morgan said with a half-hearted smile.

He relaxed as the big truck backed up and turned a wider angle so Morgan could negotiate by him. Not trying to speed by as much as he wanted, Morgan looked into the rearview mirror when he cleared. The asshole was watching his vehicle more closely than preferred. Although Morgan couldn't be sure, it appeared the other driver reached down and was writing something.

Morgan had gotten on I-75 and sped away when he realized his underwear was wet. He wanted to think it was from the hot weather and sweat. But, he knew it wasn't. He'd pissed himself. First time he could ever remember.

Now he was mad. More at himself than anything.

Damn it! That was close.

***

Back at home. It had been a safe place for so long, as long as he could remember. Not anymore. He was moving soon.

There was just one more girl to see before he did. He had to get it done before leaving. She was like his destiny. Fulfillment of that was all that mattered now.

He needed some shuteye first. Self-pleasuring about her would help in that regard.

CHAPTER THIRTY-NINE

Jimbo's mind wouldn't shut down enough to let him get some needed sleep. All that coffee consumption probably didn't help either, but maybe the Ambien he had taken a few minutes before would. It wasn't as late as usual when he normally laid his creaky body down to rest, but he knew how much it was needed for rejuvenating his energy. The gas tank only held fumes.

He had just gotten off the phone with Leo about thirty minutes ago. Their conversation had only reinforced his belief that Morgan Thomas was the main suspect in the recent assaults. How he was going to prove it was a major reason for Jimbo's insomnia.

The discussion had centered on Leo's wife, Dee, and her tentative identification of Thomas in the nightclub videos. Jimbo had asked Leo whether Dee was sure, and he had heard her response that was less than positive.

It looks like him to me.

Since Dee watched those tapes, Jimbo asked Leo if she had seen the one from the grocery store as well. It was reported to him that she indeed had observed it, but couldn't say with any degree of certainty that it showed Thomas.

Leo had proposed that Jimbo might prepare a photo lineup that included Thomas in an effort to seek possible connection from the victims. It was an idea that had crossed Jimbo's mind, but there were problems with that approach that he shared with the prosecutor.

First, he didn't know where to find a recent picture of Thomas. Second, even if he could, it would be difficult to put it in a collection of others that would appear similar.

Typically when putting something like that together, Jimbo would assemble several booking photos that included the suspect. You had to be careful not to make it obvious just who that suspect was. Otherwise, any defense lawyer worth his or her salt would be able to suppress such evidence because it could be ruled as too suggestive if a positive ID was obtained.

There were other problems as well. None of the victims had been able to give enough of a description of the assailant that would narrow down the field. The fact the victims were often blindfolded and the rapist kept his face covered in some fashion prevented recognition.

The almost total lack of forensic evidence was maddening to Jimbo as well. There was one bit of a partial print that couldn't be matched to any database. The detective wondered if he could somehow get Thomas's prints and see if a connection existed. He resolved it was worth a try and would work on that tomorrow.

That was his last thought as his wife snuggled against him, and sleep overtook everything else.

***

Leo and Dee cuddled together after the sweetness of their coupling. It was amazing to the lawyer that they still found pleasure in each other's bodies after their years of marriage. The sex could still produce the intenseness of the early years, but now the familiarity with each other more often brought a feeling of complete satisfaction with everything, not just with the act itself.

"Tomorrow's going to be a long day, Leo," Dee sighed.

Although the bedroom was dark, faint light allowed Leo the ability to see Dee's half-opened dark eyes. He knew she was right.

"Yeah," he said as his heartbeat continued to slow.

"It'll be worth it when I get to sleep with the solicitor-general," she said with a little giggle.

"Only if that's me," Leo laughed.

They were quiet for a minute, and Leo felt himself drifting toward a sunset on a beach in St. Somewhere. He loved dreams like that.

"Do you think I should tell Maxie about my suspicions?" asked Dee causing him to come back to reality.

"I don't think so, not yet. We need to let Jimbo do his job. From what he told me tonight, he's looking at the guy hard. I've got faith in Jimbo," said Leo before yawning.

Dee kissed him and then Leo was on the sand again. It was beautiful, but there was a dark cloud on the horizon. Dreams were like that sometimes.

CHAPTER FORTY

Leo awoke feeling like a kid on Christmas morning. It had been a night filled with visions that made him feel hopeful. He was refreshed by the almost full eight hours of sleep and looked forward to the promises of the day. Dee barely moved as he rolled off his side of the bed and padded toward the bathroom.

He relieved himself and then headed to the kitchen. Because he had pre-set the coffee maker's timer the night before, the pot was ready and he poured a steaming mug full. A little half and half was added, and then he walked to the front door. Almost magically, Tiki appeared from some other area of the house and waited for Leo to attach his leash to the red collar around his neck.

Dawn had broken as the master and pet stepped out on the front stoop. Surveying the area, it was obvious that the house across the street was showing some signs of improvement, which made Leo happy. The yard had been manicured and the shrubbery no longer was mangy. Although the new owner hadn't moved in yet, Leo resolved to go over soon and have a beer with the guy.

Tiki pranced a tad and was showing more energy than he had been lately. He said hello to a couple of bushes on the way as Leo proceeded toward the newspaper lying on the end of the driveway. The Jack Russell's tongue hung out, and he grinned back at Leo as he hiked his right rear leg to water nearby plants. It was almost as if the animal knew things were getting back to normal soon.

Leo reached down and grabbed The Telegraph wrapped in a clear plastic bag. It was much thinner these days, as it had become less of a homegrown news source. Just about all of the reporters and editors Leo had once known were no longer employed there. He wondered if the publication would remain a viable concern much longer. More and more people were getting the news, trustworthy or not, from other places, and Leo had heard subscriptions were dwindling.

Unfolding the front page, headlines reminded readers there was an election today. The main article covered not only the major races, but several of the local ones, too. Leo was especially glad to see that his was one of the featured at least to some extent. The paragraphs dealing with the race didn't include any new information about the candidates' qualifications and mainly described the positions they were seeking.

Leo was summarized as, "Assistant Solicitor, Leo Berry III, is a Macon native with twenty years trial experience. His platform includes a promise to remain active in the courtroom and pledging the implementation of new pretrial programs designed to help young offenders keep clean records. Three years ago, his involvement in exposing an illegal drug ring resulted in his recognition as a citizen hero."

A frown crossed his face. The last sentence had resurfaced off and on throughout the campaign. Leo had not used anything about that incident in his literature or ads and had generally tried to avoid the subject. He really didn't like to remember that period of his life, especially involving the justifiable homicide committed. While many people had passed on accolades to him, Leo was not proud to know he had taken another human life even in self-defense. It had taken some professional counseling to deal with his involvement, and he still had nightmares about the episode.

As Tiki sniffed around the front yard exhibiting behavior Leo recognized as a precursor of doing a number two, he continued to flip through the pages. He was expecting to find his last political spot, a half-page costing more than Leo wanted to spend, in a place that would catch attention. He was not disappointed when it jumped out on the second page of the second section.

The bold print and all caps pronounced, **WE SUPPORT LEO BERRY FOR SOLICITOR-GENERAL.** Enclosed in the block were two hundred and fifty names. They had been carefully screened and sought by the candidate to be included. Among those listed were people popular in every part of the community and known for their integrity. Over fifty of them were other lawyers.

Leo thought it impressive. He knew many voters probably didn't know him personally, but they may very well know at least one person contained within the box and be swayed by their alliance. The powerful endorsements were designed with hopes of attracting undecided last minute voters.

He smiled and folded the paper back to its original shape while still holding the coffee mug. Taking a big swig, Leo drained the half-full container of the tepid liquid. He then watched as the next-door neighbor backed his SUV into the street and wheeled next to where he stood.

"Mornin', Leo," rang out as the passenger side window on the land yacht slid down. At the wheel sat Cliff Massee, a self-employed engineer known for the long hours he worked.

"How's it going, Cliff? Got a busy day at work?" responded Leo.

"On the way to vote before I do. Gonna do my duty and help elect you," Cliff replied with a toothy grin.

"Thanks, I'll take all the help I can get. Spread the word."

Leo waved a salute when the vehicle drove past. He glanced at his watch and it showed 6:38 and then switched to Tiki as he finished his business in the front yard. It was already warm and humid which was typical for this time of the year, and Leo was starting to feel a little clammy.

He was about to walk back toward the house when he saw what he thought to be a small piece of trash lying in the grass near the mailbox. Leo pulled on Tiki's leash and went over to pick it up. It was a practice he had done for as long as his family had been living there. He hated to see litter anywhere, but especially near his house.

It was faded and a little crumpled. Leo almost finished wadding it up upon retrieving it with the intent of throwing it in the trashcan when he went back inside. Then something caught his eye that made him do a double take.

The receipt was for a gas purchase from a nearby convenience store. The name showing on it was Morgan Thomas.

What the hell?

The name would've meant nothing to him until yesterday, but now a light came on in Leo's brain. The previously unnoticed piece of paper must have fallen out when he had confronted the driver with a different name a few days earlier. The coincidences were mind-boggling.

Why would Thomas be over here? Surely he couldn't be stalking Dee.

Leo's mind raced with the possibilities. If he was indeed watching their house, it went against everything Leo knew about the modus operandi of the attacker. Surprise turned into red-hot anger. He put the receipt in the pocket of his shorts wondering if he had contaminated it and resolved to put it in a baggie when he got back inside.

Leo had an idea and hurried to the front door with Tiki in tow. The terrier balked initially, but gave up when Leo ordered him to, "Come now, Teek!"

After unleashing the pet, Leo went to the spare bedroom down the hall from Mindy's room. Tiki followed as Leo got down on all fours and peered under the bed. Reaching as far as he could, Leo pulled out a box. Written on the outside in black magic marker was a single word, **Annuals**.

Inside were hardbound versions of books from various schools Leo and Dee had attended. There were seven from the years Leo had spent at Mercer, four undergrad and three from law school. He discarded and stacked them to the side with little attention.

In the bottom of the box were high school editions. Some were somewhat frayed on the edges and were worn more than others. A couple of them were duplicated because of overlapped years with Leo's looking shabbier than Dee's copies. The two of them had attended Southwest High during the same period even though Leo was a class ahead of his wife.

He opened Dee's senior edition first and went to the index. Thomas, Morgan had only one picture listed there. Turning to the page given, Leo studied the face assigned to that name.

The photo had obviously been touched up to some extent probably to soften features or clear up imperfections. Nothing stood out about the rather ordinary face showing an enigmatic hint of a smile reminding Leo of the *Mona Lisa*. No teeth were visible. The eye color couldn't be distinguished because it was a black and white shot. His hair was shorter than most others on the page maybe because the hairline already seemed to be receding more than most teens at that age.

All in all, there was nothing that stood out to make Leo think this was the face he remembered from the encounter in front of the house. Neither did he think there was anything that cried out rapist. Of course, the picture was dated since Dee had graduated over twenty-five years ago.

Part of him was disappointed there was not an "aha" moment and warned Leo about not rushing to judgment. Based on his finding of the receipt, he felt it was a real piece of tangible evidence. It was definitely something he needed to pass on to Jimbo.

He heard movement in Mindy's room and knew it was time for everybody to get moving. This was going to be a long day, but he would find time to get with the detective sometime before it was done.

***

After shaving and showering, Leo offered to cook breakfast for anyone wanting something more substantial, but Mindy had already consumed a bowl of sugary cereal and Dee chose to skip as she often did, choosing instead to "ready the cabin for departure," as she called getting ready.

He fried himself an egg and placed it on a couple of slices of wheat toast that had been slathered with mayonnaise. A thin slice of cheddar cheese and a much thicker one of tomato was placed on top of the egg with a generous amount of black pepper to complete the sandwich.

Leo stood near the stove and gobbled the meal in less than two minutes. It was a bad habit that Dee often scolded him about, but one he could never quite get away from unless the family was eating at the same time. He took extra care to keep the juices from running down the front of his freshly pressed oxford shirt and the red power tie he had chosen to wear.

He was anxious to get running. People were already going to vote and heading to their workplaces. It was probably silly, but he wanted to be out there waving them on.

Dee entered the kitchen as Leo washed the pan used to fry his egg. She was dressed casually in capri pants and an oversized tee shirt with the words **YOUR CHOICE** centered above **BERRY FOR S-G**.

"Hey, Babes. Since I'm taking Mindy to your mom's, I'll catch up with you wherever you say," she said with dimples shining.

Leo admired how she looked so put together even in such attire. Her hair was perfectly coiffed and her makeup was tastefully applied. He knew she had already gotten him many votes with her looks and personality. No doubt she would get him at least a few more today.

"Okay. I'm going to start at Riverside and Pierce until about nine o'clock or so. I'm sure the traffic will be pretty heavy until then. I'll wait for you there and we can figure out what to do next. I love your outfit, by the way. Very chic," he replied with a grin.

He wanted to tell her about his find, but didn't think it was necessary at that moment. There was way too much going on today. Dee was a worrier, and he knew that she would totally freak out about the possibility that Thomas had been near their home a few days before. Leo was sure that he and Dee would be together for most of the day, if not for all of it, so she was protected. Besides, his initial assessment just couldn't wrap his head around what it all meant, and Jimbo would know what to do when the information was passed on.

Mindy joined them sporting her usual eclectic style including Doc Martens on her feet. Neither of her parents could understand her fascination with the clunky shoes, but allowed her the independence to choose what she wore.

"Let's do this," she said with an air of confidence.

"Yeah," chimed in Dee and Leo as they all bumped fists. Hugs and kisses followed before the two females left Leo standing in the kitchen. He listened as the garage door opened and Dee's car fired up.

After brushing his teeth, he walked back to the bedroom and found the shorts worn earlier. Taking the receipt now secured in a snack-sized plastic bag from that article of clothing, Leo transferred it to the right front pocket of his suit jacket lying across the bed. Because of the forecasted hot and muggy day ahead, he didn't opt to wear it now and placed it over his shoulder as he headed out the door.

When Leo got outside, he opened the rear door to his vehicle and carefully laid the jacket lengthwise on the back seat. He didn't intend to put it on until that evening when the Election Day party began.

He climbed into the driver's side and cranked the engine. While waiting on the air conditioner to do its magic, Leo took out his cellphone and punched Jimbo's number. He was disappointed when the detective's voice came on.

"This is Detective Captain James Barbour. Leave me a short message and a number and I'll get back to you as soon as possible."

"Jimbo, this is Leo. I found something this morning I think you need to see. I'm going to be out and about all day, so leave me a message if I don't answer right away. We'll have to find time to get together sometime today. Thanks."

Leo placed the phone on the passenger's seat and headed toward his first destination. As disturbed as he felt, there was enough excitement about the day to let him get past that emotion. Jimbo would take care of that problem while Leo spent the day getting elected.

CHAPTER FORTY-ONE

Morgan was up early and busy with different preparations for the next phase of his life. It had been a fitful night and he was feeling frazzled as a result, but not enough to keep from taking steps for further self-protection. This time of his life had become the most threatening and required every bit of his superior intellect to ensure preservation.

He finished packing a suitcase full of clothing suitable for a warm weather climate leaving room in one corner for a leather toiletry bag containing personal items. Morgan didn't intend to take much where he planned to go for the next couple of months knowing he could always purchase anything else he needed when he got there.

The Caribbean would not be his final destination, but he had money in an account on Grand Cayman, and he could stay as long as he needed while sorting out other arrangements. The beauty of the Internet also meant Morgan could manage other funds in banks here and his investment account with E-Trade. He had plenty of options available due to the amount of money he had saved.

Austerity had been a major theme throughout his years, but that was about to change. The plain sedan in the garage would be traded for a sporty upscale version, maybe a BMW, Mercedes, or Lexus.

He had an appointment with a realtor in a couple of hours and planned to sell the house including as much of the furniture and furnishings as was possible. He'd give away anything that didn't find a purchaser. Then when he figured out exactly where he would live permanently, he was thinking of a condo. The Atlanta or Savannah areas appealed to him, but he wasn't wed to either. An extended vacation would help him make up his mind. Morgan had plans to hit the reset button and start over again.

It would be good to get out this town, the sooner, the better. He would welcome new scenery and the challenges ahead. Away from that damn nosy detective. If it weren't for him, everything would be just fine.

The more Morgan analyzed his situation; the old confidence would try to sway his insecurities that he had nothing to worry about. He had always been careful not to leave anything incriminating behind when having fun with a pretty girl. Sure, he was obsessive-compulsive and knew it, but those traits had protected him well since his earlier forays when he was much younger.

Morgan didn't keep a journal or make notes about his conquests although he still remembered every girl he had ever bedded. Early on, various drugs whether legal or illegal, along with alcohol had helped him gain control of the chosen female. Many of those in the beginning didn't even realize what he was doing. They were so far gone by the time the sex was happening that they often slept through his pleasure. He kept everything needed in the bag carried with him.

As Morgan perfected his style, the bag's contents grew. At first, there were condoms, lubricant, and various cleaning supplies. Later, he added a vibrator and then a dildo and sometimes, edible panties. Of course, he always carried ways of disguising and hiding himself, and he was especially fond of the dark sleep mask that he often used on the girls.

He had found that the large black patches when placed over their eyes functioned to keep them from not only seeing his face, but also helped to subdue the girls from any efforts of resistance. Morgan wasn't a violent person, at least that's what he thought, and he prided himself for not physically hurting the chosen girls. They didn't know that, though. A simple threat became much more when you couldn't see what was going on.

Up until recently, his refined techniques had worked quite nicely. Morgan was convinced that hardly anyone he had been with had even reported the activities. Research had confirmed the percentage of described events was extremely small. Careful preparation ahead of time and stringent cleanup afterward took care of any other problems assuming a girl did take such a step.

Morgan frowned when he remembered that his beloved bag of pleasures was gone. Unceremoniously trashed in a common dump. It had been necessary to get rid of the items, but they could easily be replaced when he relocated. He was already thinking about how he could improve the next set.

Until he could get established again, Morgan would have to try harder to cool his jets. The consuming desires that surfaced from time to time would have to be controlled. This could be a problem since over the course of the last few months the need to find his next girl seemed to grip him more often than it had when he was younger.

The doorbell chimed, and Morgan closed his bedroom door as he made his way to the front of the house. He glanced at his watch and saw his appointment was early. That was okay. The real estate agent was expected, and he was anxious to get the process started.

When he swung open the door, Morgan couldn't hide the surprise that took over his face. There stood Detective Jimbo Barbour holding a cup in his hand.

***

Jimbo had awakened with a purpose. He was as fresh as he had felt in a while. Bren, his wife, even commented that he wasn't limping as much as usual. That was good because he had a plan.

After drinking almost a full pot of coffee, his nerves bordered on jittery. That was all right. Jimbo wanted to feel wired. It compensated for the old age, which seemed to creep in too often nowadays.

He was feeling more than a little pissed. Morgan Thomas was a big blip on his radar, but he hadn't been able to tie him to the crimes he had been personally investigating for the last few months. Both his brain and his gut told him the guy was responsible for at least three assaults on women. It was, however, very probably a lot more than that.

A few days before, Jimbo had met with a GBI psychologist trying to get insights into the psyche of the offender. Based on part of what Dr. Wally Davis said, the guy committing the attacks might be slipping.

I would surmise since he's victimized at least three women in the last few months, his compulsion is overtaking whatever restraint's been imposed on his good side. I use the term restraint loosely, and the term his good side even more so. He's probably experiencing at least some kind of inner conflict, but I would bet there's something going on in his mind that's driving him to a final resolution. That might lead him to an act of violence he's not yet done.

Since the victims are similar in appearance, I would think there is one woman he's fantasized about for a long time. Someone he feels as putting him down. If you could figure out who that person is, and if she's still in his universe, I would focus on her. He may very well try to go after her. As you know, detective, rape is more often than not a power control thing, and that's what he's doing, exerting his power and control.

Thomas had lived in Macon his whole life. Jimbo had a feeling what Dr. Davis had said was right on the money. Maybe there was a woman living nearby who was the inspiration for the guy's assaults.

Jimbo didn't know how to find out who that woman was or if she even existed. Fantasies were just that. They often made no sense in the real world. He could remember having a recurring one when he got back from Nam about having a threesome with a couple of Vietnamese hookers. Of course, he was a whole lot younger back then, and sex had permeated many of his thoughts. It also helped to forget the bad scenes he had witnessed up close and personal in combat which left scars that never healed. The point was by not acting on the fantasies made him unlike the deviant asshole he was trying to nail.

What he needed was some evidence. All he could think to do at the moment was go to Thomas's house and see what kind of reaction that might bring. It would be tricky, but maybe he could figure out a way to score some of his DNA or find some fingerprints. Even if there had not been anything left at the crime scenes he had worked, maybe there would be something to match in one of the databases.

Jimbo pulled the unmarked cruiser into the Thomas driveway halfway thinking the nosy neighbor he had met last time would greet him again. He looked around upon exiting the vehicle toward the direction of Molly Anderson's home, but didn't see her. Maybe she wasn't at home. He wasn't even sure if Thomas was either.

His garage door was closed, so Jimbo walked to the front entrance. The plan was to try and shake Thomas a little. Nothing ventured, nothing gained if he couldn't.

The doorbell was rung, and Jimbo waited, hoping Thomas was home. It seemed an eternity before the door swung open. There stood Morgan Thomas.

***

The two men stared at one another. It was a rediscovery minute for each. For a moment, neither spoke. Competition came into play.

Morgan was the first to speak, "Detective Barbour? I haven't seen you in a while. Can I help you?"

"Good morning, Mr. Thomas. Hope you're okay. I was just over at your office a few days ago and was told you were retiring. You had helped me before, so I was hoping you could help me again."

Morgan smiled and responded, "I wish I could. I don't know that I can. I don't have access to state files anymore. What are you looking for?"

It seemed like a chess match or a poker game with the men looking for a tell on the other one. Neither blinked.

"I'm working on a few cases involving assaults on women. The suspect was driving a dark sedan, and I remembered how you were able to assist me tracking down a vehicle when I had such limited information before."

"Sounds pretty scanty, Captain. If I were still working, I could probably help narrow down the fields some, but I doubt much, based on what you're saying. You might check with one of my former colleagues at the tax office. They should be able to do that for you."

A bead of sweat ran down Jimbo's face from his forehead. He mopped it away with the sleeve of his jacket. It was hot and humid even in the early morning hours, which was typical in middle Georgia.

"Maybe I will. It sure is hot out here, you mind if I come in a minute? I could use a drink of water, too."

Jimbo's plan included getting Thomas to touch something that could be dusted for prints. He had cleaned the cup before leaving his house and had been careful to hold it in a way to keep his own fingerprints in one area.

Some emotion flashed through Morgan's eyes before he responded. "Sure, Detective Barbour, but I must tell you I'm expecting a guest any minute. Come in and I'll get your water. You want some ice?"

Jimbo followed inside and handed over the plastic tumbler. He watched as Thomas grasped it toward the bottom away from Jimbo's hold.

"Yes, ice would be nice," Jimbo laughed as he followed up with, "and I'm a poet and don't know it."

"I'll be right back," said Morgan smirking as he walked away from the detective.

Jimbo did a quick check around the room. It was decorated sparsely and old-fashioned. There was a piano with a bench underneath on one wall and a floral printed sofa pressed against the opposing side of the area. A winged-backed chair with the same print was angled nearby with a table and lamp beside it. A couple of landscapes in ornate gold-flaked frames were hung on the walls. No family photos were present. Blinds on the front windows were drawn tight and had dust visible on them.

Jimbo's impression was that the furniture had been there for decades and that Thomas spent very little time in the stuffy place. Jimbo wished that he could explore the rest of the house.

That wasn't going to happen absent probable cause, and no judge he knew would ever find pc on just hunches he had.

Morgan came back into the room cradling the cup with a dishtowel. He was rubbing the outside as if buffing something precious.

"Filled up your water and got you some ice, too, Detective Barbour. I'm sorry I got it wet, so I dried it off for you. Good as new," he said with a half-smile.

Jimbo took the beverage from Thomas without showing the disappointment he felt from being outsmarted. He took a sip and smacked his lips.

"Thanks. Got to stay hydrated. Nice house you got. Live here long?" he asked.

Thomas showed his teeth in a fuller beam, and Jimbo noted more clearly the way his front two slightly overlapped. They were not as crooked as Jimbo thought his own bite was, but he remembered that one of the victims had described her attacker in such a way. The other thing that caught Jimbo's eye was no toupee on Thomas's head, which was shorn close.

"All my life except for dorms in college. Not a bad neighborhood, but I've got to admit that I'm about ready to change. As a matter of fact, I'm meeting a real estate agent today. That's who I thought you were when you got here. I'm ready to travel and have a little fun," Morgan said still grinning.

"Hmm, I might know someone interested in buying this place if it's going on the market. Mind if I look around?"

Morgan's face clouded for a fraction of a second before he replied, "It's a little messy right now I'm afraid. I should have it ready soon, however. Maybe you can come back and make an appointment for a showing if I do decide to sell."

"I might just do that. It would make a nice home for a family. I guess for a single man like yourself the place might get a little lonely, huh?" Jimbo prodded.

"Oh, I'm used to being by myself, growing up as an only child. Just never found the right one to settle down with," replied Morgan as his smirk returned.

"Probably have all kind of women chasing after you," said Jimbo while studying the other man's face.

"I wouldn't put it that way," said Morgan.

There was a discreet knock at the storm door separating the front entrance and both men turned in that direction. There stood a matronly woman holding a portfolio under her arm and pressed against her sizeable breast. Morgan walked a few steps and let her inside.

"Good morning," she said pleasantly extending her right hand. "Mr. Thomas?" she asked.

"Yes, ma'am. I've been expecting you. You're from SSK Realty?"

"Sure am. My name's Nan Thompson. I hope I'm not interrupting anything."

"Not at all. This gentleman was just leaving," Morgan said turning toward Jimbo.

"Yes, I am. Thanks again for the water, Mr. Thomas. Hope to see you again soon, " Jimbo replied as he headed out.

Both doors closed behind him as Jimbo walked to his car. He felt frustrated, but even more convinced that Morgan Thomas was the culprit he had been searching for.

He picked up the cell phone he had left in the console and saw he had a message. Playing it, he heard Leo's voice asking him to get in touch.

Jimbo pressed the button to return the call and got Leo's voice mail. "Tag, you're it, Leo. I know you're busy with the election and all, but give me a call back when you get a minute."

Driving away, Jimbo recreated the encounter. Morgan Thomas was smart, but he was going to get him.

CHAPTER FORTY-TWO

Leo and Dee stood at the corner of the busy intersection grinning and waving at passing traffic. Many people travelling past their location blew their horns and waved back while some let down their windows and shouted encouragement. Leo had been there for better than an hour with his wife joining him for the last thirty minutes. He had worked up a sweat in the summer heat and saw her starting to look uncomfortable as well.

"It seems like most people should be at work by now. Maybe we should move on to another spot or take a little break," said Leo.

Dee nodded in assent and wiped her damp forehead with a tissue removed from her Louis Vuitton. She had changed pocketbooks the evening before and had enough supplies inside to cover any contingency that might occur. Purses were one of her passions, and Leo knew Dee often chose to carry a particular one based on some reasoning only she alone understood.

They walked to Leo's car and got inside. He cranked up the Lexus and the vents started providing cooling air to both.

"You appear flushed, Wink. Are you okay?" he asked.

She pursed her lips causing the ever-present dimples to take a downward turn. "You know I can't take this heat for very long. I'm fine, but I could use something cold to drink."

"Yeah, me too. Do you want to run your car home and get something there?"

"No, I'm going to need to go to my office for a little while. There's a project I've got to finish today. I'm thinking we can meet up later before the party, if that's alright."

"Of course, Wink, but I was just hoping we'd get to spend all day having this kind of fun together."

"I love you and would do just about anything you asked, but I'd probably end up in the emergency room if I had to stay outside much longer. I'd also have to redo my makeup," Dee said while looking in the mirror on the visor.

They smiled at one another and then kissed lightly. It was a moment that made Leo realize how lucky he was.

After more discussion about Leo's plans for the rest of the day, Dee got out of his car and went to hers. Before driving away she pointed at herself, then at him, and then drew an air heart with her fingers.

Leo put the car in gear and got back on Riverside Drive toward town. He was feeling fine despite being somewhat sweaty and jacked up the satellite radio station known as Margaritaville. Jimmy Buffett always made him happy.

Jimmy sang about a déjà vu experience, and believing made it all come true. The lyrics spoke to Leo, and he told himself it was happening today. He truly thought he was going to win even though he knew there were folks who didn't think he would.

Crossing over the interstate where construction seemed never to end, Leo got to Spring Street and made a left turn going to the east side of town. He made a quick stop in the drive-through lane of the Nu-Way and got the largest size drink over their famous shaved ice before continuing on his route away from town.

He had decided to spend the morning travelling to some of the precinct spots. Campaign laws prevented going inside where the voting was taking place or even getting too near the property, but Leo knew many candidates for various offices often placed signs close by the polls. He doubted that got many votes. He wondered, however, if it might if he showed himself in the area. He just wanted to stay busy, and it was worth a try.

His first stop was near a large church on the main thoroughfare. It was one of several Leo and Dee had attended during the campaign. Randall Lance, the oldest son of an African-American leader in the community, had arranged for them to be recognized during regular services in several congregations. They had been impressed with the pastor's message and the friendliness of the people. It just happened to be the place where many on that side of the county voted.

Leo parked the car as close to the entrance as he dared and got out in the humid air. Signs in different colors dotted the landscape. A fair amount of cars were parked in the lot near the entrance, and he saw a steady stream of voters going and coming.

He popped the trunk open and took out the sign he had been waving earlier. A few cars passed as he began the routine again and a couple of the occupants responded with similar gestures.

A few minutes later a black stealthy sports Mercedes with signals flashing pulled over in front of Leo's vehicle. The license plate was personalized and read 'STOOK 1.' The driver's side window drew down as Leo walked over to see who was behind the wheel.

"Hey, Mr. Berry. Whassup?"

Leo peered inside and saw a blast from the past. The occupant was a handsome black guy dressed in navy slacks and red polo with *S. Williams* embroidered above the pocket. His perfect teeth gleamed in a huge grin. Sticking out their hands, each man grasped the others with a firm grip.

Way back in the private practice days, he had represented the man inside. His name was burned into Leo's brain, Stookey Williams. It was impossible to forget one of his first clients who had an infectious spirit. The kid back then had big dreams that must have come true.

"Stookey, haven't seen you in forever. You look like you're doing better than okay. What are you up to these days?"

Back before Leo had become a prosecutor and was on the other side of law practice handling criminal defense, Stookey was charged with a multitude of various criminal offenses. Most had been drug related and had begun when he was a fifteen-year-old juvenile. Leo was right out of school and doing a lot of indigent defense at the time. The teen had gotten involved with a bad crowd. Some around town called that crowd a gang.

Their courses in life had led them to one another when Leo was appointed to represent Stookey. The lawyer had been successful in keeping him from being incarcerated at least twice. The last time Leo had seen Stookey was nearly twenty years ago when the kid had graduated from kiddie court to the superior court at the tender age of seventeen and was saddled with a felony conviction for selling. Leo had told him it was the last chance he would get since he'd been sentenced under the First Offender Act, which gave Stookey the opportunity to allow the conviction to disappear and be discharged if the five-year probation was completed.

Looking at the expensive automobile his former client was driving, Leo couldn't help but wonder about the source of income for the now grown man. He hoped it was not illegal.

"I'm doing great, Mr. Berry. Appreciate you asking. I've got my own business and don't worry, it's legal," he said with a laugh.

"I'm going to vote today, can you believe it? Never thought that would happen. You made that possible," Stookey continued.

At that moment, Leo couldn't describe how proud he felt of the young man sitting in the car. Overcoming problems that Stookey experienced as a teenager often didn't have good results. Downward spirals into a life of crime were not unusual under those circumstances.

"Man, you just helped make my day, especially if you're voting for me," Leo said with a grin.

"You better believe it, Mr. Berry, along with all my extended family and a bunch of my friends, too. I've been talking you up since I heard you were running. Got a good feeling about you winning."

Leo never tired of hearing those kinds of comments, and he had heard several lately. It was one of the reasons he was so confident.

"Thanks so much, Stookey. Please call me Leo, okay? I'm not much older than you. Hey, I'm having a little party for my supporters at Michael's beginning around 7:00 this evening. I'd love to see you there."

"I appreciate the invite and might just do that, Leo," replied Stookey with another smile and paused.

He took a card out of the console and offered it to his former lawyer. Leo looked at it that read, **ESS ENTERPRISES**. Underneath it said **INDUSTRIAL CLEANING SERVICES** and **SHAWN WILLIAMS, PRESIDENT**. There were a couple of telephone numbers listed as well.

"Only my oldest and closest friends call me by my nickname nowadays, but I keep it on my license plate to remind me where I came from. You know about all that as well as anybody, Leo. I guess I'd better be going so I can help you reach your dreams like you did for me," he said in a more somber tone.

"Thanks again for stopping and everything else," Leo said suppressing a more emotional response.

Stookey bumped his chest with his hand and showed a peace sign before driving down the road. Leo watched as the vehicle steered into the church parking lot and the good feelings flooded through his soul.

What a great day, he thought.

CHAPTER FORTY-THREE

It was mid-afternoon before Leo checked the messages on his phone. There were three that mattered to him. One was from Dee advising the project she was working hard to complete had hit a snag, and it was taking longer than expected. The second was from Mindy letting him know that Grandma Shelley and she had made some delicious goodies for the party and that they were going to ride together to the event. The voicemail from Jimbo reminded Leo to call the detective immediately.

"Hello, Leo. Working hard getting last minute votes?" said Jimbo through the phone speaker.

"Yeah, haven't let up for a minute since I got up this morning. I'm sorry I haven't gotten back to you before now. Are you down town? I've got something I need you to look at," replied Leo.

"I'm actually at my office. I've been pretty busy today, too. Where do you want to meet up?"

Leo glanced at the clock on his dashboard. Already two-thirty and the day was getting away. His car was parked in the Board of Elections lot with the engine and air conditioner running yet he felt warm. His contacts inside the office had told him moments before the voter turnout looked to be heavy. That made him even more jumpy.

"I'm less than fifteen minutes from there, why don't I just come by your place?"

"Sounds like a plan. I'll be looking for you and alert the media the newly elected solicitor-general is expected to meet with law enforcement officials," Jimbo said dryly.

Leo laughed and said, "From your lips to God's ears."

He put the car in drive and made a loop through the huge lot in front of the now mostly vacant Westgate Shopping Mall. At one time it had been a thriving place of business in Macon with competing grocery stores on each end and every other type of retailer imaginable in between, all contained in a climate controlled environment. Leo remembered for a moment Hefner's Bakery where he enjoyed hot doughnuts and wedding cookies as a kid. Now the shells of the once prosperous area were a sad testament to the side of town where he had grown up.

Driving on Pio Nono Avenue toward town, the nostalgia continued as he thought about the former Shoney's that had now been gone for years. It had also been a place where people flocked to, and he recalled their Slim Jim ham sandwich and strawberry pie for dessert. Leo was feeling hungry and realized he had been so busy that he had forgotten to eat any lunch.

He decided to cut through the Mercer campus since it was on the way knowing there would not be many students during the summer months. The pride swelled for his alma mater as he tooled by the football stadium and then by the baseball field. The school kept growing and gave him hope for his city to offset his bad feelings for the blighted area he had just left. It was a much different and even more beautiful place than when he had attended college there.

Upon arrival at Jimbo's office, the detective ushered Leo inside. He closed the door behind them as the prosecutor pulled the baggie out of his jacket pocket and handed it over to the detective. Jimbo studied it with a furrowed brow. Leo had placed it inside the clear plastic so that the information contained could be seen.

"Where did you find a receipt with Morgan Thomas's name on it?"

"Outside my house near the spot I talked to that guy I told you about. The one you were checking on, remember?"

"You mean the one who gave you an ID? Richard Jones? You think that was Thomas outside your house?" Jimbo asked in rapid succession.

Leo could almost see the wheels turning in Jimbo's head. It was a similar process he had made when finding the receipt.

"I don't know if it was him or not. I found a picture in an old high school annual, but I couldn't say if it was the same guy I saw that morning. I guess that's why eyewitness testimony is unreliable sometimes. If I could see a more recent picture, maybe I'd recognize him. All I know is I found the receipt in the same area where that car was parked. If it's him, Jimbo, what the hell was he doing at my house?"

"A damn good question, counselor. I'm thinking it has something to do with your wife, or I guess even your daughter. Neither fit the profile of known victims, or at least I don't think so.

The others are, let's call them, less protected. Single women living by themselves. I just don't know, but maybe there is some form of obsession with Dee," replied Jimbo while absently rubbing his chin.

Leo could feel his blood pressure rising as his usual even temper bubbled. Nothing could bring a rise out of him like a threat to his loved ones.

"It's been outside in the heat for the last few days, but at least it hasn't rained during that time. Do you think there may be prints on it?" Leo questioned hopefully.

Jimbo nodded, "I'm going to find out right away," he said before pausing.

"I should tell you I talked with Thomas this morning. That's where I was when we started playing phone tag. The guy is slick. I was trying to get some prints, and he figured out what I was doing. I think he's a little spooked and getting ready to leave Macon. If he was or still is a threat to your family, I'll personally make sure they're protected, Leo."

"Thanks, Jimbo. I appreciate that. Look, I'm going to get out of your way and let you work. Let me know what you find out. By the way, are you coming to my get together this evening?"

"I'm planning on it, Mr. Solicitor-General. Hopefully, I can get the crime lab busy on this right now, and I'll let you know what they say as soon as I find out," Jimbo replied.

Leo drove away feeling conflicted, but glad for the meeting with his old friend. He still had a little more campaigning to do before focusing on the particulars of Morgan Thomas.

CHAPTER FORTY-FOUR

The atmosphere inside the restaurant was electric and building into an explosion of multicolored fireworks. There were at least a hundred people milling around. A few hung around a television set up in one corner awaiting local stations to cover the night's races. Some were enjoying the heavy hors d'oeuvres, some the adult beverages, and others both as they engaged in the main topic of conversation. *Would Leo win tonight without a runoff?*

He nervously worked the room while thanking everyone for all their support. The polls had been closed for over an hour yet the results came in at a snail's pace. The early results had been good so far, and he held a lead that was significant, but not commanding, as he had hoped. Only a few precincts had reported with Leo ahead of the other two candidates at forty-nine percent.

Leo looked around and saw people he loved. There were family members ranging from his mother and brothers to cousins he rarely came into contact with. Of course, Dee and Mindy were flitting around interacting with people in the crowd.

His daughter was talking to a couple of criminal defense lawyers, and the animation she showed made him think she might have a career in the legal field about ten years from now. His wife was flashing her award-winning smile while engaging in conversation with some of the people from his office, and he knew they were talking about him when they all glanced in his direction.

He held a weak scotch in his hand that he had only sipped from once. Alcohol wasn't what Leo wanted at the moment, and he set it down on a vacant table when he spied some of his colleagues from the DA's office across the room.

Walking toward them, he was first stopped by Michael, the owner and chef of the establishment wanting to make sure everything was to his satisfaction. After giving assurance that everything was perfect, Leo's progress was then waylaid by a couple of the bailiffs who worked in the State Court. Leo joked with them warning the two older men it was getting near their bedtime.

When he finally got to the group of prosecutors, Chief Assistant District Attorney Jessica Lynn Mooney addressed him first. She was dressed in a stylish outfit with a signature scarf tied around her neck, but not in the stilettos that always were a part of her attire. Instead, she had a funky pair of tennis shoes on her feet, which made her at least three inches shorter than normal.

They had been friends for years and had a mutual admiration as attorneys. It occurred to him she would be a good source to discuss potential charges against Morgan Thomas when the time came. Jessica might even assign herself the case since it would be a high profile one, and she had handled many over the past few years. The time was not right to talk about the matter now, and could wait. Besides, he could not be sure Thomas would ever be charged, much less prosecuted.

"Leoooooo," she strung out the last letter of his name so that it sounded like an echo falling down a canyon.

"Thanks for coming, JLM. Wow, I don't think I've ever seen you shorter than me," he replied grinning.

"Don't get used to it Cranberry. I've been on my feet all day in trial, so I slipped on my Mr. Rogers' shoes before walking across the street," she said with just a tinge of sarcasm.

"I'm honored by your presence, no matter your height. So, was justice served before you got to my little soiree? I know it had to be a bad case for you to be involved."

"You know it, Blueberry. Another scumbag bites the dust and will spend a long time trying to protect his ass from others like him. I hear child molesters don't fare too well in the prison system," her tone changing only slightly while raising her cocktail in a toast to him.

He cringed at the thought but knew she was right. There was not a lot of sympathy toward such offenders.

"Um, sorry I asked. Enough of such shop talk for now. I really appreciate you being here, Jessica, and also bringing your cohorts and disciples," Leo said as he shook the hands and greeted the others in her group.

"So, does this mean I won't get to interact with you when you become the boss? Will I have to be more respectful, too?" she asked with a Cheshire cat grin.

"Oh, I doubt I could ever get away with that," deadpanned Leo.

She snorted and everyone laughed as much at her response as at Leo's. As the laughter died, a stocky lawyer standing near the front of the restaurant boomed out in his country twang, "Can I have everybody's attention, please?"

Charles Langley had been one of Leo's strongest supporters from the very beginning of the campaign. He had contributed a sizable amount of money, placed signs on several properties and been listed in endorsements. His trademark outgoing personality was on full display as he repeated the question in an even louder baritone.

The room quieted as Charles began to speak. He gestured in Leo's direction while holding his phone.

"I just got off the line with my partner David who is down at the Board of Elections watching the results of every precinct as they're posted. He told me all but three of them are on the board, so well over ninety percent of the vote is in," he said pausing for dramatic effect.

"Are you going to tell us or are you waiting for an academy award, Chuck?" someone yelled.

There was nervous laughter before he continued, "Berry in the lead with fifty-four plus percent, the other two combined have forty-five. At this point none of the rest really matter. Let me be the first to congratulate our new solicitor-general, Leo Berry!"

Cheers and clapping rang throughout the restaurant as several people slapped his back and others grasped his hand. Dee and Mindy appeared and a group hug followed their kisses.

With so many people crowding around him, Leo took a step up onto a sturdy wooden chair in order to elevate his viewpoint and be in a better position to address them. He felt his face might crack because of the huge plastered grin.

"You 'da man, Leo," somebody yelled.

He looked around and everybody Leo saw made him feel good. There were coworkers, associates, lawyers, police officers, court officials, neighborhood friends and people he had met since starting the campaign waiting to hear what he had to say.

"Thank you, everybody. I couldn't have done this without each of you."

There was applause and a whistle from the back. Leo pointed toward the sound and gave a thumbs up.

"When I started practicing out of law school, I never saw this coming. I didn't think about running for any office or for that matter I'd become a prosecutor, but both happened. I'm convinced that things happen for a reason. I've got people to thank who believed in me along the way.

"First on the list, my parents. They brought me into the world and then made sure I did what I should.

"Second, my grandfather, Leo Berry, Sr. The lessons he taught me as a kid still resonate today. I only wish I could accomplish a fraction of what he did during his lifetime.

"Third, the colonel. He changed my life when he gave me a job as an assistant solicitor. I found my niche, and I'm absolutely sure this is what I'm supposed to do."

Leo was choked up, and the emotions running through his body were difficult to check. This was one of those moments in life that would never go away, no matter how age entered into the equation.

"Everybody in here helped me. I wouldn't be in this position without each of you, and I want you to know how much I appreciate your support. I promise I won't let you down for trusting in me, and I'll work hard in this new job. Okay, the night is still young so let's keep the party going."

Sustained ovation followed as Leo took it in. Just before stepping off the chair, he observed Jimbo come inside the restaurant with an inscrutable expression. Their eyes met, and the detective nodded at him.

The two men walked toward one another, but progress was slow as Leo was receiving attention from attendees along the route. When they finally met in the front of the room the noise was deafening to the point that they went outside in order to hear one another.

They shook hands and Jimbo spoke first, "Congratulations."

"Thanks, Jimbo. So, what have you found out?"

"It's him, Leo."

"Have you gotten a warrant?" Leo asked hopefully.

"Well, not yet. The prints from the receipt you found match some points on the partial from the glove recovered at one of the victim's residence, but the lab tech says it's far from a complete match. Since that's all we've got, I haven't tried to get a warrant yet," Jimbo said shaking his head.

"Damn it," Leo replied.

"My sentiments exactly, but I'm going to confront him about the receipt. Find out why he was at your house and why he gave you a false ID. Maybe I can rattle him. The problem right now is I think he's wise to me and getting ready to leave town. He might have already gone. I went by his house before coming here and I couldn't tell for sure, but I don't think he was there. A for sale sign is in the front, too."

"Jimbo, I don't even know at this point he was the guy. If I could see his face again, I feel like I could make identification."

The detective pulled out something from his coat pocket. Leo recognized the plastic card as a government badge worn by employees.

"Do you recognize this man?"

Leo held the card and brought it closer to his eyes. He studied the face and saw the name underneath. There was no doubt in his mind now.

"Sonofabitch, that's him. Don't let him get away, Jimbo,"

"I won't. Morgan Thomas is going down."

They talked a little more before the detective left. Leo couldn't let the news bother him right now and returned to the party. Based on what Jimbo told him, he was at least confident Thomas wasn't a threat to his family at the moment.

CHAPTER FORTY-FIVE

Morgan was elated, at least for a moment. The house was on the market. He had shut down that old fart detective. All evidence that may have implicated him had been eradicated. Plans were in place. The old confidence was restored.

First thing in the morning, he would leave Macon for good. Until then, his mind jumped with possibilities for the evening.

He could go to a club and see what could be found. Maybe cruise the downtown scene. Lately, that area had been happening. Pretty girls could be found anywhere. He could even go stroll through the Kroger and take a look. One final celebration was in order.

The fact of the matter was that opportunities were anywhere and everywhere. Morgan could wait until the right situation before making a move.

As he contemplated the choices, there was one that kept coming up. *Dee.*

No rational thought should allow him to think of her. The problem was his irrationality whenever he did let her image come into mind.

He thought back through the years. There had been a time when Morgan wanted what everybody else wanted. That seemed so long ago now.

Back before things changed, Dee was the source of his dreams. She was just so perfect. Those brown eyes that matched her hair and the outfits she wore would grab his attention every day. And those dimples, they made her smile complete.

But, she had rejected him and it took time to get over the feeling of not being good enough. He had worked hard to forget those sentiments and believed he had until lately.

As memories flooded, Morgan remembered most, if not all, of the pretty girls he had been with were mere substitutes. Some had similar features; maybe it was the hair, or the same general body size, or even once or twice a hint of the same smile.

Substitutes were just that and not the real deal. The more he thought about that, the more he was drawn to the inevitable conclusion that there was only one way to satisfy the need within his soul.

He would have to find a way to be with her. But, all of his disguises and other props were gone now. He wanted to show her how much she meant to him, however, he didn't want to subject himself to another rejection.

There was a battle raging inside him, and the part that was in control didn't want to give up. Not yet. He wanted to see her just once more before leaving town.

That's why he sat in his car not far from the Berry home. It was turning dark and no lights were on there. He guessed they were celebrating somewhere. The radio had confirmed Leo Berry was the winner of his race. He didn't give a shit about that. Morgan Thomas wanted to win his.

***

The party had started to wind down, and Dee was starting to flag. The tensions were gone now that Leo had been declared the winner, and she was relaxed after the long day. She finished the glass of wine she had been nursing for the last hour and put the glass down on the table where she sat observing the diverse crowd that remained. Across the room, Leo was beaming while talking to a nice looking black guy she didn't recognize. There were other groups milling around, but they paid little attention to anyone other than those they were talking to.

She glanced at her watch and saw that it was after nine o'clock. It wasn't terribly late, but she was tired. She looked for Mindy and found her cornered in deep conversation with a group of teens she went to school with. Dee supposed they had crashed the party at Mindy's invitation and were catching up on the summer activities.

Since she had driven to the affair in her own car, Dee had the option of heading home. The idea appealed to her because the party still had some life, and she didn't want to keep Leo from enjoying the moment.

Dee walked over to her husband and touched him on the arm. He turned to her and smiled.

"Shawn, I'd like to introduce my better half, Dee. Honey, this is my friend, Shawn Williams. I ran into him today and invited him. He's a former client of mine and is a supporter," said Leo.

Before Dee could say anything, the man replied, "Nice to meet you Mrs. Berry. You can call me Stookey, if you like. My closest friends call me that, and since you're married to Leo, you certainly qualify."

"Thanks, Stookey. Any friend of Leo is mine also. We appreciate your support and coming tonight," said Dee stifling a yawn.

"I saw that. You've got to be one tired lady," he said with a grin.

"Busted. I was just coming over to tell the new solicitor-general I need my Tempur-Pedic," replied Dee.

Leo studied her face while she looked up at him. "I'm about ready, too. If you want to go ahead home, I'll be there in a little while. Just let me tell everybody goodbye," he said as he hugged her.

"Take your time, just bring Mindy with you. She's over there with her buds," she said gesturing in their daughter's direction.

"Will do, and we won't be long. It's been a long day, and we're all beat. Be careful on the road," he said mimicking what his mother always said when they were leaving her house.

Dee winked and then kissed him lightly on the cheek. She went back to her table, gathered her purse and made her way outside the restaurant without being stopped by anyone else.

Her compact red car was parked nearby and the lights blinked on with a beep as she pressed the key fob that unlocked the doors. She slipped inside and placed her heavy purse on the passenger's seat. Dee couldn't help herself as she yawned again while starting the engine.

There was not a lot of traffic while driving home. The soft rock sounds coming from her favorite satellite station soothed her already relaxed feelings that came from Leo's victory. Everything was great in her world.

She wound down the twisting road for a mile off the major highway that led to the house while singing along with The Eagles. She had the same peaceful easy feeling they were harmonizing about. The neighborhood seemed the same way, too and most of the houses were dark as if sleeping already. That's what she intended to do very shortly.

Dee drove onto their driveway and stopped until she could activate the garage door to open. It was a noisy creaking process that she hoped didn't disturb their neighbors located diagonally on the hill next to their house. Only a single light could be seen inside Cliff and Kathy's residence when she glanced in that direction. The other house directly across the street in their cul-de-sac still looked vacant although she knew it was being renovated.

When she pulled into the garage, Dee waited until the song ended before turning the engine off. She rummaged around before retrieving the keys from the pocketbook beside her and used a control located on the ring to disarm the burglar alarm. She knew it had been deactivated when she heard a short piercing sound similar to a stormtrooper's blaster.

Dee walked directly to the doorway leading inside the house from the garage and inserted the key. As she started through the entrance, she hit a button located near the doorbell that let the garage door down.

Someone grabbed her left arm above the elbow from behind, and she stumbled inside dropping the pocketbook and almost falling. The vice-like grip kept Dee upright, but she was surprised and disoriented by the pressure exerted when his other arm reached around her right arm pinning it to her side.

She tried to turn around, but the force was relentless. "Wha…"

Before she could finish her question, a low, menacing voice said, "Stay where you are, be quiet, and you won't be hurt."

CHAPTER FORTY-SIX

"You're already hurting me. What do you want? I've got money in my purse," Dee croaked.

She couldn't see anything about the man other than the silky black clothing that covered his upper torso and white latex gloves on his hands bringing to mind pictures she had seen of mime artists. His breathing was unnerving in her ear, deep and animalistic.

"I don't want your money," he said while adjusting the arm around her so that it pressed underneath both breasts.

"You need to stop and get the hell out of here. My husband will be home any minute," she said getting mad and scared at the same time.

"Maybe, but I doubt it. If he does, he might get hurt along with your daughter, too. I don't think you want that, right?" he said in the same low tones that made her believe he was trying to use a voice unlike his normal one.

Dee squirmed at the threat and thought about the self-defense course taken a few years ago. She remembered a move involving kicking an assailant's shins. The way he was holding her prevented such an attack at the moment, but might present itself if his legs weren't so wide apart. As if he knew what she was thinking, he widened his stance even more and pushed his pelvis underneath her behind. She could feel his erection through her cotton slacks and it made her sick in the pit of her stomach.

"I bet you know what I want now," he growled as he grinded.

Panic was growing exponentially as it became apparent the man's intent. There was no telling when Leo might get home, and the thought this stranger might cause him or Mindy harm scared her even more than getting hurt herself. Dee felt helpless and thought about her friend Maxie. She had expressed those same feelings after the attack she had experienced. Dee needed a plan in order to fight back, or at least to obtain evidence against the culprit.

She tried to will herself to relax a bit. Dee needed to get a look at his face. The lack of identification had so far been a fatal flaw in finding the guy who assaulted Maxie, and Dee was determined she wouldn't let that happen here.

"If you get what you want, you'll leave me and my family alone?" Dee asked without knowing whether to believe what he would say.

He pushed her toward the bedroom down the hall where they had stood since first entering the house. He didn't answer, which led to more doubt. Dee struggled to think what to do next.

She tried to remember everything she had ever read or heard about rape. The one thing that kept coming to mind was that the crime was about power. If she could find a way to flip the guy's power trip over her, maybe she could get away. That's all she was thinking as he pushed her forward over the bed. Dee still couldn't get a look at him as her head faced in the direction of the master bathroom.

Only a few feet away was her nightstand. Inside it was a pair of scissors she often used to trim her hair and possibly could be used as a weapon. At one point, Leo had kept a pistol there, but she had insisted he move it. The gun was now locked up in their closet and wasn't even loaded. If given the chance, she would probably change her mind about that decision, but she would love to get her hands on the sharp pointed shears.

He removed his right hand from under her and left the other above her elbow. He then warned her in that same voice, "Don't try anything. I don't want to hurt you, but I will."

She could hear him behind her as he fiddled with something. The pressure he exerted on her never changed while she heard the sound of paper tearing.

***

Morgan was so close to achieving his lifelong goal. The pretty girl of his dreams was bent over the bed with her ass so close he could almost taste it. He had dropped his elastic sweat pants and was rolling a thin-skinned condom onto his purple veined penis. The packaging had been torn open with his mouth. Next he would slide her pants down.

It wouldn't take long to find his pleasure because this was his dream fulfillment. Once it happened, he was out of here. *In and out,* he thought grinning to himself.

Morgan was only taking advantage of the situation as he had done many times before, but this time would be the sweetest. He had to hurry, though. No telling how little time he had to complete the moment and get out without jeopardizing everything he had worked for.

He just couldn't let the occasion pass when he had seen her drive past him. She was alone and seemingly not paying attention to his presence. It was a split-second decision he made to jump out of his car, put on the tight head covering that made him look like a villain wrestler, and slip on the surgical gloves in his pocket. Morgan had studied the other houses before her car arrived and had seen no evidence any neighbor was at home or at least aware that he was lurking.

The whole operation had to be what was meant to be. It was just perfect in every way imaginable. Before seeing her, he had thought masturbating outside the house would be enough to satisfy the dream. Not now.

He reached down and grabbed the top of her britches. Just as he started to pull them down, there was a snarling sound to his right. There was no time to react as a brown and white monster lunged at him with all of his sixteen pounds aimed at his groin.

Its teeth sank into the most sensitive part of him, and Morgan let go of Dee with both hands. The pain blinded him and he fell down to his knees while his pants were around his ankles. A howl came from way down inside him as he tried to disengage the dog's bite. He felt a tearing of his testicles as he gripped the animal around the throat.

As he squeezed the dog with all the strength he could muster, a couple of things happened Morgan had no control over. Dee had slipped away from him, and blood was flowing out of the area where he struggled. The loss of DNA crossed his mind, but trying to save his balls was more paramount at the moment. He thought he heard his name mentioned and for him to stop. He couldn't afford to stop, though.

Just as he thought the dog might be loosening its grip on his tender area, he felt a new piercing pain just above his right shoulder. Morgan tried turning his head in that direction and saw two handles jutting from the spot. There was an involuntary loss of feeling in his hand and the dog twisted away taking a part of Morgan with him. As he removed them, the bloody blades fell beside his even bloodier exposed privates.

He was in real trouble. All Morgan could think about now was that he needed to get the hell out of there. No longer was he in control. He grasped the clothing around his feet and pulled it up. Looking down, there was blood on his gloves and all over the front of his body.

Morgan got to his feet and started moving back down the hall where he had entered. Pain was everywhere.

***

Dee's panic was almost unbearable. Then she heard Tiki. The rumbling growl sounded ominous and ferocious.

Until that moment, she had not even thought of him being around. Lately, he had been rather listless and had even slept through louder disturbances than the current one. Right before this maniac was going to have his way with her, the lovable pet that had never bitten anyone she was aware of, decided to make an entrance. What an entrance it was, too.

When the guy let her go, the first inclination was to run. Then, he was trying to hurt her little protector, and she couldn't let it happen. The scissors she had thought of before provided the weapon needed to make the attacker let Tiki go.

Right before she stabbed him, Dee had an epiphany with the shears grasped above her. Even though his head was covered with some kind of ridiculous mask, all of the videos replayed in her head.

"Morgan, stop!"

When he didn't, she plunged the points with all her might inside his back below the right shoulder until the handles stopped further progress. He screamed and after a moment, he reached with his other hand to snatch them out and then let them drop to the floor. Tiki made his getaway and his toenails could be heard scurrying across the kitchen floor away from the bedroom.

She watched with some disbelief as the man gathered himself and stumbled down the hall away from her. The fear had subsided a bit, but white-hot anger had taken over.

In one corner of the bedroom sat Leo's golf clubs that were used only infrequently. Dee took a few steps there and grabbed an iron. She hurried after him.

Dee was not a violent person, but now she wanted to hurt this guy even more than she already had. She heard the garage door open and him go out. It was Morgan Thomas, she was sure. He couldn't get away again.

CHAPTER FORTY-SEVEN

Leo wrapped up the party by telling the remaining attendees he appreciated their attendance and support, and promised to work hard. Most everyone had left shortly after Dee had, and the rest did soon after his final speech. He was tired, and it was a workday for the ones who stayed, so they didn't need much reminding.

He and Mindy were only fifteen or twenty minutes behind Dee. They talked about the campaign and the future as they drove home. Mindy spoke nonstop about the people she had met and how interesting they were. Leo loved the fact she had been engaged.

They drove into the neighborhood with little on their minds other than the night's success. As they got to the driveway, nothing could have foretold seeing Dee chasing after someone with a golf club. The bright headlights illuminated the surreal scene causing both occupants to gasp.

Leo slammed on the brakes and jumped out of the vehicle after throwing the transmission into park. He told his daughter to stay inside the car and call 911.

The man being pursued by his wife was limping and holding on to himself. He had on some weird looking mask. There was a dark stain down the front of his clothing.

Leo ran toward the guy at full speed. Lowering his shoulder like he was a linebacker, Leo rammed into the fleeing man's torso lifting him from his feet and then knocking them both to the hard concrete. Leo's hands were wrapped around the guy and burned from the friction caused by the surface when they hit. The man's air whooshed out of his body at the same moment, and the back of his head bounced off the cement unnaturally.

Leo brought his hands from behind the now still body. He barely noticed the bloody scrapes on them as he reached for the mask. It was somewhat difficult to remove the neoprene material, but Leo succeeded. Dee had made it to the scene wielding the golf club just as the covering came off.

Even in the much less than perfect light, there was no doubt this was the man each of them had suspected. Leo wanted to pummel the slack jawed face, and he thought his wife might do the same if he got out of the line of fire. She looked disheveled, but otherwise okay.

"Are you okay, Wink? Did he hurt you?" Leo asked still straddling the body.

She started to sob and then replied, "He tried to rape me, Leo. Tiki stopped him."

Leo thought again about hitting the guy repeatedly. It would be easy enough in the unconscious state he was in. Ragged breathing let Leo know Thomas was at least alive, but he was bleeding from the back of his head as well as from his lower body.

Climbing off Thomas, he stood and made sure the prostrate figure didn't move before taking the seven iron from Dee's hands ensuring she wouldn't de-brain him. Leo then took her into his arms and comforted her with soothing assurances that everything would be okay. Sirens could be heard in the distance as Mindy appeared and joined the hug.

An unmarked car screeched around the corner down the street from the Berry house. It continued to their location and Jimbo got out. It was the fastest Leo had seen the old detective move in several years.

Jimbo took in the details while the sounds of other police cars got closer. Every dog in a half-mile radius was howling at the approaching cruisers' high-pitched wailing.

"You were right, Jimbo. Thomas has to be the rapist. He attacked my wife and tried to rape her. Our dog saved her. I got here as he was trying to escape," said Leo.

"Damn, don't tell me the crazy fool came back here. Thank you, God, for stupid ass criminals. I had a feeling he might, so I was on the way just to check when I heard the call go out. I didn't think he'd try and attack anybody else before he left town. Did you kill him?" said Jimbo while reaching down to check Thomas's pulse.

Three cruisers drove into the cul-de-sac with lights flashing. Officers surrounded the group while Captain Barbour arose and addressed them.

"I can't advise this subject that he's under arrest and read him his rights until we get him evaluated at the hospital. His name is Morgan Thomas and will be charged with multiple felonies. Get an ambulance and I'll ride with them. I'll need security set up around him until we can get him processed. There's a dark Ford sedan down the street that should be his that I want impounded. I'll get a search warrant, so I don't want it inventoried by you guys."

The people on the scene were dealing with the situation as they saw it. The ending is often like that.

EPILOGUE

A few months later, there were some developments.

Jimbo finally retired and moved to Lake Sinclair with his wife. He loved drinking coffee while sitting on the deck watching the sunrise. They fished a lot, and he thought about writing a book based on his career. Life was stranger than fiction, and others would probably find his tales entertaining.

After Morgan Thomas was released from the hospital, he sat in jail for months while awaiting trial. The sitting judge refused to grant him bail because evidence showed he was an escape risk.

He hired the premier defense lawyer in middle Georgia, Hogie Franklin, and it cost Morgan a substantial amount of his money. Franklin's trademark was his ponytail. It seemed that most high profile defense attorneys tried for something that would get them some recognition in their field, and he had borrowed that hairstyle from somebody in Atlanta.

Hogie was professional and very good at his craft, and he used every legal trick allowed in Morgan's representation. He quickly determined the best defense for his client was based on a theory of mental incompetence. There was some medical evidence of brain damage due to his client's head being slammed on a driveway. Morgan had developed involuntary facial ticks that he couldn't control from that encounter.

When that defense failed to work, Hogie took the next logical step. Morgan had a mental disease that he couldn't help or control, and hence he should be found not guilty because of it. Insanity defenses only work sometimes, however.

The prosecutor, Jessica Lynn Mooney, had heard all that stuff before. She wasn't buying it and was willing to let a jury decide the issue.

As a result of the publicity associated with the case, several women claiming to be victims in the past came forward. Because of the lack of evidence to substantiate the claims, they were not used as potential witnesses or to file additional charges.

At the last minute before trial, a plea deal was struck. Morgan pled guilty to one count of rape and one count of attempted rape with a negotiated sentence of twenty-five years. It was a lot better than a potential life sentence behind bars.

There was a possibility of parole in eight years, but most people familiar with the process thought the defendant would serve a lot more than that due to the nature of the crimes. Several other charges were dismissed as a result of the deal. Maxie and Dee were consulted and agreed to the resolution. Neither wanted to testify, but agreed they would if they had to and thought it was a fair sentence. They both were dealing with anxiety issues from their attacks. Ultimately, both became strong advocates for victims of sexual assault helping to empower other affected women.

Morgan went into the prison system with physical and emotional problems suffered from his last foray. He only had one scarred testicle, and couldn't achieve erections as he once did. More than that, schizophrenia tore at his brain. Recurring bad dreams about dogs often kept him awake in his cell.

The one good thing that came from his mental health issues was that other inmates steered clear of him. He was obviously screwed in the head and that kept him reasonably safe from attack. Nut cases were often avoided in that world.

Leo loved the new job. Because the election was over after the primary and his illness prevented him from working, the Colonel had retired early. Leo was appointed by the governor to finish the remainder of the Colonel's term and was sworn in a few months early. Rob left without saying goodbye, choosing to go into private practice. Leo felt regrets at the loss of his former associate, but thought maybe it was for the best. At least Rob seemed to be thriving, and Leo was happy about that.

He named Sandy as chief assistant and hired a new assistant, Becky. Women ruled in his office, and Leo was only there to supervise. That's what he thought anyway. Leo remained active in the courtroom, as he had promised to do throughout the campaign.

Cases continued to roll in and out. Leo revised his retirement date and planned to serve four terms. In the meantime, he would do what he could to seek justice and help folks as much as possible within that framework.

Mindy was growing up and her parents knew she would do well in life. She loved her new car and was turning into a good driver. It was hard to believe, but they knew one day she would marry and have kids of her own. Leo and Dee wondered how it would be when they became grandparents.

Tiki, despite his age, seemed delighted in the return to normalcy following the election. There was no indication his brush with danger had affected him. The devoted canine, once again, reveled in the early morning walks with Leo, after which he frequently sought patches of sunlight within the house in which to nap the day away. The family's affection for him only grew more intense and often resulted in a few extra doggie treats from Dee.

Life went on. Most people liked Leo, or so it seemed, at least for the time being. It was a good thing. He had made the right choice.

THE END

Acknowledgements

After several starts and stops due to delays that were both under and outside my control, I was able to complete this book with assistance from friends and family. They make it possible for me to pursue writing, so I give them my appreciation and love.

First, to my wife, Donna, and my daughter, Mandy, you are always my foremost inspirations, even if I don't make it known as much as I should. Your love has given me the greatest happiness in life.

Second, to the rest of the family including my mother, brothers, and super cute grandchildren, the experiences we have shared have helped me in ways you probably don't realize. I am a better person for having you along for the ride during my time on the planet.

To all my friends and fans that have read my books and encouraged me to keep writing, you all have warmed my heart with your kind words. If you're lucky in life, as I have been, you make friends along the way who stick with you through good times and bad. Thank you all for sharing my journey.

Special thanks goes to Dr. David Wallace, a smart psychologist and sometimes better golfer than me, for giving me technical advice on the subject of sexual deviancy. Anything he told me that I chose not to use in character development for this book should be blamed on me and not him.

Thanks to my many friends in law enforcement for their many contributions. I especially want to acknowledge retired Captain Jimmy Barbee for friendship extending over four decades; for your military service to the country; and for the many years protecting citizens in our hometown. You are an inspiration and should write a book. My fictionalized accounts could never live up to the real stories.

Once again, I also want to thank Carl Graves of Extended Imagery for his creation of the front cover and Cheryl Perez of yourepublished for the layout and remaining work.

Finally, I absolutely could not have completed this effort without the undying assistance of my core group of beta readers. Darryl Bollinger, Cindy Adams, Mandy Scarbary, Misty Peterson, and my life partner, Donna, are brilliant and bring different insights to the process every time I write a story. My deepest appreciation goes to each of you.

Any mistakes remaining are mine.

Thank you, readers everywhere. I hope you enjoy this one.

40870809R00198

Made in the USA
Columbia, SC
13 December 2018